IN THE NAME OF FAMILY

IN THE NAME OF FAMILY

CYNTHIA COPPOLA

First published by Brown Stone Publishing, 2024

Copyright © 2024 by Cynthia Coppola

All rights reserved. No part of this publication may be reproduced, stored or transmitted in any form or by any means, electronic, mechanical, photocopying, recording, scanning, or otherwise without written permission from the publisher. It is illegal to copy this book, post it to a website, or distribute it by any other means without permission.

This novel is entirely a work of fiction. The names, characters and incidents portrayed in it are the work of the author's imagination. Any resemblance to actual persons, living or dead, events or localities is entirely coincidental.

First edition

This book is dedicated to my amazing wife, Deborah.

*Thank you for your unconditional love,
your endless belief in me,
and for always seeing the best in me.
You are the best part of me.*

PART I
SECRETS

ONE

JANUARY, 1950
TONY

TONY REACHED INTO his closet and pulled down a wooden box from the shelf. He sat on the side of the bed holding it for a few minutes and let his mind circulate through thousands of memories and images of his previous life. He slowly opened the box and took a deep breath as he retrieved a wedding photo. He rubbed his thumb over Carmella's face and felt the familiar tug on his heart as he took in her beauty. He let out a long sigh and shook his head as his eyes filled with tears.

"I miss you honey," he whispered. "I feel like I've made a mess of things these past five years. I was a wreck after you died and could barely function. Thank God for Mom and Pop. They really got me through it all. I'm back on my feet again, and I promise you I will make things right. As right as they can be, I guess." He wiped his eyes and shook his head again.

"Carm." He hesitated. "I really couldn't imagine having another woman in my life after you passed. Not seriously, that is. I admit I took some girls out, mainly just to have a good time. I think I might've chosen to date girls I knew I would never have a future with because I didn't wanna have a life with anyone but you. But now, I, I've developed feelings for someone." He rubbed his thumb over her image again. "Strong feelings, Carm. Her name is Ruth. She works part-time for me down at the shoe factory. She's a real nice girl." He chuckled. "Not as feisty as you but she's just as kind. I feel ridiculous, really. I haven't even asked her out on a date yet. But, just thinking about her stirs emotions in me that I haven't had in a long time. I have to admit it feels good, but at the same time I feel guilty ... like I'm being unfaithful to you. I didn't feel this way with the other girls because they didn't mean anything to me. But Ruth, she's different." Tony propped the picture on his nightstand and started nervously playing with the wedding ring still on his finger. "Honey, I remember how adamant you were that I find happiness and love again. At the time I didn't think that could be possible. But now I'm not so sure. Maybe there is more happiness in the world for me and for the first time, I feel like I'm ready for it." He took his ring off and kissed it. "I will always love you. I promise you that. You will never be forgotten. I just think it's time for me to live life again." He put the ring and picture in the box and returned it to the closet.

Tony looked at his watch and realized that if he didn't leave for work, he would be late. He grabbed his coat, keys, and wallet and went out the door still thinking about his wife. As he walked down the front steps toward his 1947 black Fleetmaster, he noticed a red flash in the tree by the curb. He stopped and looked up to see a red Cardinal sitting in the branch seemingly making eye contact with him. The bird bobbed its head slightly, blinked at Tony, and gracefully took flight.

"Huh." He smiled and felt a light peace flow through him. He watched the Cardinal fly away. "Thanks, Carm."

Tony thought about how he might ask Ruth out for dinner during his ride into work. Being the Plant Supervisor at The Hoffman Shoe Factory, he knew he must remain discreet and had to find just the right opportunity. As he pulled into the parking lot, he felt a lump in his throat when he saw her.

"Good morning," Ruth said cheerfully as she walked over to greet him.

"Good morning," he replied quickly and hoped she didn't notice his voice crack. As they walked through the parking lot together, he looked at her and admired her petite stature and the bounce that she always had in her step. She reminded him of Rosie the Riveter with her hair wrapped in a red bandana and her navy-blue coveralls. It was clear to him that she really enjoyed working at the factory and she wasn't like most of the other women who worked there. The pleasure she took in every task she was assigned was a marvel. Tony suspected that the other women's main purpose was to find a husband. But not Ruth – she was more focused on her job. Sure, she returned flirtatious smiles and giggles when he would try to impress her, but she didn't come across as desperate as the others. She was easy to be around, and her light-hearted demeanor was refreshing.

"How does the schedule look today? Do you need me working on the line?" she asked casually.

"Yeah, we've got a tight deadline on a large order, so I am gonna have to have you work assembly today."

"No problem." Ruth slowed down her pace and touched Tony's arm. "Are you okay? You seem a little off."

"Yeah, I'm alright." He stopped walking and tried to hide his shaking hands. "I, I wanna ask you something." He stammered, "I know I'm your supervisor ... and maybe you're not even interested ... but I would really like to ... I mean would you wanna?" He took a deep breath as Ruth smiled up at him. "Would you like to have dinner with me tonight?"

"I would love to." Her smile lit up her face.

Tony let out a big sigh of relief and smiled back at her for a few awkward moments. "Ok, great. How about Giovanni's at 6? It's a little Italian place on 86th Street in my neighborhood, Bensonhurst. It's not a fancy place, but the food is 'delicioso' as we say in my family."

"Can we make it 7? I have something to take care of at home, and I would like to freshen up beforehand."

"Sure, that would be fine. What's your address? I'll pick you up." Tony looked down and tried to hide his eagerness.

"Uhm, no it's ok. No need to go out of your way to pick me up; I'll meet you there. I'm all the way out in Bedford Stuyvesant." The tilt of her head and spark in her eye told Tony there would be no changing her mind.

"Fine, ok, but please let me at least pay for a cab." Tony hated the idea of not being able to escort her on their date and started to feel protective at the thought of her going out to Bensonhurst alone at night.

"I appreciate that. Now let's get to work before the supervisor writes me up."

He held the door open for Ruth and followed her inside the factory. He felt as excited as a schoolboy and couldn't hide his smile all day.

Tony arrived at Giovanni's at six to give the waiter a little pre-tip and ensure they got really good service. His Pop taught him this trick. He always said to make sure you take good care of the waiters on a special evening; they can either make it a great night or your worst night ever.

"Good evening, Mr. Russo. It's good to see you tonight," Tony's favorite waiter, Lou, greeted him as he entered. He chose this small restaurant because it had a warm feeling and great food. He'd always loved this place with its black and white floors, rickety tables, and red checked tablecloths. The dark wood paneling and paintings of the Tower of Pisa and the gondolas in Venice created a comfortable, relaxed atmosphere.

"Hi Lou." Tony shook his hand and smoothly slipped the tip into his palm. "Is that nice table by the window free?"

"It is. But don't you want your usual table?"

"Nah, I think the bright table by the window would be better than the corner booth tonight." Tony scanned the dining room to do a quick comparison of the tables and nodded his head.

"Of course, right this way."

As he settled himself at the table, he nervously repositioned the chianti bottle candle holder several times and finally decided to put it back to its original position. His heart started thumping and his hands sweating as he peered out the window waiting for Ruth to arrive. He wiped his hands on a white linen napkin and then attempted to refold it as it was before. After several failed attempts, Lou appeared at his side, took the napkin, and replaced it with a fresh, clean, well-folded one.

"Oh, thank you," Tony stammered.

"You seem nervous tonight. This isn't like you."

"I can't even remember the last time I was out on a date… with a nice girl that is."

Lou raised his eyebrow. "Haven't I seen you here for dinner with a few pretty girls?"

"Yeah, you have, but truth be told, I would be embarrassed to introduce them to my family. This girl is special. I really wanna make a good impression." Tony looked up and Lou saw the concern in his eyes.

"I know just the thing. How about I bring you a bottle of our best Chianti for the table and maybe a shot of your favorite whiskey to calm your nerves?" Lou nodded and walked off before Tony could thank him.

He took a few deep breaths and started shaking his right leg up and down. A habit he'd had since he was a child. Usually he tried to control it, but tonight he allowed the rapid beat to soothe his nerves. Only moments after Tony downed the shot of whiskey, Ruth's cab pulled up in front of the restaurant and Tony raced out to pay the driver.

Tony smiled at Ruth as he leaned into the cab to pay her fare. But when he turned around, her beauty took his breath away. He was used to seeing her dressed simply for work at the factory in baggy overalls and a bandana covering her hair. But tonight, she looked as elegant as a movie star in a form-fitting burgundy pencil dress with a matching short, fitted jacket. Tony even noticed that her black stiletto pumps, gloves, and handbag were all accentuated with a small bow. Standing in the bright moonlight her warm amber eyes and dark brown curly hair that framed her soft oval face glowed. Tony unconsciously smoothed his gray, tweed sports coat and straightened his narrow black tie. "You look beautiful tonight," he said nervously. "You know who you look like? You look just like the beautiful Elizabeth Taylor."

"Oh, you're just saying that." Ruth laughed.

"No, I mean it. I never say things I don't mean."

"Well then, thank you." Ruth said humbly.

Tony proudly led her through the restaurant to the table. He locked eyes with Lou, who was walking toward them with menus, and relaxed slightly as Lou nodded his head.

"This place is lovely," she said as she slipped into her chair and accepted the menu. Her face brightened as she looked around and took in the atmosphere.

"They have great food here. Of course, it doesn't compare to my mother's cooking, but it's really good."

"Everything looks delicious. Can you choose for both of us? I really don't know what to have."

"Sure, I promise you won't be disappointed." Tony met Lou's eyes and nodded.

"Are we ready to order?" Lou stood tall as he approached and gave Tony a slight smile.

"Yes." Tony nodded and said confidently, "Tonight we will share the cold antipasto as an appetizer, and for dinner two plates of the chef's special Pasta Bolognese."

"Excellent choice," Lou responded as he collected the menus.

Ruth hesitated, "Uhm, I'm really not familiar with Italian food. What exactly is Pasta Bolognese?"

Tony chuckled in delight at Ruth's innocence. "It's pasta made with a red meat sauce." He quickly added, "I hope that's alright?"

"Oh yes, it's fine."

After the antipasto was delivered to the table, they fell into comfortable conversation.

"Tell me, was it difficult for you to move to a new country?" Ruth leaned in with interest.

"My father moved us here when I was ten. At that age, I made out ok. I made friends almost immediately with the other kids in the neighborhood. Some of them moved to New York from Italy also so they knew what I was going through. It was really because of them that I was able to learn English and adapt so well. When I started school, there were a few boys that tried to pick on me. My buddies taught me how to defend myself. I think their lessons were a little too good because I have a right cross better than Rocky Marciano's."

"Really?" Ruth looked alarmed.

"Don't worry, I only use it when I absolutely have to, and I've never raised a hand to a woman. Never have. Never will," Tony said as he reached across the table and placed his hand on hers. "In my book, real men don't hit women."

Ruth smiled lightly, looked down at Tony's hand and rubbed her thumb across his. When she looked up into his eyes, he got the feeling that she wanted to say something, but Lou distracted her as he approached with the entrees.

"Here we are, I informed the chef that the order was for you, and he took extra care in preparing your meal." He placed the plates on the table and stepped back with a slight bow.

"This looks wonderful." Ruth's eyes brightened.

"Enjoy your meal, Bon Appetit."

"Thank you very much." Tony smiled broadly at him in a gesture of thanks.

Ruth was about to start cutting up her food but quickly put her knife and fork down when she saw Tony swirling his pasta around his fork with the help of his spoon. She tried her best to copy his smooth navigation of the utensils but ended up with a large ball of pasta too large to eat wrapped around her fork. Tony was enamored as she attempted to conquer the pasta on her first try. "You know, us Italians make eating pasta look easy. But it's an art learned over a lifetime of eating it multiple times a week."

"I just don't know how you do it." Ruth giggled and held up her hands in defeat.

Tony held up his fork and spoon and demonstrated. "Here's what you do. Move the pasta around with your fork so you can grab only a few strands, use your spoon as support and twirl."

"Hmm, ok let me try this." Ruth leaned in over her bowl with determination. After a few tries she squealed in excitement, "I did it!" and took her first taste of Pasta Bolognese.

Tony enjoyed watching her fun tenacity and admired her expressions of delight. "Do you like it?"

"I do. It was a lot of work for a forkful, but it was well worth it."

"Practice makes perfect." He smiled. "By the time you're done eating, it won't be so much work." He placed the breadbasket next to her. "Here's a little secret. Grab a piece of bread and scoop up some of the sauce with it. Every bite won't disappoint."

Ruth quickly grabbed a chunk of bread, smothered it with a large portion of sauce and closed her eyes in delight with her first bite. "Oh, that's so good."

"You, you have a little bit of sauce on your chin." Tony reached over and gently ran his thumb along her soft skin. They locked eyes, hesitated, and then laughed like children.

As they finished their meal, they shared stories about their favorite foods and debated over which bakery had the best bread. Tony took comfort in the conversation, but also felt a pang of nostalgia as he realized the last time he felt this way was with Carmella. After clearing the dinner, Lou served two cups of Espresso and a plate of Biscotti.

"We have your favorite Almond Biscotti tonight and I took the liberty of pairing it with your usual order of Espresso. Would you also like anything more decadent for dessert?"

"What do you think? The Cheesecake and Tiramisu are excellent here." Tony raised his eyebrows and smiled as he tried to entice her.

"Oh, no. This is just fine," she said as she looked curiously at the Espresso cup then casually sat back and asked, "Do you have a big family?"

"Not really. As you know, my wife Carmella died five years ago. Here in New York, it's just me, my Pop, my Mom, and my sister, Louisa. She's married to a decent guy, Bob, although I don't know how he puts up with her. They're raising three kids. Other than that, there is my cousin, Frank, who's like a brother to me. He and his mother came here from Italy with my family just after his father died."

"How nice that they came to New York with your family. That must've been hard for them."

"Yeah, it wasn't an easy time. They really aren't blood relatives, though. Frank's father was my Pop's best friend and business partner. When he died, my parents insisted they move to New York with us. We were always closer to them than any of our other family." Tony was captivated by Ruth's smile and her genuine interest in his stories. "So, what's it like living up in Bedford Stuyvesant?" He offered her a piece of Biscotti and noticed for the first time how delicate her hands were.

"It's a nice neighborhood. I live with my parents and brothers in the brownstone I grew up in. We live in a tight-knit Jewish community and my father is prominent in our synagogue."

"If I remember correctly, your father's a doctor, right? I didn't know you had brothers though."

"Yes, two brothers. There's Isaac who is five years older, and

Ethan, who I'm closer with, he's three years younger. It wasn't always easy being the only girl. I had a modest upbringing and was only permitted to be friends with a few girls from respectable Jewish families." Ruth sipped her coffee. "Joan is my very best friend who is like a sister to me too. Our mothers have been lifelong friends, so she was one of the very few girls I was allowed to spend time with." She leaned in and giggled, "Joan married a great guy, Alan. But if our parents knew how liberal Alan and Joan have become, they would be furious."

"It sounds like you had a strict upbringing?" Tony asked gently.

"You can say that. As a female in my family, I haven't been able to make too many decisions for myself. The men pretty much make the money and the rules. The women keep house and raise the children. Family and community are most important. I guess that's why I wanted to work so badly at the shoe factory. In spite of my father's strong objections, I needed to experience more of the world outside of our five-block radius. It took a lot for me to convince him that working a few days a week at the factory wouldn't corrupt me." Ruth looked down and Tony struggled to read Ruth's emotions.

"I can see some similarities with my family background as well." Tony leaned in. "My mother kept house and raised us kids while my father made the money. The difference is my father tried to make the decisions but more often than not, my mother wouldn't have it." He chuckled, "Sometimes she put her foot down and sometimes she let him think he made the decision. They are a pair, my parents."

Ruth smiled and took a sip of Espresso. She immediately scrunched her face at the bitterness.

"Is this your first Espresso?" Tony tried not to laugh.

"Yes!" she laughed. "How can such a small cup of coffee be so strong?"

"It takes some time to get used to. Take a bite of the Biscotti. Would you like something else?"

"Maybe just some regular coffee?" She blushed as Tony waved Lou over to the table.

The rest of the evening passed quickly as they continued to share stories of growing up and discussed religious and cultural differences they've experienced. Eventually, Lou cleared his throat quite loudly in a signal that it was closing time. After Tony paid the bill, he pressed his hand on the small of Ruth's back and guided her through the restaurant past the waiters who were eager to clean off the remnants of the table.

"I don't think I've ever been the last customer in a restaurant before." Tony said as he led Ruth into the cold night air. "I've really enjoyed myself. If you wouldn't mind, I would like to take you out again real soon."

"I would like that very much." Her eyes sparkled in the moonlight while the cold air turned her button nose and ivory cheeks red. Tony wondered if she could sense both his relief and child-like excitement over her answer.

"How about we take in a movie next week? The new Spencer Tracy flick sounds like it would be good."

"Oh, yes. That sounds great."

Tony leaned in to kiss her cheek, but she turned her head ever so slightly and his lips landed on hers. Their kiss was soft and tender. As Tony wrapped his arms around her, their bodies fit together perfectly, and they both delightfully exhaled at the same time.

"Now Ruth, I'm gonna drive you home personally, I don't trust any taxi drivers this time of night."

"I will be fine; you really don't have to go out of your way. Besides, my family will already be in bed, and they are light sleepers.

It would be rude of me not to invite you in for some coffee," Ruth playfully tapped Tony's nose with her pointer finger.

"No need to invite me in. I understand. But I insist on driving you home," Tony returned the gesture and playfully tapped Ruth on the nose, grabbed her hand and led her to his car.

TWO

JANUARY, 1950

RUTH

RUTH WOKE UP the next morning feeling giddy as a schoolgirl. She floated into the kitchen and was disappointed to see that her family had not yet gone out to run their usual Thursday morning errands.

"Good morning," she said cheerfully.

"Well, good morning to you. Was that humming I heard coming from your room a little while ago?" Her mother insinuated as she sipped her coffee.

Ruth stood up straight and said, "Yes, as a matter of fact it was."

"Humming?" her father snapped not looking up from the newspaper, "What is there to hum about? Looks like there might be a war breaking out over there in Korea, and I'm afraid Truman is going to involve us in that conflict."

"Papa, it's a beautiful day today." Ruth was not going to let anyone spoil her mood today, especially not her parents. Jacob and Esther Klein had very little tolerance for conflict of any kind, and pretty much demanded submission and conformity in all facets of their lives. She'd recently started to wonder if her obedience to them was out of fear of their domineering and controlling ways or out of habit.

"Beautiful day? Huh, they are predicting snow for tomorrow. Esther, call and tell Isaac to bring home some rock salt after work tonight and then I want to get going. We have a lot to do today."

"Yes, of course." Esther jumped to her feet and scurried out of the kitchen.

Ruth spent the rest of the morning and early afternoon taking care of laundry and cleaning up the house a bit. She anxiously waited for her friend Joan to stop by so she could finally talk about her wonderful night with Tony. There's nothing that Ruth wouldn't tell Joan; she'd been there for Ruth through the best and worst times of her life. Ruth hoped she would've been able to come by sooner so they could have more time to talk in confidence, but Joan had a meeting at her son, Paul's, school. She heard Joan come through the front door just as she put a kettle on the stove.

"You're beaming! Tell me all about your dinner, and don't leave a thing out!" Joan exclaimed as she rushed into the kitchen.

"Sit down. Let's have some tea." Ruth laughed and placed butter cookies on the table.

"Your family will be home within an hour, and I want to hear everything." Joan said while she mixed milk into her tea.

"We had dinner at a little Italian place, Giovanni's. I was relieved when Tony ordered for both of us. After all, what does a Jewish girl know about Italian food?"

Joan nodded. "I wouldn't know what to order either. What did you have?"

"Let's see, we shared a bottle of Chianti, a basket of garlic bread, an appetizer called Antipasto, and we each had Spaghetti Bolognese."

"Antipasto? Isn't that a platter with meat, cheese, and olives?"

"Yes, but it also had some marinated mushrooms, peppers, and artichoke hearts." Ruth leaned in and whispered, "Don't tell anyone but I ate Provolone Cheese, Salami, and Ham!"

"Ruth, you rebel." Joan laughed. "Don't worry. I've been eating cheese on my hamburgers since high school. And actually, Alan and I eat pork when we go out to eat every once in a while, too. How was it?"

"It tasted so, so good. But the Bolognese was even better."

"Now what's Bolognese?"

"It's a tomato meat sauce that they served on spaghetti. Although Tony called it pasta. I know it had ground beef in it, but I think it had sausage also. I'm telling you Joan, I've never tasted anything like it. It had garlic and hint of onion mixed with tomatoes, the meat and something else that was a little sweet. I wanted to eat everything on the plate, but I got so full."

"It sounds wonderful. But let's get to the good stuff. Was Tony as handsome and charming as ever?"

"He was! You know how much I love his thick, dark, wavy hair and deep brown eyes. Last night I had a hard time not staring at him too intensely because he looked even more dashing than usual." Ruth sat back and smiled as she remembered the feeling in the pit of her stomach she got when their eyes met outside of the restaurant. "But you know what I found to be most delightful? Tony looked all calm and cool on the surface, yet I could see he was just as nervous as I was." She giggled. "He kept trying not to shake his leg and every once in a while, he would reposition his knife and fork like he didn't know what to do with his hands."

Joan smiled and sipped her tea as Ruth looked into the distance replaying the image.

"You know," Ruth said. "I've never had such a wonderful dinner with a man before. As the evening went on, our nerves relaxed, and our conversation was comfortable and easy."

"If anyone deserves a romantic evening out, not to mention some adult time, it's you." Joan placed her hand on Ruth's as both of their eyes welled up with tears. "So, what did you talk about?" Joan said lightheartedly.

"We really got to know so much about each other. He told me about his early years in Italy and the challenges of moving to New York as a young boy. He still lives with his parents in the same apartment they settled in when they came here. Oh, and he has a sister, although he didn't speak much about her."

"And what did you tell him?" Joan asked looking deep into Ruth's eyes.

"I told him I also live with my parents in the brownstone that I was born in and how infuriating it can be growing up with two brothers. You know, we discovered that although we have cultural and religious differences, there are many similarities to the way we were raised and the values that have been instilled in us. We both hold family to be very important. I'm telling you, the night just floated by. We laughed at the stories of some of the pranks my brothers would pull on me and his stories of trying to learn English as a kid. We were so caught up in talking and laughing that we didn't realize it was past eleven o'clock by the time we finished our coffee."

"Speaking of learning English, what will your family say when they find out you are seeing an Italian Catholic ... right off the boat?"

"Right off the boat? He's been in America since he was ten and got his citizenship at least eight years ago. My goodness, it's 1950! Don't you think it's time we evolved as a society? Scratch that, don't answer ... I won't tell them." Ruth nervously stirred her tea.

"Come on," Joan said. "We've been like sisters since we were out of the womb. There's no way you can keep this from them. They are bound to find out. Especially with your turbulent past. They've got one eye on you at all times."

Joan was right. She was always right when it came to these things. To say Ruth's past was turbulent was an understatement. Yet, she felt a strong connection to Tony from the minute she walked into the Hoffman Shoe Factory last year hoping to get a job. While Tony interviewed her it was all she could do to focus on his questions rather than his wavy black hair and expressive eyes. But it wasn't his good looks that won her over. Tony had compassion and wasn't too macho to show it. If he perceived someone was in trouble or was downtrodden, he was always quick to lend a hand.

"Well, it's too early to start worrying about my family. And besides once he hears my story he may turn around and run."

"Just be careful about what you're getting yourself into. Maybe you should be the one to turn around and run."

"Maybe I should, but I just can't. Tony's different than the typical Jewish men I've known throughout my life. He's genuinely interested in my opinions and what I have to say and is not so overbearing. I watch him at work, and he's very kind to everyone, not just the men. And when he talks about his mother, it's always with pride. It's obvious he loves her and has no problem showing it. Do you know any men like that, besides maybe your husband? Because I sure don't, between my father and many other men from our community, I have yet to see any of them have a serious conversation with a woman about matters of substance, let alone compliment them."

"You know, not all of the men in our community are as domineering as the men in your family. You've had a tough time of it, so I do understand your attraction to Tony."

"I really do like him. I have a strong feeling he is my future ... if only I can break away from my past."

"Your future? This you know after only one date?" Joan dropped her half-eaten cookie into her plate.

"I know it sounds crazy. It's just a feeling. A sixth sense if you want to call it that. To be honest, it scares me. I fear letting anyone get close to me again, and yet, I agreed to go see that new film *Adam's Rib* with him next week."

"Take it slow and be careful. You've got a lot going on." Joan whispered as the front door blew open and Ruth's family bustled in with their packages.

THREE

JULY, 1950
TONY

TONY CRADLED TWO loaves of bread as he walked swiftly down the street humming to himself. He volunteered to go to the store when he got home from work so he could get a little fresh air and calm his nerves. It'd been six months since he and Ruth started dating, and he was a little apprehensive about introducing her to his parents. Although they both suggested that he find himself another nice girl and settle down again, he wondered if they would embrace Ruth just as they did Carmella. She was Tony's high school sweetheart and had been thought of as a member of the family long before they were married. No two women could be any more different than Carmella and Ruth. Being the fifth out of six children, Carmella was raised in a loud, bustling home. She had a very animated personality and lit up a room as soon as she entered it. Ruth, on the other hand, had a much more conservative upbringing. Although she would often slip into a room quietly, her genuine warmth and down-to-earth personality immediately drew people in once they've met her. Tony took a little comfort in the fact that he had never known his parents to be anything but kind, and they were both very enthusiastic about meeting her. His mother had been cooking all day as if it were a Sunday rather than a Tuesday, and his father bought a special bottle of wine just for the occasion. As he rounded the corner, he saw Ruth getting out of a taxi with a small bouquet of flowers.

"Hey, let me get that," Tony called as he jogged up to the taxi and tried to get his wallet out of his back pocket with two loaves of bread in his hand. "I really wish you would let me come out and pick you up."

"Thanks. I will absolutely not let you come all the way out to my neighborhood just to drive all the way back here." She smiled and took the bread from Tony's hands.

After paying the driver, Tony embraced Ruth and said, "There's my girl." He breathed in her sensual fragrance, *L'Air du Temps*, closed his eyes and smiled.

"I think we're crushing the bread." She giggled and gave him a gentle, lingering kiss on his cheek.

"We can't have that." Tony took the bread. "Are you ready to meet my parents?" He asked as he took her hand and led her up the steps and into the large four family brick apartment building.

Ruth immediately felt comfortable when she entered the Russos' home. The three-bedroom apartment was larger than she thought it would be and felt warm and welcoming. The living area was understated with a red velvet sofa and matching wing back chairs. The oak coffee and side tables matched an entertainment unit which housed a new television set along with a radio and turntable. To the left of the living area was a dining room, complete with an intricately carved mahogany table and hutch. Ruth's stomach made a slight gurgling noise as she was greeted with a delicious aroma of a roast combined with the scent of a fresh apple pie.

Tony tilted his head, raised his eyebrows and whispered, "Was that you?" while he tried to contain his laughter.

"I'm afraid so. I was so nervous today I couldn't eat, and the food smells wonderful," Ruth whispered back as she clutched her stomach.

Tony's father, Sal, rushed over to greet them followed by his wife Anna. "There they are. You must be Ruth, I am Salvatore Russo, and this is my wife, Anna."

"Hello, it's very nice to meet you. Your home is lovely. These are for you, Mrs. Russo." Ruth smiled warmly and handed the flowers to Anna.

"Please, honey, call me Anna, and Tony's father Sal. We're very informal here. These flowers are beautiful. You know, I never pick up flowers for myself, and I can't tell you how long it's been since this one gave me flowers." She jabbed Sal in the ribs. "They will make a perfect centerpiece."

Ruth watched as Anna made her way to the hutch in the dining room and stood on her toes to reach a clear glass vase on the top shelf. Ruth hesitated while she contemplated if she should offer to help Anna with the vase, but before she could speak, Anna had it in hand and rushed through a swinging door into the kitchen. Sal and Anna were exactly as Ruth pictured them to be. They were a picture-perfect example of an older Italian couple. They were both short and stocky and had endearing smiles. Although Sal lost much of his hair, Ruth noticed he didn't resort to the long comb over that she had seen on so many men his age. Anna's beautiful, thick light brown, curly hair complimented her round face and bright eyes.

"Come, sit down." Sal said as he led her to the living room. "I'll get the wine. Tony, give me that bread and sit down next to your girl." He tapped Tony on the back and shuffled off to the kitchen as he inspected the bread.

Tony laughed, "Well, that's my parents."

"They seem very nice."

"They are. What you see is what you get. They don't hide their feelings and they speak their minds. But I will say, they are always kind. If they have a criticism they deliver it with tact, and they would give you the shirts off their back if they had to."

"That's a wonderful way to be. Now I know where you get it from." Ruth said, thinking about how opposite her own parents were to the Russos and how her brother Isaac had taken on their traits. Yet she, herself, and her younger brother, Ethan, were compassionate.

"They are definitely good role models."

"I thought they would have thicker accents than they do."

"Yes, my parents made a conscious decision when we moved here to embrace everything America has to offer, starting with the language. Every once in a while, they speak Italian with friends who haven't mastered English yet, and we will all speak Italian from time to time in the house just to keep up with it."

"Here we are." Anna bustled in carrying a platter of sliced beef. "Dinner's ready, come take a seat here at the table."

"Oh, let me help you." Ruth jumped to her feet and took the platter from Anna's hands.

"Come on, son, let's get this wine poured while the gals bring in dinner." Sal raised the wine bottle in a salute before he removed the cork.

They talked and laughed over their meal while Anna recounted her favorite stories of Tony and his sister, Louisa, growing up. Ruth got the impression that Louisa was a bit more stubborn than Tony, and that while Tony was clearly his mother's favorite, she was Daddy's little girl. After a pleasant dinner, dessert and coffee Sal and Anna changed into bowling outfits.

"I'm so sorry that we can't visit with you longer." Anna took Ruth's hands in her own, "Tonight is our league championship, and we are trying to keep our first-place spot and win that trophy. We just can't let our team down."

Ruth smiled brightly. "It's no problem. I enjoyed the dinner and company greatly. Good luck, tonight."

"Luck has nothing to do with it." Sal winked. "Our team's got the talent."

"Now don't wait up honey." Anna kissed Tony's cheek. "You know how late championship night can be. By the time all the games are played, totals are tallied, and the awards are handed out, we're all ready to kick back and celebrate with some cocktails down at Freddy's."

"You're not driving tonight, are you?"

"No, no, we've got a taxi on the way. Let's go Anna, he'll be pulling up anytime now. Ruth, please come back for a visit soon." Sal pulled Tony aside and said, "I like her. She's one of the good ones."

Tony closed the door behind them as they left and took Ruth into his arms. "So, what do you think?"

"I love them. I really do. Your parents are just wonderful."

"They really took to you too. I can tell." Tony pulled Ruth closer to him and they kissed passionately as their bodies pressed against each other.

"Let's take this into my room," he whispered as he gently bit her ear.

She pulled back. "I love being with you and want nothing more than to get closer to you. But you have to know, I am not the kind of person who sleeps around. I think we're getting caught up in the moment."

Tony took Ruth's hand in his. "Today was wonderful just like every day we're together. Being with you intimately means far more to me than just a moment. I don't wanna be with someone who sleeps around, I wanna be with you. The sweet, loving woman I'm falling in love with."

"You're falling in love with me?" Her eyes beamed.

"Yeah, Ruthie, I love you. I want us to start thinking about making a future together."

She looked up into his eyes. "I love you too." She hesitated, "But a future together may be a little complicated."

"Let's not worry about that just yet. Give me some time. For now, all I can do is give you some stolen moments while my parents are out. I'm working on some business plans which will help me get my own place. Then we'll talk about how complicated our future will be. Is that a deal?"

"Yes, it's a deal." Ruth hugged Tony and buried her hesitation in his neck.

He squeezed her into him, started kissing her gently from the top of her head, onto her forehead, down her cheek, and then slowly and deeply on her mouth.

Her body relaxed as she groaned. "Which bedroom is yours?"

FOUR

OCTOBER, 1951
RUTH

IT'D BEEN ABOUT nineteen months since Tony and Ruth began their relationship, and it was the happiest time of Ruth's life. Tony was everything she thought he was and more. She knew they had some serious conversations that needed to take place, but she kept putting off the serious for the romantic and fun. Why ruin good times with conversations about family and religion? She hated having to whisper over the phone when she called Tony to tell him she had to go to the doctor to see about this flu she caught, but she wasn't up to having a conversation with her parents about Tony just yet. She knew exactly how the conversation would go and hadn't gotten up the nerve to bring it up. Tony was so sweet and concerned about her when they spoke, he even offered to take her to the doctor himself. She often wondered what she did to deserve a man like Tony and worried about how he would react when he learned the truth behind her family.

At the doctor's office, she fidgeted with her dressing gown and swung her bare legs while she sat on the examining table. "I never should've let myself get so close to Joan's son, Paul, last Saturday," she thought to herself. "That kid was sniffling and sneezing all over the place, and now I've got the flu." She straightened up when the doctor and his nurse entered the room.

"Well, let me be the first to congratulate you. You are going to be a mother." Dr. Fischer patted Ruth on the shoulder and beamed brightly.

"Pregnant? Are you sure?" Ruth looked back and forth between them.

"Yes. Without a doubt. In my estimation you're about four months along now."

"Four months? But I had my period."

"How heavy?" The doctor looked at Ruth briefly while he wrote in the chart.

"Maybe not as heavy as some I've had, but there was definitely blood."

Dr. Fischer nodded his head, "That's not uncommon in the beginning of a pregnancy. I do want to keep a close watch on it, though. If it continues after these next few weeks or gets heavier, I want you to contact me immediately."

"I thought I had the flu," she whispered.

"Many women think the same thing. Pregnancy and the flu often have the same symptoms, I'm afraid. Now I'm going to have my nurse here, Jodi, set you up with some vitamins and schedule your next appointment. I know this is an unexpected surprise. Do you have any questions?" Ruth silently shook her head and placed her hand on her stomach as tears rolled down her face.

She spent the rest of the day walking around the park in a daze, and by the time she made it home it was getting dark. The house was empty and still. She spent the next hour sitting in the dark living room and tried to figure out how to break the news to Tony. She promised she would call him tonight to fill him in on her doctor's appointment, so she picked up the phone receiver and dialed his number with her trembling fingers.

"Hello?" Anna's bright voice answered the phone.

"Hi Anna. This is Ruth. Is Tony home by chance?"

"Well, hello Ruth. It's good to hear your voice. Tony's here. Before I put him on, I want to invite you for Sunday dinner. I've been after Tony to invite you for a long time now, but he doesn't want to overwhelm you with the family."

"Oh, Sunday dinner?" Ruth tried to hide her emotions. "I, I'm not quite sure."

"No worries, honey. Let's make it a standing invitation. When you can make it, we would love to have you."

"Thank you. I'd like that."

"Here's Tony now. It's always so nice to speak with you, Ruth."

"You too, Anna." Ruth inhaled a large breath and closed her eyes.

"Hey Ruthie. How are you feeling? How'd it go with the doctor?"

Ruth let out her breath. "The doctor's visit was not what I had expected."

"What do you mean?"

Ruth struggled to speak.

"Are you there?"

"I'm here." She whispered.

"What's happening?"

"We need to talk."

"Ok, I'm here."

"No, I mean in person."

"I'm on my way over."

"No, wait! Don't come over," she pleaded and regretted calling him.

"You're really scaring me. Just tell me what's wrong."

"I don't want to have this conversation over the phone. We have a lot to talk about."

Tony began to lose his patience. "You have to give me an idea of what this is all about. My mind is racing, and I'm jumping to all sorts of conclusions. If you don't have the flu, then what is it? How seriously sick are you?"

"I'm not sick. I'm pregnant." Ruth shocked herself when she blurted out the news.

Tony was speechless.

"Pregnant? Are you sure?"

"The doctor is certain. I'm about four months along."

"That, that's wonderful," Tony's voice broke. "Don't you think that's wonderful?"

"I think we have a lot to talk about."

"This is definitely not how we planned things, but we'll work it out. Now I know you said your parents will have a tough time about the religion, but I'm determined to win them over. Tomorrow I'm gonna come for dinner, and we'll all talk about it."

"Oh, I don't think that's a good idea."

"It's time we got to know each other."

"No, really. Tomorrow is Shabbos. It won't be the best time."

"Nope. I insist. I wanna meet your family and get them to see that I can embrace your religion. Besides, if not tomorrow, then when? We need to start planning the future."

"Well, alright," Ruth said reluctantly. "But, please, let's take it slow. Let's not mention the pregnancy. Not yet. Let's get my parents to see how wonderful you are before we make the announcement."

"Ok, that's a deal," Tony said, more excited than Ruth had ever heard him.

FIVE

OCTOBER, 1951
TONY

THE NEXT MORNING Tony woke up feeling a happiness he almost forgot existed, but his mood became tense on his way to meet his sister, Louisa, for lunch. He always got tense before meeting up with her. She always meant well, and he knew she loved him and wanted nothing but the best for him, but she was always so opinionated and judgmental that he often walked away feeling angry. He took a deep breath as he approached her just in front of the coffee shop. She always looked elegant and today was no different. Looking like she just stepped out of Vogue, her shoulder length dark red hair was held up with a modest rhinestone clip, and her form fitting navy silk dress fell just past her knees and made her look even slimmer and taller than she was. As he leaned in to kiss her cheek, he noticed that she seemed to tower over him.

"Hi, you look nice. Dressed up for a special occasion?" Tony asked as he led them to a table.

"Dressed up? No, I'm going to stop by and see Bob's mother while I'm out here."

"How is Maggie doing after her knee surgery?"

"She's fit as a fiddle with no thanks to Bob. I was the one who waited on her hand and foot during those first few weeks."

Tony grabbed a lunch menu and while he glanced at it, he thought to himself that it sure didn't take Louisa long to start complaining. He often struggled to understand his sister. They were both very different from each other. Tony by nature found the positive in situations and never thought twice about helping someone else. Louisa, on the other hand, always felt like a victim and was often resentful when she felt someone had more than her.

"Bob said he was shorthanded at the deli and it's been busy, but I think that's just an excuse."

Tony put the menu down. "I guess business is good then?"

"I suppose we're doing alright," she mumbled as she looked over her menu.

"And the kids?" Tony was trying to delay the inevitable conversation about his relationship with Ruth.

"They're kids. Rena is starting with the back talk. Nine years-old only! Bobby is taking after his father more and more every day, I swear. At five he's already telling Bob how to run things at the deli. Always keeping us laughing that one. And Sophia, Sophia has a spark in her little three-year old eye that I just cannot make out – part angel, part devil. It wouldn't kill you to drop by the house more often you know." She put her arm on the table and leaned in.

Tony felt his annoyance flair, but quickly dismissed her remark. He didn't want to get into an argument.

"I will try to drop by sometime this week. It's not always so easy for me," Tony said and felt relieved as the slight waitress hurriedly delivered their coffee.

"That's because you're spending too much time with that girlfriend of yours."

There it was. It was no secret that Louisa didn't approve of his relationship with Ruth. She was very close with Carmella and had compared the two women since the first time she met Ruth, and she simply refused to get over the fact that Ruth was Jewish.

"I'm gonna stop you right there. I'm gonna ask Ruth to marry me."

"Marry you!" Louisa demanded in a disgusted tone that made the people at the next table turn to look at her.

"Lower your voice. Yes, marry me. We've been together for almost two years now, and I don't wanna wait any longer."

"Oh, how can you do this to our family? May I remind you that she is *Jewish*!"

"Jewish? Is that all you see when you look at her? She's a caring, forthright woman who will be a great mother and wife."

"*Mother* and wife? Oh, that's a good one. What does she know about being a mother? Make her spend some time at my house if she wants to see motherhood." Louisa pushed away her coffee cup.

Tony leaned in. "Ruth is pregnant."

"Oh dear God. How did you let that happen? Are you sure it's your child?"

"Yes, it's my child. How dare you even ask me that?"

"I ask because I don't trust her. When I met her, she was obviously hiding something. She wouldn't talk about her past, just glossed over it with a flare for changing the subject before I realized that the subject had been changed."

"You're being ridiculous." He wouldn't let Louisa raise any doubts about Ruth. She had told Tony that she was involved with a man who was selfish and cruel just before meeting him, and she didn't like to revisit the past. "I'm gonna marry Ruth! Not just because it's the right thing to do, but because I'm ready to start a new life."

"This is the last thing you need right now. How can you afford to take care of Ruth, a baby, and all your other responsibilities? These are tough times, and you certainly are just getting by on what you are making now at the shoe factory."

"I've got some things lined up. Frank and I are looking into starting a little something."

"Frank? Our Frankie Visconti? Oh Tony, I don't know. I've been hearing stories about some of the people he's associating with. I don't think it's a good idea to get into any kind of business with him."

"Frank is Pop's Godson and he's like a brother to me. Sure, he's made some choices that I wouldn't have, but I'm a smart man. In another year I'll be 32 and what do I have to show for it? It's time for me to start working for myself. I can't rely on the shoe factory. I'm hearing rumors they may shut down. And then what? Frank has a connection that may give us a loan and I've got some business smarts. We can't lose."

"Well, I don't like it! I don't like any of this one bit! I don't trust Frank and there's something about Ruth that I just don't trust either. All I can say is, good luck. You're going to need it."

That was the best Tony would ever get from Louisa. He tried to shake off his aggravation and managed to change the subject. They ate their lunch politely talking about how excited the kids were for Halloween, and by the time they finished, they were reminiscing about their own childhood Halloween adventures.

Tony thought about how he and his sister had never been particularly close as he drove to Ruth's house from the coffee shop. Tony always considered himself easy going and adaptable while Louisa was always very serious and rigid. She wasn't as appreciative of things like Tony was. Her expectations were very high, and she became quite judgmental when people or things were not how she thought they ought to be. Sometimes he felt bad for her in spite of her difficult nature. He remembered her personality changed when she was twelve and their parents brought them to America. She had a very hard time leaving her friends behind, and an even harder time making new ones. She was teased terribly by the kids in school and never fit in. Now, Louisa still found it hard to fit in with people, and most of her time is spent with the kids. Tony thought that maybe her cold persona was a shield she used to protect herself from being hurt by anyone, and wondered if she would've been different if they hadn't moved from Italy to New York.

It was still a mystery how Sal and Anna could afford to bring them to America and provide a good life for them through the years. From what Tony could gather by piecing together the little snippets and tales he was told, their parents made an impulsive decision to leave Naples just after Sal's business partner, Bruno Visconti, went missing in 1930. Before his disappearance, Sal and Bruno owned and managed a dinner club which Tony came to suspect was a money laundering front for the Camorra. They lived a comfortable life in a modest home where Anna would host elaborate Sunday dinners each week for Sal and his friends. Their door was always open and Sal, his friends, and business associates would come and go at all times of the day and night.

Louisa said that one morning, Bruno's wife, Maria, came to the house hysterical saying that Bruno went out the night before with three of his business associates and never returned. Anna gave Sal a long, cold stare and he immediately left the house for the entire day, not returning until well into the night. Two days later they were on a ship with Maria and her son, Frank, headed to America. Whenever Louisa and Tony would question their parents about their life in Naples, the conversation would get halted abruptly, and they knew better than to push the subject. Now that he's older, Tony thought maybe he would try again to get the full story when the time felt right.

But for now, he needed to mentally prepare himself to meet Ruth's parents.

SIX

OCTOBER, 1951
RUTH

RUTH PACED AROUND the kitchen and cleaned the already immaculate surfaces. Both Tony and her parents would be arriving soon, and her nervousness was almost too much to bear. Tony insisted that he come to the house tonight for Shabbos dinner with her family.

"What do I do? What do I do? What do I do?" she asked herself. She was anxious because Tony only knew part of her story and had only met her parents once when they ran into him in the lower east side of Manhattan on their way to Yonah Schimmel's for knishes. It was a brief encounter, but her parents knew immediately that Tony was more than just a friend from work. They were polite enough to him, but they made it abundantly clear to Ruth that she had to immediately stop seeing him socially. They had even gone so far as to make her younger brother, Ethan, keep tabs on her. They didn't know that Ethan was more interested in pursuing his own love interest, Rachel Horowitz, and he never checked up on her comings and goings. Ruth feared how her parents would react once they found out she continued to see Tony and was pregnant. She told them that a friend was joining them for dinner, and she desperately hoped that when they saw Tony, they would reserve their anger and politely follow through with the visit. If her parents saw past the fact that he was Italian and Catholic and actually realized he was a good man, Ruth's situation might not be so bleak.

Ruth knew that her relationship with Tony could be disastrous on so many levels and she considered breaking up with him on a few occasions. Each time she made up her mind to end it, some little thing happened to prove to her once again that she and Tony were kindred spirits and the thought of not having him in her life was more than painful. She knew she couldn't continue their relationship as it was without telling Tony her full truth but never felt the time was right to have such a serious and deep conversation. The last thing she wanted was to get pregnant, but maybe on a subconscious level she allowed it to happen. After all, it gave her the strength and courage to finally be completely honest with him.

The chime of the bell sent chills throughout her body, and Ruth tentatively opened the front door.

"There's my girl." Tony beamed and leaned in to kiss her while trying to balance a bouquet of flowers and a bottle of wine.

"What's all this?" She uttered completely confused.

"These are for your mother. The guy at the flower stand said that Gerber Daisies are the best choice because they represent new beginnings. I hope I made a good choice with this wine for your father."

"You shouldn't have done all this. It's completely unnecessary." She took the flowers and wine and led him into the front parlor.

"I wanna make a good impression for your family. I sensed tension when I met your parents that day we ran into each other, and I want this time to be perfect. Let's sit down I wanna talk to you." Tony took a seat on the leather sofa.

Ruth hesitated before she placed the flowers and wine on the coffee table and joined him.

"Ruthie, you've made me a very happy man. After my wife died, I never thought I would love again. From the first time I met you, I knew you were special, and you have filled my heart and life with such love and happiness. I wanna take care of you and build a life for us. Marry me and make me the proudest man on earth."

"No." She shook her head. "I can't marry you. It's not that I don't love you. Because I do with all my heart and soul. But I can't marry you because, well, I'm already married." She let out a long deep breath expelling all the tension and anxiety that had built up within her since she fell in love with him.

Tony's face went blank. "What, I, I don't understand?"

"It's true. I've tried to tell you so many times, but I just couldn't bring myself to."

"You've been stepping out on a husband?" Tony whispered in disbelief.

"No. It's nothing like that. He was abusive. We've been separated since long before you and I met. I've been trying to get a divorce."

"You've got to explain. I need to know everything."

"Yes, ok." She nodded and took Tony's hands in her own. "Six years ago, my parents decided it was time for me to be married and start a family of my own. They arranged a match with the son of one of my father's close friends, Harvey Goldberg."

"A match? You didn't know him?"

Ruth shook her head and her voice wavered. "I knew him, but we didn't date and fall in love like many couples do. In our community it's not uncommon for parents to arrange marriages for their children. My father, Jacob, and Harvey's father, David, have been friends since they were young and it was, in their eyes, the perfect match for both of us. They sealed the deal and made the announcement over Shabbos dinner. My mother, Esther, could not have been happier and immediately started chattering on about wedding plans. Harvey's mother, Sarah, on the other hand, was respectfully civil. Although our families celebrated many holidays together, Harvey and I were not close as kids. My older brother, Isaac, was very close friends with him. I was often considered to be the kid sister who was always getting in the way. Harvey's outspoken, bold personality took up every room he entered, and he often made me feel shy in his booming presence."

Tony pulled his hands from Ruth's, rubbed his face and leaned in. "Go on," he said.

"We were married within three months. I entered the marriage as any 19-year-old girl would, filled with giddiness and optimism mixed with nervousness over the wedding night. I was incredibly young and naïve and wanted to be the best wife that I could. At the time, I wasn't good at reading people's demeanor and completely missed the fact that Harvey wasn't as enthusiastic as I was about our marriage."

Tony shook his head. "Why didn't he tell his father he didn't wanna marry you?"

"It's not always that easy," Ruth whispered. "Harvey was 24 going on 25, and he hadn't had a serious relationship with a suitable girl yet. He went around with a lot of girls, and most of them he couldn't introduce to his family. His father knew Harvey wasn't the type to settle down with a woman and have a family on his own, so he did what many generations of fathers before him did. He put his foot down and demanded that Harvey comply."

"And just like that, he did?"

"Well, that's the thing, his father funded his accounting practice, paid for all of his living expenses, and even gave Harvey a monthly allowance. Harvey didn't want to lose any of that."

"Unbelievable. Did you know this was going on?" Tony stared at Ruth blankly.

"No, in my young mind, he was a handsome, successful man. I didn't learn the truth until after the wedding." Ruth looked down and continued slowly. "While I survived the wedding night, Harvey turned out to be a callous, and condescending man. Nothing was ever good enough for him and he criticized my appearance, my housework, and my cooking. One night he threw a platter of food against the wall in a fit of rage. He was disgusted that my cooking didn't measure up to his mother's." She took a deep breath. "He then dragged me by my hair across the kitchen toward the stove and swung a cast iron pan at my head. Luckily, I was able to duck just in time before it flew out of his hand making a large hole in the wall."

Tony leaned back into the sofa and rubbed his hands together.

"These outbursts became more and more frequent, and I was overwhelmed and shattered." She shook her head as her eyes welled up. "My parents were of no help to me. My father dismissed me as a dramatic female who was exaggerating, and my mother advised me that it's the role of a good wife to serve her husband and keep peace. Even my brothers didn't recognize the extent of the abuse because Harvey would be charming in their presence."

"So how did you get out?"

Ruth cleared her throat. "About two years into our marriage, I found myself pregnant. By this time Harvey was spending less time at home and more time God knows where. He would often stay out all night and when he returned, he would be drunk and miserable. Needless to say, this child wasn't conceived out of love, but from abuse."

"Pregnant? You got pregnant?"

"Yes." Ruth looked down, took a deep breath, and continued. "Harvey turned explosive when I told him about the pregnancy. He kicked and beat me so badly I thought I would miscarry. When it was all over, he spat on me, called me a pig, turned, and walked out of the apartment. My parents came and moved me back home, and six months later we welcomed my daughter, Miriam. Since then, they've helped raise her."

"So, you've got a child?" Tony stared at her blankly and shook his right leg up and down.

"Yes. I didn't mean to deceive you. I was going to tell you," Ruth whispered. "I've tried asking for a divorce. He won't give me one. Even my parents won't help me with it. They say I made a commitment to the marriage and must remain in it. Even after everything he's done and all of this time."

Tony sat in silence for what seemed like a lifetime. "I'm sorry. I need some air. I can't do this now." He stood up and shook his head.

"Wait! Don't leave. Can't we talk about this?" She pleaded.

"I just can't talk right now. I need to think." He quickly kissed her cheek and walked out the door.

Ruth stood staring at the door, paralyzed. Her breath came in spurts as tears poured down her cheeks. She supposed she couldn't really blame him for leaving the way he did. It must've been a shock to him to find out she was married and had a daughter. She told him only a little about how domineering her parents were and how isolated she was from the rest of the world. She knew she should've been completely honest from the start. He wasn't like Harvey. Tony always showed her respect and above all he made her feel that it might be ok to feel safe and secure.

Deep down, Ruth was hoping he would take her into his arms and tell her everything was going to be ok. But she knew that that kind of thing only happened in the movies, and she just delivered a huge piece of reality to him.

SEVEN

OCTOBER, 1951
TONY

TONY'S THOUGHTS AND emotions had been spiraling in every direction since he left Ruth's place. He never felt more like a fool than he did now. Why did Ruth keep something so important from him? Did she think she couldn't trust him? She said she loved him and wanted a future with him. Was that all a lie? Yet, Tony considered how abusive her husband was and how domineering her parents were. What kind of fear and anxiety was she bottling up? How could a man like that Harvey have been so heartless to a sweet, young girl like Ruth? The more Tony processed his thoughts the angrier he got at Harvey, and the more he even started to doubt himself. Did he make it hard for Ruth to confide in him? Did she think he would've reacted with fear and intimidation like Harvey?

    He drove over to Caruso's Lounge and hoped that a few drinks with Frank would help him clear his mind and think things through. Caruso's had become Frank's favorite hangout and he was there every Friday night. Tony had been there a few times, but always got a strange vibe from the regulars. These were men who were uptight and rigid as they sat in dark corner booths whispering to each other while they scanned the room. Tonight, Tony wouldn't pay any attention to these guys; he needed Frank's ear. Since they'd been kids, Frank was always the person that Tony could rely on. He told it like it was whether Tony wanted to hear it or not. Yet Frank, himself, didn't take it well when people offered him the same blunt advice. Frank had a wild side growing up, and as an adult, Tony had heard around that he'd been drawn into some dangerous situations. Deep down, Tony wanted to believe the rumors weren't true, but he could never tell with Frank.

As he entered the bar, Tony immediately saw Frank in a back-corner booth involved in a deep conversation with a few men Tony had never met before. When Frank looked up, he stood and waved Tony over.

"Carmine, I would like you to meet Tony Russo. Tony is a good friend of mine. Tony, this is Carmine Esposito," Frank said with a pride in his voice that felt a bit unnerving.

"I'm pleased to meet ya, Carmine." Tony said, trying to appear genuine and offered a handshake in an attempt to hide his mood. Tony knew of Carmine and his sway throughout the neighborhood but never met him. It was clear that he was a man of importance and his firm grip and piercing eyes confirmed that Carmine Esposito commanded respect. His silver-streaked black hair, thick eyebrows, and tailored navy-blue pin-striped suit reminded Tony of his father's friends back in Italy. There was something about him that made Tony feel like they've met before.

"Tony Russo?" Carmine questioned with a slight hint of accusation. "Is your family from Naples? My family has business associates back there and I'm just curious if there's any relation."

"I'm sure there's no relation. Russo is a very common name." If there's one thing Sal taught Tony, it was not to reveal too much about yourself to anyone that wasn't part of your inner circle. There was something about Carmine that made Tony uneasy, and he wondered what Frank's association with him was.

"I'm sure." Carmine nodded slowly. "Let me introduce you to my friend, this is Joe Bonanno."

"Hi Joe, how ya doing?" Tony had become impatient and was not in the mood for small talk.

Frank sensed tension in Tony's mood and was quick to put an end to the discussion. "Tony, why don't we have a few drinks? Thank you, Carmine, for meeting with me tonight. You've given me a lot to think about."

"I'm sure we will talk again soon," Carmine said dismissively.

"You look like hell. Let's have a seat at this table. Gino, get us a couple of bourbons and keep them coming." Frank nodded at the bartender who took in every detail of Tony's exchange with Carmine. After getting an approving nod from Carmine, Gino brought over a couple of glasses and a bottle of Glenmore.

Caruso's was not as crowded as it usually was on a Friday night. There were some couples who sat at small tables along with a handful of regulars at the bar all dressed smartly and refined. The dark cozy atmosphere was welcoming as Tony Bennett's "Because of You" played in the background. A couple of boisterous young guys who sat at a table next to them was the only blemish to the respectable place. The men didn't fit in with the other customers and were obviously not from the neighborhood. Their work pants and rumpled shirts led Tony to believe that they probably stopped in after a hard day at work and have been taking up space for quite some time.

"What's going on?" Frank asked as he poured the drinks.

Tony took a deep breath and downed his drink. The smooth, oaky warmth of the bourbon was just what he needed. "Ruth is married! *Married!* And with a child! How could I not have known?"

"Whoa, hold on. How do you know? Tell me what happened." Frank swiftly refilled his glass.

"She turned down my proposal. Said she couldn't marry me because she's already married and has a daughter."

"Geez! You said that Ruth didn't like to talk about her past ... something about it being abusive." Frank leaned in.

"You know, Louisa said she was hiding something. She said she didn't trust her. I just didn't wanna see it." Tony shook his head.

"Louisa?" Frank snorted. "Forget what she thinks. Louisa loved Carmella so much that I don't think she'd ever accept any other woman for you. All that matters right now is you." Frank raised his right eyebrow and said, "Have you been completely honest with Ruth about your past?"

Tony knew exactly what Frank referred to. "Well, not completely. But my wife's dead. Ruth's still legally bound to another man and now there's another child involved." Tony motioned for another refill of the bourbon.

"Doesn't everyone keep secrets?" Frank mused as he refilled both glasses.

"This is all too much for me to take in at once. I knew our different religious backgrounds would be difficult for Ruth and me. Both of our families have been known to have prejudices in the past, but it wasn't anything I thought we couldn't handle. But an abusive husband? Why would she keep that from me?" Tony turned his head as the guys at the next table had gotten louder and he felt his patience run thin.

"I don't know. But what I *do* know is that everyone's got a history, and no one's perfect. There's nothing you can do about her past just like there's nothing she can do about yours. All you can do is focus on the present and the future. What do you want for your future?"

"You know what I want? I want everything to not be so much of a struggle. Money, family, the job – its' all a never-ending battle to do the right thing and survive. Being around Ruth was never a struggle, it was always a welcome diversion. And now that diversion is tainted."

"That's reality my friend. What would life be without conflict? Boring if you ask me. You know I'm not one for sitting still and waiting for good things to happen on its own. You have to get out there and make things happen. Knowing you, the child isn't the main issue. So, Ruth has a husband? There's nothing in life that can't be fixed one way or another," Frank said as he raised his eyebrows.

The conversation was interrupted as the younger, red-haired drunk from the next table attempted to stand and stumbled into Tony's chair. He knocked over the bottle of bourbon, spilling it into Tony's lap. Both Tony and Frank swiftly jumped out of their chairs.

"Watch out!" The red head bellowed, and his spit flew into Tony's face.

"Look, we don't want any trouble, why don't you go on home now. I think you've had enough." Frank reasoned and tried to get a hold of the situation.

"No, I'll take care of this," Tony said calmly. He landed his fist across the guy's left eye and dropped him to the floor instantly. Tony wasn't looking for a fight, but the weight of the past few hours boiled up like hot lava and released with one hard punch. "I recommend you drag your friend out of here. Don't let me see either of you in this neighborhood again." Tony warned the red head's buddy as he poked his finger into the man's chest with a fierce look in his eyes. The man stuttered a quick, "Yes, sir," helped his companion off the floor, and the two stumbled out of the bar.

Carmine's nod of approval from across the room caught Tony's eye and he wondered what Carmine whispered into his associate's ear as he held up his glass in a subtle toast. His burly comrade instantly approached Tony.

"Carmine likes the way you handled that. He could use some good security guys from time to time. If you ever need a job, Carmine may have some opportunities for you."

"Thank you, but I'm good." The last thing Tony needed was to complicate his life any more than it was already. "Please tell Carmine I appreciate the offer," Tony said and rubbed his knuckles as they started to turn purple.

"If you change your mind, come back here to Caruso's, ask for me, Tommy."

"Think this over. This is a great opportunity," Frank whispered in Tony's ear.

"Maybe it is, but now's not the time. Thanks for the talk and the drinks. I need to go sort out my life."

EIGHT

OCTOBER, 1951
RUTH

GETTING THROUGH THE rest of the weekend was tough for Ruth. She hadn't heard from Tony since Friday, and her eyes burned from crying. After Tony left Friday afternoon, she told her parents that her friend who was coming for dinner had fallen ill, and that she too was not feeling well. She didn't know what else to say. This was the best excuse she could come up with to get out of having dinner with her parents and avoid them for most of the weekend. Although she managed to keep up the charade and was grateful that the family were at the Synagogue most of the weekend, Ruth sensed her mother's suspicion. Esther's dubious gaze made Ruth nervous, and she started to think that maybe her mother somehow knew everything.

On Monday morning, Ruth stared out of the kitchen window as she haphazardly washed the breakfast dishes. She tried to figure out what to say when she saw Tony at the factory. What was there to say? Would I'm sorry and I love you be enough? Although she knew deep down that getting involved with anyone was a bad idea, she was drawn to Tony both physically and spiritually. Before she knew it, she was in too deep and just didn't know how to open up to him about her marriage and her daughter.

"What was I thinking?" she mumbled to herself. Ruth never really thought that keeping the truth from Tony was a betrayal, it'd just been that she wasn't ready to share. She thought that if she told Tony the truth, she would lose him. She realized she was being selfish, but she wasn't ready to let go of the one good relationship she'd ever had in her life. Ruth shook her head. "I should've told him sooner." All weekend she contemplated the circumstances and tried to get a grip on her emotions, but the tears and the overwhelming heaviness that took over her body didn't let her think straight. She wouldn't blame Tony if he just turned his back on her and their child. "Will he ever be able to forgive and trust me?"

Ruth dropped a glass in the sink, startled by her brother Isaac's sudden appearance in the kitchen. "You're awfully clumsy this morning." Isaac's blue eyes seemed to pierce her thoughts. "In fact, I've noticed you haven't been yourself lately. You're irritable, distracted, and you look awful." He looked Ruth up and down.

"I'm fine, just have a lot on my mind." Ruth continued washing the dishes.

"I bet you do. Harvey told me you've been asking him for a divorce," he said flatly.

"Yes, did he also tell you the ugly things he said to me?"

Isaac's friendship and allegiance to her husband had long been a source of pain for Ruth. While she could forgive Isaac's belief in the traditional customs, she couldn't forgive her brother for condoning Harvey's physical abuse that nearly killed her.

"Oh, come on." Isaac dismissed as he sat at the table and opened the newspaper.

"That he would never give me a divorce because that would make me happy? That I'm a deranged pig? And that I am a failure as a human being?" Ruth turned around to face him.

"Now you're being dramatic." He rolled his eyes.

"Are you telling me that you don't believe he said those things to me?" Ruth put her hands on her hips.

"No, actually, he told me what he said. And you know what I say? I say, it's time for you to be a proper wife. It's time for you to go back there and do your duty! You've been coddled here long enough. I don't understand why Papa has let it go on as long as he has."

"Coddled?" Ruth was horrified. "Harvey almost killed me and the baby. If we go back who's to say what would happen?"

Isaac slammed the paper down on the table, crossed the room, and grabbed Ruth by her arm. "He almost killed you because apparently you were not a dutiful wife."

"I wasn't *dutiful*?" Ruth countered. "I did everything I could to be a good wife. The house was immaculate, his clothes were clean and crisp, I served him hot meals at all times of the day and night. He wanted for nothing with me, and I wanted nothing more than to make him happy." Ruth shook her head vigorously. "Nothing was good enough. Oh no! There was no making Harvey happy." Ruth paused a moment and narrowed her eyes. "He was an awful husband. He forced himself on me and beat me regularly. Yet, I stayed and kept trying to make the marriage work. If that's not dutiful, then I don't know what is! I don't love or respect him. I fear him. I should *not* be expected to live like that."

Isaac leaned in close to Ruth's face and tightened his grip. "You belong to Harvey! You don't need to love him, but you must respect and obey him. I've been told you've been socializing with that grease ball, Tony Russo. You better knock that off before you bring even more shame to this family." Isaac twisted his arm and pushed Ruth onto the floor. "Now get your act together."

Isaac stormed out of the kitchen while Ruth pulled herself up and willed herself not to cry.

"Be strong." These two little words had become her mantra these past years and had become a close friend to her. She then prepared for work and spread makeup on the bruises Isaac's grip created on her arm.

Ruth took a deep breath as she clocked in at the factory. She didn't know what to expect from Tony, and she saw in his distant stare that he was still feeling troubled. Working on the assembly line was a great distraction for her, and she managed to be more productive than she anticipated. Throughout the day, both she and Tony caught each other's eyes, and his expression considerably softened each time he looked at her. At the end of her shift, he sidled up to her and tapped her shoulder.

"Hey," Tony said tenderly as he looked down at his shoes.

"Hey yourself." Ruth's voice got stuck in her throat.

"Would you like to have dinner tonight? Maybe talk about everything?" Tony looked up and met Ruth's eyes.

"I would like that very much," Ruth whispered as her body relaxed with relief.

"Good, how about Giovanni's? I have some things to take care of here that shouldn't take too long. Let's say at six?"

"Six is perfect." Ruth placed her hand on Tony's arm and said, "Thank you."

Giovanni's had come to be their special place. It's where they had their first date, and it's where they found themselves enjoying dinner most Thursday nights. Ruth was relieved that their usual corner booth was free, and that the dinner crowd was thin so they could talk with some privacy. Their usual server, Lou, set down their drinks along with a basket of bread.

Ruth touched Tony's hand. "Look, I'm sorry. I never meant to deceive you." Tears threatened her eyes as she tried to rationalize the situation. "There never seemed to be the right time to explain everything. All this time, I've been trying to get a divorce. Harvey wouldn't consent, and my parents refuse to help. They adamantly believe that marriage vows should never be broken. Not under any circumstances. Especially when children are involved."

Tony closed his eyes for a brief moment and when he opened them, they were filled with sadness. He slowly took a mouthful of whiskey and said, "Tell me about your daughter."

"Miriam? Miriam is the sweetest, most precocious four-year old you'll ever meet. She has curly brown hair just like mine and green eyes just like her father. She has a vivid imagination and loves to make up her own fairy tale stories and sing and dance. You would never know she was conceived under hateful circumstances. My parents and I make sure her life is filled with kindness."

Tony smiled. "I can see how much you love her by the way your face beams when you talk about her." He lifted his glass and took another sip of whiskey. He hesitated, "What's the situation with Harvey? It's been four years since you left, and she was born. How much is he involved in your lives?"

Ruth could feel the heat as it rose through her spine and into her face. Just the thought of Harvey Goldberg has sent her into a panic that had lasted for hours or even sometimes days. She straightened her back, let out a deep breath and told Tony about the last time she was in Harvey's presence.

"Just after Miriam was born, Harvey, his parents David and Sarah, and Rabbi Epstein came to the house in an attempt at forcing a reconciliation. After the Rabbi gave Miriam a blessing, my mother, Sarah, and I prepared lunch. Harvey just stood on the outskirts staring at Miriam. His face was stone cold. He didn't pray during the blessing. He didn't even attempt to touch her."

"Really?" Tony was surprised and sat up in his chair.

"He didn't show an ounce of love or concern for his daughter. I didn't expect to see any remorse or kindness toward me, but I thought he would have some tenderness for his child. His frigid demeanor scared me so much that I remember every detail of that day."

Tony took Ruth's hand.

"During lunch, my mother and Sarah tried to break the tension by nervously carrying on small talk about Miriam being a gift from God. Finally, Harvey's father, David, slammed his fist on the table and shouted, 'Enough!' He pointed his finger into Harvey's face and demanded, 'You must get your house in order!'"

"How did Harvey respond?"

"Harvey shouted right back and said that his house was in perfect order, and he would not be told how to behave in his home or how to treat his wife. Then his father got even angrier and reminded him that he nearly killed me and the baby. He reminded Harvey that he wasn't raised that way, that they saw to it that he had everything he needed."

"I bet he was angry," Tony said. "It sounds like he tried to be a good father to Harvey."

"You know, David was always kind to me, but Harvey never liked it when he didn't get his own way." Ruth shook her head and took a sip of wine.

"What did Harvey say to his father after all that?"

"Harvey was just as enraged as David, if not more. He started to shout back at his father and said that he didn't ask for any of those things, that he never got to be a part of the decisions made about his life, and yet he remained respectful to both of his parents. He then got heated and slammed his hand on the table like his father had and shouted that he would not be told how to run his household."

Tony let out a large sigh and shook his head. "It sounds to me like Harvey doesn't like to be controlled. I guess I can see how frustrated he was about not being able to make his own decisions about his life, but he should've controlled his anger better and not directed it toward you."

"This is how it is for some of us." Ruth shrugged. "Our fathers make most of the decisions. Sometimes sons will get to play a small part in the choices, but the daughters," Ruth looked down, "the daughters are sometimes thought of as just possessions, who don't get to have many choices."

"I knew your family was strict, but I didn't realize it was this bad."

"It really hasn't been easy for me," Ruth whispered.

"But the physical abuse? That's not expected, is it?"

"That's a good question, that I haven't quite figured out yet. I know some men in my family think it's their right to physically punish their wife if they think she is disobedient. While others only use their words as their weapons. Yet, I also know other families where the men are kind to their wife and daughters." Ruth shook her head. "I *will* say that the Rabbi wasn't in favor of Harvey's behavior and even tried talking to him that day. He told Harvey that the Bible said that marriage is a holy covenant before God. He said that Harvey sealed that covenant with his signature on the Ketubah on our wedding day, and by doing that he made a commitment to care for my physical and emotional needs. He then said Harvey had a moral obligation before God to do so. But Harvey got even angrier when the Rabbi asked if he really wanted to continue to break his promise to God. He pushed away from the table and told the Rabbi that it was his business and then he stormed out of the house."

"Oh, wow," Tony sat back in his chair. "He is something else." Tony said sourly. "So that's it? He just walked away?"

"It was decided that Miriam and I would stay with my parents until Harvey became rational. But he *never* became rational. While both his parents and my parents agreed that Miriam shouldn't be raised in a volatile environment, they held firm that divorce was not an option. Harvey sends Miriam small gifts on her birthday – on his parents' insistence, I'm sure. Arrangements were made that Harvey would send money monthly and my parents invite the Goldberg's to the house a few times a month. Their friendship hasn't changed despite the circumstances, and as a result, Miriam has a good relationship with them. I've begged my father to arrange a divorce, but when it comes down to it, he will not budge. Harvey has stripped me of my dignity, battered me physically and emotionally, and still controls my life." Ruth sat back and let out a long sigh.

"Ok, ok." Tony heard the misery in her voice and realized how tough it's been for her. "Here's what we're gonna do. We'll meet with your parents. We'll tell them that we intend to be a family together. You, Me, Miriam, and the baby. Surely once they know you're having a child they'll come around. I just don't see any other way."

"Are you sure?" Ruth momentarily allowed herself to feel hopeful.

"I admit, I was angry when I left your house on Friday. I felt deceived and confused. I did a lot of thinking over the weekend, and even talked about it with Frank and my parents."

"Your parents? What must they think of me?"

"It was my mom who helped me see the depth of your predicament. She explained how hard it had to be for you living in such a harsh situation."

"That's a great way of putting it. Do you know, my brother Isaac demanded that I return to Harvey and be a dutiful wife *just this morning*? It got ugly." The tears she tried so hard to hold back streamed down her face with speed. "I, I, just don't want to live like this anymore."

"You won't have to, Ruthie." Tony pulled her close to him and put his arms around her. She leaned into his chest and sobbed.

"You don't understand. It's not going to be easy. They'll never agree with the plan. My parents will be shamed in their community. I can't see a way out of this."

"We have to try."

"I'm afraid of what they'll do. You don't know them like I do."

"We'll find a way to make it work, I promise."

The next Thursday afternoon, Tony arrived at Ruth's house ready to talk to her parents. They quickly prepared lunch while her parents were at the park with Miriam.

"Are you ready for this?" Tony asked as he placed a platter of sandwiches on the table.

"I'm a ball of nerves," Ruth said as she stepped into Tony's open arms. His firm embrace helped to strengthen her resolve to stand up for herself and her future. "My biggest fear is if my parents don't agree."

"Your father's a doctor. Surely a man of science can see reason."

"My father is a man of the Jewish faith first and foremost. This is what drives his every decision." Ruth insisted as they heard the front door open. Her breath was taken away as she saw Miriam enter the house with her parents closely behind.

"Mommy!" Miriam squealed as she ran into Ruth's arms.

"Did you have fun at the park, honey?" She squeezed her daughter tightly and took in the scent of the fresh air infused within her hair.

"Yes. We had pink cotton candy." Miriam wiggled out of her coat and noticed Tony in the parlor.

"Hi." Miriam waved her hand at Tony, and Ruth saw by his expression that he was smitten.

"Well, hello Miriam. My name is Tony. I'm a friend of your Mommy's. It's very nice to meet you." Tony leaned over into a bow and gave Miriam an enormous smile.

"What's this?" Ruth's father, Jacob, demanded.

"Bubeleh, why don't you go on up to your room. You can have a tea party with your dolls." Ruth's mother, Esther, said as she led Miriam toward the stairs. Ruth watched as Miriam gingerly climbed the stairs toward her room. As soon as she heard Miriam close the door, she turned to face her parents.

"Momma, Papa, I would like to reintroduce you to Tony Russo. You've met once before, but I am afraid that was such a brief encounter quite a while ago." She nervously looked at Tony and said, "Tony, these are my parents Jacob and Esther Klein. I thought it would be nice for us to have lunch together today."

"It's very nice to see you again, Mr. and Mrs. Klein." Tony leaned in, hand extended, for a handshake.

"It's Dr. Klein and why don't you tell me the real purpose for this visit." Jacob snapped and ignored Tony's outstretched hand.

Ruth moved to Tony's side. "There's something especially important we want to talk to you about. Please, let's sit at the table."

"Come on, Jacob, let's hear her out." Although Esther moved toward the table, her glaring eyes were fixed on Ruth. Jacob took his usual seat at the head of the table and Esther sat at the other end.

Tony and Ruth exchanged nervous glances as they tentatively filled in the side seats across from each other.

"Ok, now that we are seated tell me what is so important." Jacob slowly turned his head to Tony and stared straight into his eyes.

With as much determination as Ruth could come up with, she said, "You know how unhappy I am being trapped in my marriage to Harvey. I am asking you again to please arrange a divorce."

Jacob snapped his head toward her and thundered, "Absolutely not! You made a commitment, and you will honor that commitment."

"But this is not a marriage. You speak of honoring commitments? Harvey made a commitment to protect and care for me. Has he honored his commitment?" Ruth reasoned.

"Oh Ruth," Esther interjected. "You cannot be a divorced mother of a young child. Think of the disgrace that will bring upon all of us. Miriam included."

"Miriam will be fine. She will have a family and parents that love and protect her."

"Parents? What do you mean parents?" Jacob demanded.

"She means, sir, that Ruth and I intend to be married once we're able to do so." Tony stated strongly.

"Married?" Jacob's anger rose with every syllable.

"You were not to see this man, and now he speaks of marriage?" Esther charged.

"I am a woman with my own mind and my own will. Yes, I disobeyed your instructions, but Tony is a good man. If only you took some time to get to know him, you will see that. I did not intend to fall in love, but I have. Tony makes me happy and will provide a safe, loving home for us."

"No! You will not marry! I forbid it! God forbids it!" Jacob nearly knocked the water pitcher off the table as he jumped to his feet.

"Would a good man come into my home talking of marriage to my daughter when she is already married?" Jacob accused as he pointed a finger at Tony. "You disrespect me, my family, and my faith!"

Tony slowly rose from his chair. Ruth saw his face had turned red. "I mean no disrespect," Tony restrained his anger as he spoke, "I love your daughter and I vow to respect and honor her and our growing family. I promise to provide for their needs and make a good life for us. A life filled with virtue and faith."

Immediately, Esther interrupted, "Growing family? What do you mean, growing family?" She looked wild-eyed between Ruth and Tony. "Ruth?"

"Yes, it's true," Ruth whispered as she placed her hands on her stomach. "Tony and I are expecting a child."

Esther's head slowly dropped into her hands and her sorrow emitted low moans while Jacob's shock took hold of his face and transformed it to a blank stare.

"Now you know why getting a divorce from Harvey is even more important than ever."

Jacob slowly shook his head and swiftly struck Ruth across the face and knocked her to the floor.

"Kurveh! You are nothing but a common whore," Jacob bellowed as Esther's moans quickly escalated to loud, screeching wails.

Tony moved in to strike Jacob, but he stopped as Ruth stood and shouted, "Six years! Six years I have endured the pain of being a dutiful daughter and wife. And for what? What did that get me? Physical and emotional abuse! No more! I *cannot* take it anymore! I will not live like this."

Jacob stood up straight and tall while he pronounced his last words to Ruth, "You have made your choices, and you are dead to me! Get out! Get out of my house and don't ever come back. You are *not* my daughter."

Dumbfounded, Ruth turned to her mother. She placed her hands on Ruth's cheeks and took in every detail of her face. After a few moments she simply said, "You must go but Miriam must stay."

Panicked, Ruth looked from her mother to her father and back. Each had turned their backs to her. "No! No! You can't take Miriam from me!" she cried. "She's my daughter. She's my baby." Ruth tried to run toward the stairs, but Jacob stepped directly in front of the stairwell blocking the way. "This can't be happening. You can't do this," she wailed. Tony grabbed her as her legs gave way and carried her out of the house as she sobbed uncontrollably.

NINE

OCTOBER, 1951
TONY

RUTH WAS LIMP in Tony's arms as he carried her to the car. She was inconsolable and sobbed throughout the entire ride to his home. He really thought they would convince her parents to arrange a divorce. Ruth tried to warn him, but he never believed they would be so cruel. The whole encounter had shaken him up almost as much as it did Ruth, and on the drive home, he thought about how lucky he was to have such a great relationship with his own parents. He admired them and their natural fortitude and concern for everyone they cared about. Sal was a hard-working man and bringing his family to America wasn't easy for him. He was lucky to have found work as a mason through people he met in the neighborhood, and he learned the trade quickly. Before retiring, he worked many long, hard days but it was his personality and ability to charm people that helped him make some great connections. Sal eventually became a supervisor and was well liked and respected by everyone he worked with. He would come home each night tired, his calloused hands often bleeding. Some nights, Tony found him sitting alone sipping a drink as he stared out the window. Tony could never quite comprehend the look in his eyes. They were filled with a mixture of remorse and sadness, and Tony couldn't figure out what it was he was looking at or looking for. Only Anna's touch could bring him back from that place he went to, and her smile softened his face filling it with tenderness and gratitude.

Anna adjusted to her new life in America the best she could and quickly bonded to her new Italian neighborhood. She always enjoyed cooking and caring for her family, but she especially came to life each Friday night when she and Sal gathered with their friends to play cards. Tony thought about how her lifestyle changed completely here and going from living in a nice house on a hillside to living in a three-bedroom apartment in a crowded city had to be difficult for her, but she never complained. She always said there were more important things in life than material objects and that family above all was most important. Tony reminded Sal and Anna of this attitude as he told them all about him and Ruth. They were both initially concerned when Tony told them about Ruth's background, her marriage, and her daughter. They felt uneasy about the challenges Tony and Ruth would face, but they quickly grew happy over the thought of a new grandchild.

By the time they made it to Bensonhurst, Ruth's uncontrollable sobs transformed into a silent stream of tears that saturated her blank stare. Tony wasn't sure if Ruth even knew where she was.

"Ok, Ruthie, it's ok," Tony soothed as he gently helped her out of the car, and into the building. When he opened the door to the apartment, Anna quickly jumped to her feet, grabbed Ruth's arm, and helped her into the kitchen.

"Odio! What happened?"

"It was awful. Ruth's parents were just awful." Tony said while he tried to wriggle Ruth's arms out of her coat.

"Get her some water." Anna guided Ruth into a chair and affectionately touched her hands to Ruth's cheeks.

"What's going on?" Sal appeared in the doorway and dropped the newspaper he was reading on the counter.

"We just came from Ruth's parents' house. We tried to talk to them about us, and it turned ugly. They threw her out and refused to let her take Miriam. I think she's in shock." Tony handed the water to Anna while he tried to make eye contact with Ruth.

"Here honey, drink this water. I just made a nice pot of soup. You need to eat." Anna wasted no time wrapping Ruth's hands around the water glass and dashed throughout the kitchen as she pulled together a quick meal.

"Water will not help. She needs something stronger. Ruth, drink this." Sal poured a large amount of wine and replaced the glass in Ruth's hands.

"Th-th-thank you." Ruth stuttered as she blankly looked at Sal and slowly sipped the wine.

"No, you need to guzzle it right down. Let the warmth take hold. It'll help." Sal looked back and forth from Ruth to Tony.

"Salvatore, don't push her. If she doesn't want to drink it, let her be."

"I'm just saying now is not the time for sipping."

"Oof, old man. It's never time for sipping as far as you're concerned. Now, make yourself useful and grab the bread out of the box. Tony, help me put these soup bowls on the table."

"Please don't fuss on my account. I, I, I'll be alright." Ruth managed to whisper.

"Fuss?" Tony chuckled nervously, "Mom is happiest when she's giving Pop and me orders while making a meal. You'll see."

Anna smirked and gave Tony a sideways glance as they served the soup.

"Here honey, eat this. It's filled with vegetables. It's good for you." Anna placed the bowl in front of Ruth and squeezed her arm as she moved around to sit in the chair next to her. "And after you eat, you will take a nice, long nap."

Ruth nodded in agreement, and they all sat in silence while they ate, awkwardly exchanging glances as they tried not to notice the tears that streamed down Ruth's face. After she managed a few sips of broth, it wasn't difficult to convince Ruth to lie down. While Anna helped her to Tony's room and got her settled, Sal took the Sambuca bottle out of the cabinet.

"I can't even imagine what she must be feeling. To be rejected by your family and your child kept from you."

"This was not at all what I thought would happen." Tony dropped his head into his hands.

"Well, what did you expect, son? She comes from a conservative Jewish family. In their community, they could be shunned. This is their way." Sal shook his head.

"I knew it would be hard, but I never wanted to bring this much pain and sorrow to her."

"Surely Ruth knew the consequences better than you did." Sal raised both eyebrows, "Don't focus on feeling guilty. That'll do no good. Focus on what you're going to do."

"I agree," Anna said as she returned to the kitchen. "As a mother myself, I feel for her. I do. But these are the circumstances and you both have to start thinking about that child she's carrying. Maybe in time, her family will come around. But you don't have a lot of time to sit back and wait. How are you going to manage?"

"After everything that happened today, I suppose I'm gonna have to quickly work things out. Frank and I have been talking about going into business together, and I'm thinking we may have to try to make that happen sooner than planned."

"What kind of business are you thinking?"

"We wanna open a restaurant similar to Giovanni's, but only a little bigger and it'll have entertainment on weekends. Nothing as big as your place was, Pop, back in Italy. Just a nice spot for the locals to come have a nice meal, dance a little, and enjoy some music." Tony noticed that his parents exchanged glances.

"That's quite a big deal to pull off. How's Frankie planning on making this happen? He spends his money before he even makes it."

"Frank has a lead on a loan. I'm now thinking maybe we'll ask to borrow more to get us started sooner."

"Frankie has a lead? What lead is this?" Sal fired.

"He has a friend that can secure us a loan."

"What friend?"

"A businessman from the neighborhood. Carmine is his name. I met him over at Caruso's."

"Carmine? Caruso's? No Tony, absolutely not. You don't want to go into business with that man. It's too dangerous. It's rumored that Carmine Esposito was connected with Lucky Luciano and is also close to Joe Bonanno, among other crime bosses. Leave it to Frankie to get himself connected to the wrong people."

"I've heard the stories about Carmine. But this could be a solid opportunity. This neighborhood needs a nice place like this. It'll be a gold mine. Within a few years, we'll have the loan paid off, and will start seeing some profits. With all I learned about business from the factory and maybe input from you, I know we can make this work.

Frank'll just get the loan for us. It'll just be a loan, nothing more. People do it all the time."

"You don't know nothing about nothing. This loan Frankie will get, it'll never be paid off. I know people like this Carmine. They never let you off the hook. You'll always owe them. If it's not money, it's favors. I will say, the idea of the place may be a good one, and you may just be successful. But this funding, this is no good," Sal shook his head adamantly.

"Listen to your father. He's right." Anna waved her hand.

"I don't have any other options right now. The factory is closing, no one is hiring, Ruth's pregnant. I have to do something," Tony said in desperation.

Sal and Anna looked at each other for quite some time and nodded slowly. Sal raised his pointer finger and said, "Give us a minute," as they walked into their bedroom.

Tony sat back and closed his eyes. The full impact and meaning of the day's events were bearing down heavy on him. The plan for the restaurant was the only solid idea he had, and if he couldn't make it work, he didn't know how to take care of Ruth and a new baby. Sal and Anna were gone for what felt like an eternity and came back to the kitchen holding hands. Anna wiped tears from her eyes and shoved the tissue in her apron pocket.

"Ok, here's what we're going to do. You and Ruth. You will stay here. It'll be tight, but we'll make it work. We'll give you the money to get this thing started with one condition. You will *never* borrow money from Carmine or any of his associates. No matter how bad things get, you do *not* go to them for money."

"I appreciate the offer, but you don't have that kind of money." Tony looked back and forth at his parents' faces as he tried to comprehend their expressions.

"I suppose it's time you knew." Anna kissed Tony on his head.

"Knew what?"

Sal cleared his throat and refilled the glasses of Sambuca.

"We moved here from Naples because it was time for us to start a new life. You remember Frank's father, Bruno, and I owned a beautiful dinner club where the most powerful, wealthy men would wine and dine their wives and girlfriends?"

"Yeah, of course."

"We offered only the best in booze and entertainment, but above all we provided discretion." Sal pointed his finger to make his point. "But Bruno and me, we didn't have the money to open such a place. So, we took a loan from the only person we knew who could give us the money, a man by the name of Marco DeLorenzo. Now, Marco was very influential within the community and would look out for the students at St. Bridget's, the Catholic School he helped to build. We came to know Marco when we were students and would earn some spending money by doing odd jobs for him. It was Marco who offered to lend us the money for the club, and we thought it was a good idea." Sal shrugged. "The deal was the club was ours to run so long as we made our payments on time and looked the other way while business meetings were held in the private rooms every once in a while. Everyone was happy and it paid off. We were making a decent living, and no one was getting hurt."

"That's my point, I just know Frank and I could do the same."

Sal shook his head. "Things were good for quite some time. Then one night I walked in on Marco having a heated discussion with Bruno. Marco stormed out just after he looked me dead in the eyes and snarled, *'this ain't over.'* Bruno rolled his eyes and said it was just a misunderstanding that he would clear up. I never gave it a second thought and things went on as usual for a few months." Sal paused. "One day I came into the club to find Bruno laying on the floor of the office. He'd been badly beaten. He insisted that I not call the authorities or get him medical help. I finally got out of him that the misunderstanding he had with Marco months before was because he hadn't been delivering our full payment each month. Turned out, we owed Marco almost a half a year's worth of payments in addition to our regular monthly payments." Sal sipped the Sambuca. "Bruno realized there was no way he could make up the difference, so he agreed to work for Marco on the side until Marco felt the debt was paid in full."

"Hmph," Anna shook her head.

Sal looked at Anna, touched her hand and continued, "I was furious! Every month I gave Bruno the exact amount of cash to make the payment and he was to deliver the money to Marco. I demanded to know what he did with the money he'd been taking. Bruno finally confessed that he was involved with a young woman, Theresa, outside of his marriage to Maria. Theresa had become pregnant, and he was now trying to support two households. He had skimmed some of the money from each payment to cover the expenses of the second household."

"Oh my God, Uncle Bruno?"

Sal nodded and sighed. "The beating was a warning from Marco to keep Bruno in line and to make sure our monthly payments would arrive in full and on time. I then decided to meet with Marco, myself, and explained that I would personally take over making the payments and he had my word we wouldn't come up short again. He understood that I didn't know what was happening, but business was business, so he doubled our monthly payments."

Tony's eyes grew wide. "Double the payments? How'd you make that work?"

"While this was a hardship for our family, we cut back and made it work. We didn't have a choice. Bruno on the other hand, he was sinking and was having trouble providing for Maria and Frankie, let alone Theresa and their baby daughter. To make the extra money, Bruno started getting involved in some illegal things with a few of Marco's associates – without Marco's knowledge or permission, of course. This went on for close to another year, but as time went on Bruno was getting in deeper with Marco, while he was also trying to manage his own side hustles. He was spending a lot of time taking care of Marco's dirty work to pay off his debt, and when he wasn't doing that, he was sneaking around trying to make his own extra money. Bruno was my dear friend so I would pick up the slack at the club and make excuses when Marco would come around asking for him."

Tony could feel his father's pain as he looked into his eyes. "I had no idea."

Sal dropped his head and continued. "We should've known this couldn't go on forever. Marco was a shrewd and ruthless man. He started to spend more time at the club, having his business meetings there almost nightly. It didn't take him long to notice Bruno's absence and he wasn't buying the excuses I was making. We didn't know it, but Marco had one of his associates follow Bruno to see what he was up to. Bruno had gotten sloppy in covering his tracks and Marco started to suspect that I might somehow be involved in Bruno's extra business deals. I could sense tension in Marco's scrutiny and also in my interaction with his associates."

Sal put his head in his hands as Anna placed her arm around his shoulder. "Then one morning, Maria came to the house, worried that Bruno went missing. I spent the entire day looking for him and asked everyone who came into the club that night about him. No one knew anything; even Theresa hadn't seen him for days." Sal's voice broke. "That's when I knew Bruno was never coming back." His voice lowered to a whisper. "At the end of the night when the club was empty, Marco came in with two of his more robust associates. He said he knew all about Bruno's side work and had to take matters into his own hands."

Sal looked at Tony, his own eyes turned glassy.

"He warned me that it would be a shame if the same thing had to happen to me if he found out I was somehow involved."

Tony stared at his father speechless as Sal shook his head.

"Right there and then I knew what had to be done. Your mother and me agreed that we all needed to leave Naples as soon as possible, Maria and Frankie included. I would never be out from under Marco and knew that the debt would never be repaid. I booked passage for us to come to America because I had heard that New York would be a good place to start over. We had some money saved, but I was afraid that it wouldn't be enough for us. So, I went into the club like usual for the next two nights, but instead of making the cash deposits in the bank, I took the money and all of the cash Marco kept in the safe as an extra security measure. I reasoned that Bruno and I more than paid off our debt to Marco and this money would be like cashing in an insurance policy on Bruno's life." Sal looked at Anna and she nodded. "I gave Theresa some money to help her and the baby then packed up the rest along with our belongings and we sailed to New York."

Tony took a sip of Sambuca and shook his head. "I have so many questions, I don't know where to begin. Does Louisa or Frank know any of this?" Tony looked back and forth between his parents.

"Louisa's put pieces of the story together." Anna waved her hand through the air. "She doesn't know about the money, though. That

I assure you. If she did, she would've demanded it long ago. No, she and Bob, they're doing alright. His family set him up with that deli and they have a steady income. We don't worry so much about her."

"As for Frankie," Sal added. "Maria made us promise on her death bed that we would never tell him the truth about his father. He's been told Bruno was at the wrong place at the wrong time and got shot by a stray bullet in a gambling hall. He doesn't need to know anything else." Sal looked Tony in the eye and pointed firmly.

"Tony. You ... you deserve a second chance for a happy family." Anna wrapped her hands in his. "We loved Carmella just as much as you did, and still don't understand why she was taken from us so young. But God has blessed you a second time with Ruth." Her eyes filled with tears as she quickly shook her head, jumped up from the table, and moved swiftly toward the sink.

Sal interjected, "Your mother and me, we agreed that we would never use this money we took unless we absolutely had to. Sure, we dipped into it every now and again to help when things got tight for any of us and then of course, for Maria's funeral, but for the most part there should be enough for you boys to start your business. Now you know I love Frankie like a son. But he has grown up to be just like his father, God rest his soul. Bruno was a good man and a good friend. But he had an eye for the ladies, and truth be told, he got a thrill from his connection to Marco and the criminal life. I hear around that Frankie has started in his father's footsteps. And this I don't like," Sal shook his finger and tapped it on the table.

"I get it. I'll keep an eye out for Frank and keep him in line. But are you absolutely sure you wanna do this?" Tony looked deep into Sal's eyes, willing him to say yes.

"Hey, it's an investment. Who else will take care of your mother and me in our old age?" He winked and smiled.

"Then it'll be a family business. You, me, and Frank. I really think we can make this work." Tony's heart felt light and filled with hope.

"You know, I wanted nothing to do with the restaurant business when I came here. I needed a fresh start and working as a mason helped. Like many other masons around me, my work took on meaning. I struggled each day to let go of my anger and guilt for not helping Bruno more, and each brick I laid was in memory of him." Sal waved his arms around. "Around New York there are many monuments built by men brick by brick as a labor of love and healing. It's time I let go of my past. And now … now, we build your future." Sal lifted his glass and swallowed the last bit of Sambuca.

"A family business. This is the perfect way to honor Bruno and Maria. We'll be helping the boys to get started the right way." Anna quickly worked her way throughout the kitchen as she wiped down all of the counters.

"Uh, Mom. Frank and me … we aren't boys anymore. We're grown men if you haven't noticed." Tony chuckled, he felt relieved that maybe everything would work out.

"I am well aware." Anna stopped cleaning and put her hands on her hips. "Let me ask you. How much does Ruth know about your life with Carmella?"

Tony sighed. "She knows I was married before and my wife died from cancer."

"Is that it?" She tilted her head to the side.

"That's it."

"It's time you tell her everything. No more secrets."

TEN

OCTOBER, 1951
RUTH

RUTH OPENED HER eyes after waking from a fitful nap. The heaviness of the day's events overwhelmed her, and she curled into a fetal position as she relived the nightmare. She knew her parents' reaction would be severe, but all of her strength and confidence could not shield her from the depths of cruelty that was forced upon her. Going in, she was ready for an argument. She was even prepared for her parents to turn their backs on her, but the one thing she wasn't ready for was losing Miriam.

"How?" Ruth whispered to herself, "How can they be so heartless? My sweet, precious girl. How can I live a life without her? How could I give birth and raise another child without his or her sister? How can I ever feel whole without my daughter?" Ruth shook her head and wiped her eyes as she turned onto her back. She pondered the fact that what was done can't be undone. There's no going back now, and quite frankly going back wouldn't make a difference. She knew that being pregnant with a child from a man who was not her husband will never allow her to go back to the life she once had.

In Tony's bed, she felt safe. The dark navy walls embraced her, filling her with a sense of protection. She glanced at the half dozen or so pictures of his family neatly arranged on the dresser, and she realized just how much family meant to him. Could this neat and tidy room be trying to tell her that everything was going to be alright? She slowly got out of the bed and glanced in the mirror. She was taken back by her reflection. Who was that woman staring back at her? The deep dark rings that circled her red puffy eyes made her look almost fifty years older. She tried her best to fix her disheveled hair and then made her way toward the kitchen where she heard Tony and his parents talking.

"Well, look who's up." Anna smiled. "Did you get any rest?"

"Not too much, I'm afraid." Ruth smiled half-heartedly.

"Sit down. Are you hungry?"

"No, I'm not very hungry." She took a seat between Tony and Sal.

"How are you feeling, Ruthie?"

"To be honest, I'm feeling empty and scared."

"Oh, I'm sure. But don't worry. We have a plan." Tony couldn't contain his excitement and spoke so quickly Ruth had trouble following. "Mom and Pop are gonna give me and Frank some money they had socked away. We're gonna open up that restaurant we talked about. We can stay here with them until we can afford a place of our own. What do you think?"

Ruth squeezed her eyes shut and tried to comprehend everything Tony threw at her. "The restaurant? Stay here?"

Anna set a cup of coffee in front on Ruth and put her arm on Sal's shoulder. "What Tony is trying to say is that Sal and I have some savings we would like to use to help with the startup of your restaurant. Until you can get your own place, we would be happy if you would stay here with us."

"Oh. Wow." Ruth looked at Anna and Sal in disbelief. "It really does sound like you have a plan. You are both so kind, but we can't do that. You should hold onto your savings for a rainy day."

"This is the rainy day we've been saving it for, and if we can't invest it in our family then it's worthless." Sal winked at Ruth.

"But what will people say about you having your son's married girlfriend, who happens to be pregnant with his child, living here?"

"You know, I will admit that Sal and I were shocked and had our concerns when Tony told us you were pregnant. But we did a lot of thinking, and we came to the conclusion that this is our grandchild you're carrying, and we want nothing more than to help give this child a safe, loving home. Both you and the baby belong with people who care about you, not at some awful women's home for unwed mothers. Now let's be honest, it's not going to be easy, and people will judge. But you know what ... let them talk." Anna huffed. "We take care of our family. Nothing anyone says can change that."

"Besides, we know the people in this neighborhood. Saturday nights some of these guys are out gambling and doing God knows what with God knows who and showing up at church with their wives on their arms the next morning," Sal chimed in.

"Like it or not, you're now a part of our family. We'll do what we can for you." Anna walked over and pulled Ruth out of the chair and embraced her, wrapped her thick arms around Ruth's ribs, and kissed her forehead.

"I can't thank you enough. You're being so good to me, and please believe that the last thing I want is to humiliate your family."

"Don't give it another thought, honey." Anna pulled back from the embrace and held Ruth at arm's length. "We Russos are tough. Who knows, maybe someday the world will be more objective, but in the meantime, we won't pay gossip any mind."

"Here, here." Sal raised his glass.

Anna continued, "You listen to me now. I know things are tough with your parents and your little girl. This may be the hardest thing you'll ever have to go through. But if there's one thing I've learned, it's that things change over time. That's not to say people will change. No. I haven't yet met a person who has changed a lot through the years. But circumstances ... they change. Right now, you need to make the best of the situation for the baby. Your health and well-being are important at this point. Don't give up hope on your daughter. We'll put our heads together and maybe figure out a way you can be a part of her life. Just give it time."

Ruth nodded in agreement and let out a long deep sigh. She knew Anna was right. She now had another child to think about, and she made a vow to herself that when she was able to think clearly, she'd find a way to get Miriam back.

"Ok, that's settled. This has been an emotional day. Over the next few days, we'll switch rooms and Sunday we'll have our first family dinner with Ruth."

"Switch rooms, are you crazy?" Sal snapped his head toward Anna.

"No, Mom, that's not necessary." Tony added.

"Tony and Ruth should have the bigger room for the baby. We can't fit a crib in Tony's room, but we can in ours. I want to give Ruth some time to get settled and make it her own."

"That is so very kind," Ruth said as she the wiped tears from her eyes.

"Thanks, Mom." Tony kissed Anna's cheek and took Ruth's

hand. "Now I think it's time for Ruth and I to turn in. It's been a long day and we have a lot to talk about."

Anna locked her eyes with Tony's and nodded.

"Ok, Anna looks like you win but you're still making the lasagne for dinner Sunday, right?"

"In almost fifty years of marriage, have I ever not made a lasagne for Sunday dinner?"

"You really do look good in my shirt." Tony smiled brightly as he watched Ruth get settled into bed.

"I look awful, I'm sure. I can't believe everything that has happened today. I need to call Joan to fill her in. Hopefully, she'll be able to get some of my clothes and things for me."

"Listen Babe," Tony said seriously. "I know how upset you are about Miriam. I'm sorry it all blew up the way it did. I'll do everything I can to help you get her back."

"We just have to. She's my world." Ruth started to cry again.

"Ok, Ok. Remember, though, your world has gotten bigger. You have me, Mom and Pop, and our little bambino."

"Yes, I know." Ruth faked a smile for Tony's sake. She wondered if he could really understand how deeply she hurt. "So, tell me about this money from your father." Ruth tried to change the subject.

"Well, I told Pop about our plans of going into business with Frank, turned out he's had some money stashed away that he brought over from Italy. He thinks the restaurant could be a good idea and he wants to help get us get started. This could be the key to our future. This could set us up for life." Tony beamed.

"I just worry about using your parents' life savings."

"They say they've had the money for years and wanna do something good with it. Right now, the way I see it, it's the only chance we got. Pop says it's a bad idea to borrow outside of the family, he wants to protect Frank and me from shady business deals. It'll be a family business, and I think it'll do Pop some good to be involved."

"You know your parents better than I do. I have to say, I feel a little overwhelmed with their kindness and generosity."

"That's just how they are. They've always been giving people. I think they got that way from everything they went through leaving Italy and coming here. The neighborhood helped them from the beginning and now they're always helping other people. Sure, they fuss and argue, especially with each other, but they always put family first. You'll get used to them in no time." Tony got very quiet and stared into the distance.

"Are you ok?"

"Yeah, I am. I need to talk to you about my family, though, and it's difficult."

"What is it?"

"I've told you about Louisa's kids, right?"

"A little. You don't talk much about Louisa. She has two girls and a boy?"

"Well, yeah, but one of those girls, the oldest, Rena," he hesitated, "Rena is actually my daughter."

"What? I, I don't understand."

"When, my wife Carmella got sick it was a terrible time for us all. We didn't know she was sick. Mom was the first to notice she wasn't eating as much as she usually did. Carmella just said she was tired and didn't have a huge appetite. Then she started getting sick after eating and complaining of pain in her stomach. It took a while for the doctors to figure out it was cancer but when they did, they started her on radiotherapy. Rena was a toddler at the time, and it was impossible for Carmella to look after her anymore. So, we agreed that Louisa and Bob would take Rena in temporarily.

"That must've been so hard for you." Ruth shook her head.

"Mom was spending her days taking care of Carmella while I worked to pay the bills. As time went on it was clear Carmella was only getting worse and the doctors told us to stop the treatments and make her comfortable. Carmella died within four months." Tony looked down at his hands. "By then, I realized I needed to give up our apartment and move in with my parents to finish paying off the medical bills and the funeral. Truth be told, I was a wreck. I never felt sadness so deep that it was an effort to move and breathe." He looked back up at Ruth. "Looking back now, I think maybe Louisa took advantage of the situation. She convinced me I was not in a position to raise a daughter by myself and that she and Bob could provide a stable home for her. So, I agreed." Tony let out a deep sigh and took Ruth's hand in his and squeezed.

"Does Rena know you're her father?"

"No. She doesn't remember anything from that time, and Louisa and Bob are the only parents she's ever really known. They are Mom and Dad to her, and it hurts me every time I hear it. But, now that she's nine, I think it would be too hard on her to tell her the full story."

Ruth slowly shook her head. "Why wouldn't Louisa tell her the truth?"

"I hate to say this, but Louisa can be selfish. She and Bob had been married at least five years when Carmella got sick, and they didn't have any kids yet. Louisa was starting to think she would never have kids, so she grabbed at the chance to raise Rena. All Louisa ever wanted was to be a mother."

"But that poor child. Does she know about Carmella?"

"She knows Carmella was my wife and she went to be with the angels." Ruth could see Tony's eyes were glassy. "But she doesn't know Carmella's her mother. I try to talk about her around Rena, so she knows that Carmella was a kind, gentle, loving person. I sometimes get so angry. Rena will never know her true mother, and I failed her as a father." He leaned in closer to Ruth. "But, Ruthie, you've given me a second chance to be a father. I'm telling you right now, I'm not gonna mess this up. I'm gonna do whatever it takes to take care of us."

Ruth wrapped her arms around him. "Right now, I feel like I have also failed Miriam."

"We'll make this right. Our family will have a future filled with love. Love and happiness! That I can promise you." He gave her a broad smile and his eyes twinkled with hope.

Ruth couldn't help but smile and it temporarily felt good. Maybe she should've been more upset with Tony for not telling her the truth about Rena from the start, but then again, she wasn't forthcoming about Miriam either. Right now, it felt like her brain was hurting from the recent turmoil, and what she needed more than anything was to find some peace. She and Tony spent the next hour in each other's arms talking about how to move forward and discussed ideas for the new restaurant. Tony fell asleep easily, but Ruth was too anxious to sleep. She wanted so badly to be excited about the restaurant and a new life with Tony, but her emotions were not allowing the happiness to break through her sorrow and fear. When she married Harvey, she was a young girl in love with the idea of being a wife and mother. That dream was quickly crushed and the one good thing that came of her marriage was stripped away from her. She stared at the ceiling while her mind played a maddening game of ping pong going back and forth between feeling hopeful and the reality of how hard life was going to be without Miriam. As if he could read her mind in his sleep, Tony rolled over and pulled her close to him nuzzling his head in her neck. He filled her with assurance and faith.

ELEVEN

OCTOBER, 1951
TONY

SUNDAY HAD ALWAYS been Tony's favorite day ... the day dedicated to family and food. No matter what was going on during the week, they all gathered at Sal and Anna's for a big Italian feast. Every week Anna made her standard minestrone or pastina chicken soup, antipasto, lasagne, meatballs, sausage, and braciola. Sometimes she made either eggplant, chicken or veal parmigiana, and on extra special occasions some pasta with mussels and clams would be added to the mix. Both Anna and Sal have always opened their home to friends in the neighborhood to join them, especially those who were struggling. Every week the house was filled with wine, food, laughter, and the occasional heated discussion. When Tony was a kid, he used to think people were fighting, and he never could understand when the grown-ups insisted they weren't fighting, they were just talking. Although he tried to prepare Ruth on what to expect for her first Sunday family dinner, it was Anna who made her feel most comfortable through her chatter and Italian cooking lessons. Anna had a keen intuition, and she pulled Ruth into the kitchen and put an apron on her. She knew it was just the thing to keep Ruth's mind occupied and make her feel at home. Tony smiled as the two of them fluttered around the kitchen attempting to work around Sal who was constantly in the way as he sampled their food. Tony realized that since Carmella had passed, he's felt a bit disconnected during the Sunday gatherings. As if he was always on the outside looking in. Today he felt more complete than he had in years.

Anna could only take so much of Sal's interference before she demanded, "I want everyone out of the kitchen. Ruth and I don't need you in the way while we prepare our meal. Now, take your wine and get." She swiped at Sal with a dishtowel and raised her eyebrows at Tony and Frank who had just joined them.

"Ok, ok, we have business to discuss anyway," Sal conceded as he grabbed a few olives on his way out of the kitchen.

"Frankie, I'm glad you came over early. There's a few things we should discuss before Louisa gets here." Sal filled wine glasses as Frank and Tony settled on the sofa. "Tony filled me in on your plans for a restaurant. I think you boys have a good idea but your plan for borrowing money is no good."

"Uncle Sal, hear me out." Frank started.

Sal put his hand up. "No, I know what you're going to say. Your dad and me, we were in your position years ago. We borrowed money from the wrong people to open up the club and it didn't end well. We've tried to protect you kids from the harsh reality of the past, but I'll not let you both make the same mistakes your father and I did. I'm offering you an opportunity that we didn't have. I have some money saved from long ago, and in honor of your father's memory, I'm offering it to you both to get started the right way. I want you to take this money and make me proud. Make your parents proud, Frankie. May God rest their souls." Sal made the sign of the cross, kissed his fingers and gestured upward.

"I don't know what to say. Tony did you know about this?"

"Pop and I discussed it last night. What do you say? Let's make this a family business."

Frank leaned forward and said, "Well, alright! Uncle Sal you've always been like a second father to me. Your support and guidance through the years has always meant a lot. I won't let you down."

"I've always tried to look out for you. I know you've gotten yourself into a few tight spots, but it's gotta be different now. If we do this, we do this right."

"You've got my word." Frank put his right hand on his heart. "Thank you for this."

"That's settled, then." Sal stood and raised his glass, "To our family, alla nostra famiglia!"

"To our family!" Frank and Tony stood and raised their glasses with pride.

"Now we talk business." Sal sat on the edge of his chair. "Your sister, Louisa, she don't need to know about this money. We tell her you both saved some of it, some you got, Frankie, when your mother died, and the rest you borrowed from a business associate of mine from the masonry business. Nothing good will come from her knowing I had this money. I always spoiled her while she was growing up and she did well when she married and never needed help. She won't understand that I'm giving it to you, and she will expect it for herself. Your mother and I agree that a small lie would do well to keep the peace."

"Understood." Frank and Tony said in unison. "So, what's next?" Tony added.

"Next, we start planning. The better you plan, the more efficient the process will be. I'll make a list of expenses, supplies, furniture, and what not that will be necessary. You two need to start looking for locations and find out what's required to obtain licenses and permits. We have to come up with a menu, price list, workers, and entertainment. Now I want you both to be realistic. We'll need to establish ourselves and build a good reputation before we start turning a profit. It's better to expand as we go than invest too much up front and then have to cut back."

Sal stopped talking as the door opened. Louisa's kids ran into the apartment and Louisa and Bob trailed behind carrying bags of food from the deli.

"Pop-Pop!" Sophia squealed as she ran to Sal and hopped in his lap.

"How's my sweet girl today?" Sal's face lit up immediately.

"Fine."

"Did you say hello to Uncle Tony and Uncle Frank?"

Sophia jumped down quickly and hugged both Frank and Tony before she ran into the kitchen.

"Why don't we all see what we come up with and have lunch here Wednesday to continue our planning." Sal whispered as Louisa entered the room.

"What's going on in here? You all look so serious." Louisa put her hands on her hips. "Rena, Bobby come in here and say hello." She bellowed before anyone could reply.

Bobby skipped into the room trailing crumbs behind him from the half-eaten cookie in his hands. "Hi everybody." He smiled and crumbs fell out of his mouth as he leaned against Sal's chair.

"Hey Bobby, I sure would love a cookie. Why don't you go see if Nonna will give you another one? Just don't tell her it's for me." Sal winked as Bobby nodded his head and walked back to the kitchen.

"Nonna," he yelled, "Pop-Pop wants a cookie, I mean can I have another cookie?"

They all had a hearty laugh, but Tony's smile faded as he saw Rena hesitantly enter the living room.

"Hey Rena, how's things?" Tony said pleasantly, hoping to get her to smile.

"Fine," she said flatly.

"Just fine?" Tony asked as he looked back and forth between her and Louisa.

"Oh, you know nine-year old's, Tony. They're always so moody." Louisa waved her hand brushing him off.

"Come on over here and tell me all about your Halloween outfit," Tony said, trying to lighten her mood. After getting an approval nod from Louisa, Rena sat between Frank and Tony. They both got her to laugh as she talked about the princess costume Louisa made for her.

"Come on everyone, dinner is ready," Anna said as she and Ruth set the last few serving platters on the table.

"Everything looks even better than ever." Tony said as he held out a chair for Ruth.

"Your mother taught me her special lasagne recipe." Ruth beamed with pride.

"Lots of love went into this meal. This week a little more so than others. We have a lot to be grateful for." Anna smiled and nodded at Ruth.

"Well, I'm no more grateful today than I was three years ago." Louisa gave Ruth a quick but perceptible glare then smiled widely and said, "I am eternally grateful for all of us." She looked around the table at everyone else and made sure she locked eyes with both Anna and Sal.

Louisa's sly attitude was not lost on Tony, and he spent the rest of the day doing all he could to make Ruth feel comfortable. Each time he locked eyes with her his heart fluttered, but he was especially moved when he saw Ruth and Rena huddled together on the sofa talking about school and giggling over girl things.

"Don't worry, son, everything's going to be just fine." Anna said as she touched his arm and looked over at Ruth and Rena. "Ruth is a good fit to our family. You both have some challenges ahead of you, I'm not going to deny that, but it will all turn out for the good."

"I hope you're right."

"I am. You'll see." Anna smiled and called out to everyone that dessert and coffee were on the table.

After the dinner dishes were done and everyone went home, Ruth and Tony settled down for the night.

"So, I guess you survived your first Russo family dinner."

"I did. I enjoyed it very much. The whole day felt so much more light-hearted than family meals with my parents. But Louisa seemed uptight around me."

"Louisa is always uptight. Don't pay her any mind. She'll come around and warm up to you. Just give her time. She's always had her own ideas and opinions on how things should be, and she's very suspicious of new people. But I know once she gets to know you and see you for who you are, she'll relax and love you."

"I don't know if she will ever love me. I will settle for her liking me. Or pretending to, at least. The kids are adorable. I could tell that Sophia has your Dad wrapped around her finger and Bobby is so smart. I didn't think Rena would be as reserved as she was though."

"Yeah, Rena must be going through a phase. She's not usually as quiet as she was today, but I did see you two deep in conversation."

"I remember being her age. It's not easy for girls. I was happy that she warmed up to me."

"Were you able to talk to Joan today?"

"Yes, I spoke with her early this morning. She's going to get some of my things, and I'm going to meet her tomorrow at the diner." Ruth frowned as she looked at herself in the mirror. "I look like I've aged twenty years overnight."

"You look like perfection to me." Tony smiled, wrapped his arms around her waist and pulled her close. She chuckled and pressed her lips softly into his, groaning slightly as he pressed his body closer. Tony led her to the bed and slowly removed her clothing, kissing her gently as each part of her flesh was uncovered. She pulled him into her firmly and they made love more tenderly than they ever had in the past, expressing not only their desire but strengthening their commitment to each other.

TWELVE

OCTOBER, 1951

RUTH

AS RUTH WAITED for Joan, she found herself daring to daydream about a happy future. Her little one fluttered around in her stomach and reminded her that life was full of unexpected surprises. She began to think that maybe, just maybe, everything was going to be alright. Joan breezed into the diner, and Ruth's heart sank when she noticed Joan was empty handed.

"Ruth, oh Ruth, how are you doing?" She placed her purse on the table and started to remove her white gloves one finger at time.

"I, well, I'm ok. Where's my things? Did my parents give you trouble?"

"No, I know your parents well enough to know that they wouldn't give me a stitch of your clothing. Ethan is meeting us here and he's bringing them. Now tell me the truth, how are you doing really?"

"Oh, thank God." Tears welled up in Ruth's eyes. "I'm just a roller coaster of emotions. I'm sick over Miriam, yet Tony and his family have opened their hearts and home to me. I feel like I belong and are part of the family already." As Ruth grabbed a napkin to wipe her eyes, she saw Ethan struggling with the door. All at once Ruth saw why he was struggling so hard.

"Mommy!" Miriam squealed and ran over to the table with her arms outstretched.

Ruth grabbed Miriam and let out a large gasp. She was not expecting to see Miriam and the light in her little eyes overwhelmed her. All she could do was hug and kiss her daughter.

"Mommy, I've missed you. When are you coming home? Grandma said you have to go live somewhere else. Can I come live with you?"

Ruth looked straight at Ethan, and he shook his head as he looked down.

"Ruth, I thought you should see Miriam to talk to her. She's struggling and doesn't understand. I told Mom that I was taking her out for some ice cream to cheer her up. She doesn't know we're here."

Ruth nodded her head in understanding. "Oh baby, I've missed you so much. Now sit down here like a big girl. Mommy needs to explain some things to you."

"Ok." Miriam climbed up in the chair and folded her hands together in her lap as she looked up with her big green eyes.

"Miriam, I need you to know that I love you with all my heart, and I am very sad that I cannot be with you right now. I am so sorry that this is the way it has to be for now. Always remember that I love you and I'm thinking of you all day and all night."

"But why? Why can't we be together? I'll be a good girl, I promise. Just please come back." Miriam said through her tears.

It was all Ruth could do to fight back the flood of tears. "No, honey, don't ever think you are not a good girl. You are the best girl in the whole wide world. This is not your fault. Sometimes Mommies and Daddies need to live apart from their children for a little while, but I promise you I will do everything I can to change this. I know you don't understand it all right now, but some day you will. I need you to be brave and be good for Grandma and Grandpa."

"Ok, I will." She sniffled.

"Every night when it's not raining, I want you to look up at the sky and find the brightest star. Every time you see it, know I am looking at it too and I'm sending you all of my love. Ok? Is that a deal?"

"Deal." She smiled brightly and nodded her head.

Ruth pulled her close and hugged her tightly, not wanting to let her go. "Now maybe Aunt Joan can get you a chocolate milk up at the counter while Uncle Ethan and I have some grownup talk."

"Come on Miriam, I see a great spot for us right on the end. And look they have crayons." Joan gave Ruth a tight smile as she led Miriam away.

"Ethan." Ruth stood and hugged him extra tightly. "How can I ever thank you for bringing her today?"

"I will say it wasn't easy sneaking your things out of the house while convincing Mom that she would be safe with me. We really can't stay long, but I thought it would be good for both of you to talk. What a mess, Ruth, getting pregnant? By an Italian, *Catholic*, no less? What were you thinking? What are you going to do?"

Ruth said slowly and firmly, "I fell in love with a kind, caring man. I will admit we should've been more careful about getting pregnant. But this baby and this relationship is a blessing. For the first time, I am loved and accepted for who I am and not who I'm supposed to be. Tony and I will make this work. If I have to sacrifice my family, who by the way it's clear do not love me unconditionally, then so be it. But I am telling you right now, I will find a way to be in Miriam's life. That I will not sacrifice."

Ethan's eyes softened. "I guess I understand. I never did like or trust Harvey. I could never treat Rachel the way he treated you."

"But that's the difference, you have a choice to be with Rachel. I was never given a choice. Maybe if I was allowed to form my own relationships, I might've found a nice Jewish man and fallen in love. We'll never know. I do know that I've found a place with Tony and his family and when I'm not thinking of Miriam, I'm happy."

"My heart really does break for that little girl." Ethan shook his head.

"Please promise me you'll look out for her, protect her. Remind her how much I love her." Ruth looked pleadingly into Ethan's eyes.

"Without a doubt, I promise you. Of course, you know I've been forbidden to see or contact you. Give me some time, I will find a way to keep you two connected."

"Thank you, thank you for everything. I love you little brother." She reached over and placed her hand on his cheek.

"I love you too." He took her hand and kissed it softly. "I really need to get Miriam back. If you need me, just call Joan and she will get a message to me." Ethan gave a nod to Joan who led Miriam back to the table.

"Look, Mommy, I drew you a picture. It's a cow."

Ruth's face lit up as she took the paper placemat with an abstract scribble from Miriam, "Well, thank you, it's beautiful."

As she watched Ethan and Miriam walk away from the coffee shop, she clutched the drawing against her heart and whispered, "I will cherish it always. Bye-Bye for now, baby girl, I love you."

THIRTEEN

DECEMBER, 1951
TONY

TONY, SAL, AND Frank worked long hours bringing their dream of the restaurant to life. When it came to starting the business, they all shared a passion that brought them closer together. Even Anna and Ruth spent hours excitedly sharing decorating ideas as they compared paint colors, wallpaper patterns, linens, and fixtures. Tony had given his resignation to the shoe factory the week after Sal and Anna offered to help with the restaurant. Much to his surprise, the owner of the factory personally asked Tony to stay on through the end of the year to help with the shutdown. When he tried to refuse, Mr. Hoffman said he would double his wages for his efforts. Although he worked all day at the factory and devoted his nights and weekends to the restaurant, Tony had never felt more alive and energized. He even noticed a more enthusiastic spring in Sal's step as well. His father's passion for the restaurant business had been reignited, and Tony was amazed to see not only Sal's sharp business skills but also the finesse in which Sal negotiated contracts and deals with vendors.

It was two months since the confrontation with Ruth's parents, and Tony was hoping that her first Christmas would be a good one. He had been painfully aware of how hard she was trying to cope with being shut out of Miriam's life, especially now that the holiday season was here. He had stopped encouraging her to reach out to her parents. Every time she did, the result was relentless heartbreak that would set her back for days into a deep depression. During those dark times they all worried about her, but Anna especially empathized with her situation. Their quiet conversations sitting at the kitchen table well into the night was the one thing that helped Ruth the most. They all worried about how she would feel during their annual tradition of picking out the Christmas tree, but she was eager to pick out the nicest one.

"Are you ladies ready to decorate this tree or what?" Sal called into the kitchen as he added water to the tree stand and Tony turned on the radio. Sal smiled as Perry Como's, "It's Beginning to Look A Lot Like Christmas" filled the living room. "Now this here is a good tune."

"We're all ready, here we go." Anna sang as she and Ruth carried trays of hot chocolate and cookies into the living room.

"Oh, that really is a lovely tree. Ruth, you picked a good one. Did you boys test the lights before putting them on? You know you need to test them before you put them on."

Tony chuckled. "Yes. They're all working."

"Jeez, you'd think we've never done this before."

"Hmph." Anna rolled her eyes and turned to Ruth. "Last year when Sal made a big show of turning on the lights, half the tree didn't light. The two of them spent hours digging through the tree replacing every bulb to find the ones that were burnt out, I tell you!"

"Oh no you didn't?" Ruth tried to stifle her laugh by taking a bite of a cookie, but Tony saw the glint in her eyes.

"I swear I checked them last year." Sal waved off Anna as he opened a box of ornaments.

Tony caught Ruth's eye, shook his head and whispered, "He didn't check them." He took a red ball from the box and gave it to Ruth, "Ruthie, why don't you go ahead and put the first one on this year."

"Are you sure? Anna, maybe you should do the honors."

"I'll tell you what, let's start a new tradition, why don't we all grab one and put them on at the same time. It'll signify our bond as a family."

"Now that's a good idea." Sal kissed Anna's cheek and they all spent the next few hours decorating, laughing, and singing.

"Well, that was fun," Ruth said as she slumped into the sofa.

"It was fun," Anna agreed. "I realize today is December 23rd and the first day of Hannukah. Is there anything you would like to do as a family to celebrate or commemorate your holiday? Maybe we can get a Menorah?"

Tony shot a warning look at Anna. "Mom!"

"I'm sorry Ruth, I don't want to upset you."

Ruth put her hand on Anna's. "I'm ok and appreciate your offer. I just can't light a Menorah, sing the songs, and follow the traditions without Miriam. It just wouldn't be right for me."

"I understand, honey," Anna said.

Ruth sat up. "Although, I know you have your Christmas Eve dinner all planned out, but do you think it would be alright if I made a batch of latkes? We could have them as an appetizer if you'd like."

"Of course, dear." Anna brightened. "What's a latke?"

Ruth chuckled. "It's a potato pancake that's made in oil. This year, I'd really like to make them to express my appreciation for all of you."

"That would be wonderful."

Christmas was always a big holiday for Tony's family, and he was relieved to see that Ruth had been smiling all day. He even noticed her humming along to some Christmas songs earlier in the day as she made the latkes. He watched as she cleared the dishes from the dining room table, and he felt the warmth of the holiday in his heart. He took her by the hand and led her to a quiet corner in the living room.

"Are you enjoying your first Christmas so far?"

"I am. Everything's been lovely."

"Your latkes were delicious, everyone enjoyed them. I'm so sorry for my sister's rudeness."

"You don't need to apologize."

"Yeah, I do, she had no business saying, '*What are we Jewish now?*' That was a hurtful thing for her to say."

"I don't think anyone else heard her."

"But still, it's not right, and I'm gonna have a talk with her on the way to midnight mass tonight."

"Ok, but please don't make a scene. It's Christmas Eve."

"I'll be discreet, I promise. Are you sure you wanna go to church? You know you don't have to."

"I'm sure. Your parents have embraced me like one of their own. This holiday is important to them and to you too. I want to embrace everything that makes your family so special."

"Ruthie, you are one of a kind, and that's why I love you." Tony wrapped his arms around her and kissed her gently. "Whoa, our little bambino is saying hello." He laughed and put his hand on her stomach.

"Don't you mean bambina? She or he's been really active all day today. I guess it's the excitement about Christmas."

"Just think, this time next year there will be a little piece of us here." They both smiled and Tony pulled out a box with a red bow from his jacket pocket. "Merry Christmas. I know we agreed not to get each other gifts this year what with the baby and the restaurant, but I saw this and had to get if for you."

"I guess we both had the same idea," Ruth said as she reached behind Tony and took a small gift from the top of a pile by the tree. "Merry Christmas to you."

"So much for our agreement," Tony laughed. "You go first."

Ruth gently pulled the ribbon and opened the box which contained a sterling silver charm bracelet. "It's beautiful."

Tony clasped the bracelet on her wrist. "I got this to show you the happiness you bring to my life. The first charm is a Christmas Tree to celebrate our first Christmas, and each time we have a happy event, we will add charms to remember them."

"Thank you," Ruth whispered as she gazed at it. "I love it."

"Well, I guess it's my turn. Hmm, what could this be?" Tony smiled as he ripped the wrapping and opened the box revealing a circular tie tack with a crystal stone in the center. "Oh, you shouldn't have."

"You're not going to be working in a factory anymore. You'll need a nice tie tack to match your suits."

"I'll look like a million bucks with this one. I'll wear it every day for luck."

"Hey, Uncle Tony, it's time to open the presents. Nonna said we can't start until everyone is together." Bobby grabbed Tony and

Ruth's hands and pulled them to the sofa.

"Ok, ok, we're here. Let's get started." Tony smiled at Ruth and touched the tie tack against his heart before he put it in his jacket pocket.

"Go ahead and pick out your gifts," Louisa said to the kids. "You know the rules, you can only open one gift from Pop-Pop and Nonna, one gift from Uncle Tony, and one gift from Uncle Frank tonight. The rest you'll get to open tomorrow morning after Santa comes."

Tony loved to see each of the kids inspect their brightly wrapped packages carefully. He remembered how special his parents made each Christmas for them, and he could still feel the excitement as he would write a note and leave milk and cookies for Santa. One year, he swore he heard the sound of Santa's sleigh bells. It wasn't until Rena was born that Sal confessed that it was him who rang the bells as he set out a few gifts from Santa and ate the cookies. Tony dreamed of creating the same magic for Rena as she grew up, but by the time she was old enough to understand about Santa, she was living with Louisa. He looked over at Rena and noticed how she quietly picked out her gifts and made a small, neat pile. He wondered if her Christmases were magical. Each of the kids squealed with delight as they opened their new treasures. Louisa gave Frank a sarcastic glare as Bobby banged on a drum Frank gave him, Sal cradled the dolly that Sophia insisted he hold while she opened her other gifts, and Anna sat down on the floor close to her grandchildren so she could ooh and aah over each gift.

"Rena, what did you get?" Tony asked. He wanted so much to hug his daughter.

"It's a yo-yo," she exclaimed. "Thank you, Uncle Frank, this is a nice one."

"You're welcome, Rena. After you finish with your gifts, I've got a few good tricks to show you."

"Uncle Tony, this one's from you and Ruth, I saved it for last because it's so pretty."

"Ruth picked it out special for you." Tony beamed as Rena very carefully and slowly opened the package.

"It's a diary! And look it has a lock and a key. Thank you very much."

"I was hoping you'd like it," Ruth said. "When I was your age, I would write down my special memories."

Louisa grabbed the diary from Rena's hand, looked it over, and tossed it into Ruth's lap. "She's too young for a diary."

"Oh, come on, Louisa!" Tony stood, picked up the diary, and handed it back to Rena. "It's just like a notebook."

"She has plenty of notebooks, she doesn't need a fancy one."

Ruth stood next to Tony and said calmly, "Louisa, I didn't think ..."

"No, you didn't think. What gives you the right to pick out a gift special for Rena? I've got news for you, you are not her mother, and you never will be."

"That's enough! In the kitchen, now!" Anna stood and pointed to the kitchen.

"You heard her, Ruth, my mother wants to see you in the kitchen."

"No Louisa, I want to see *you* in the kitchen. Tony, Ruth, you might want to come in and hear what I have to say too."

"Well, you heard your mother." Sal stood. "Let's head to the kitchen."

"I've got this Sal!" Anna's eyes met his and he immediately sat back down.

"Uncle Frankie, why don't you show us some of your yo-yo tricks," Sal said to ease the tension.

"Now, I've had about enough of this, Louisa," Anna started trying to remain calm. "You owe Ruth an apology. Not just for the diary, but for every rude comment and glare you've delivered every chance you got these past few months."

Louisa looked at her mother in shock. "What? Did you think I didn't notice? I did! And I have to tell you, I am ashamed of you. You were not raised to be so disrespectful, and I won't have it. Not in this house, not in my presence, not ever." Anna stepped in front of Louisa and held her by the shoulders. "God rest her soul, Carmella is gone. I know you loved her like a sister, and she and Tony had a good life together. We will always keep her in our hearts and in our memories. But Ruth," Anna reached out for Ruth's hand, "Ruth is now a part of our family. She's not Carmella, and she shouldn't be compared to her. If you took the time to get to know her, you will see she is a loving, genuine, kind person. The type of person I thought you were."

Louisa looked down, "I'm sorry, Mom."

"Well, that's a start, but you're nowhere near the finish." Anna nodded toward Ruth.

"Ruth, I'm sorry. I do mean it. Tony is my baby brother, and sometimes I feel like I need to look out for him. I don't ever want to see him hurt like he did when Carmella died. I guess I lost sight of the fact that he's a grown adult, and if he loves you then you must be a good person."

"Thank you. I'm not trying to replace anyone, yourself included. And I'm sorry about the diary, I guess we should've checked with you about it."

"It's fine, I suppose."

"This is good. Remember, we are a family." Anna squeezed Louisa and Ruth's hands together. "Family is more important than anything. We accept each other and look out for each other. Do you understand?"

"Yes ma'am," they all said in unison.

"Good, now we have to get ready to go to church. I want to get there early and sit up front together, proudly."

FOURTEEN

MARCH, 1952
RUTH

RUTH FOLDED AND refolded the napkins as she set the dining table. It was Ethan's idea to get together so he could meet Tony personally. He told Ruth that he wanted to be a regular part of her life, and it was time that he and Tony got to know each other. Her doctor said the baby could come any day now, so Ruth knew well enough not to fight Tony, Anna, and even Sal when they insisted Ethan come to the house for dinner. The past few weeks they hadn't let Ruth lift a finger and had been watching her like a hawk. She had been looking forward to the distraction that Ethan would bring, but now that the time came, Ruth's nerves were starting to get the best of her. She loved her brother and wanted so much for him to love and accept Tony and his family. She hoped he could see that she was now a part of a loving family; something she had always wanted.

Ruth spent a lot of her free time reflecting and she was determined to provide a peaceful, loving environment for her new child.

As much as it pained her, she realized she hadn't been able to provide that to Miriam. Living with her parents, her world was filled with tension. Ruth could now see that within the few months before she left, Miriam wasn't the bubbly, cheerful little girl she used to be. Her singing and dancing had all but dissipated and she had become moody. Anna helped Ruth realize that it was inevitable that her little girl would be directly impacted by her own moods, and that the constant hostility between Ruth and her parents was not healthy for Miriam. The last time she saw Ethan, he said that she had become more like her cheerful self again. Ruth knew that the most important gift she could give her daughter was a peaceful childhood, and for now that meant coming to terms with being separated.

"There's the door, Ruth, would you like me to get it?" Anna asked.

"Oh, no, I got it, thank you though." Ruth waddled her way to the door and found that Tony got there first.

"Ethan, come in. It's so good to finally meet you."

"Hi, Tony. Same here. Hey Ruth, you look very ..."

"Pregnant!" Ruth said as she pulled Ethan in for a hug.

"No, you look great." He chuckled nervously.

"You're being kind as usual little brother. Come in and meet everyone. These are Tony's parents, Anna and Sal Russo."

"It's nice to meet you. Here are some flowers for you, Mrs. Russo, and Ruth thought a nice fresh loaf of bread would be a great addition for dinner. It's still warm from the bakery."

"Lovely. Thank you, Ethan. Please take off your coat and make yourself comfortable."

"Would you like some wine?" Sal asked. "I got a couple of bottles of Manischewitz."

Tony, Ruth, and Ethan shared a small grin as Ethan said, "Yes, that would be very nice."

"Why don't you all sit at the table. Ruth have a seat, honey, you shouldn't be on your feet. I have some nice Minestrone Soup, a tossed salad, and a platter of fresh mozzarella and tomatoes for starters and then I have some Manicotti and Eggplant Parmigiana."

"Oh, this is a feast. Thank you for your hospitality, but you didn't have to go to all this trouble."

"My wife doesn't know how to make a light meal." Sal gestured for Ethan to sit next to him. "But I'll tell you what, she's the best cook in the neighborhood. Nobody's Manicotti can compare."

Throughout dinner, Ruth found she didn't have much of an appetite and didn't want to alarm anyone about some cramping she's had. She was enjoying how easily Ethan bonded with Tony and Sal and was particularly amused with their debate over which Yankee was a better ball player, Phil Rizzuto or Yogi Berra.

"Tony, Sal, why don't you help me clear this table. Let's give Ruth and Ethan some time to talk."

"You heard the boss. Tony, grab a plate." Sal winked at Ethan as he handed Tony an empty platter and walked into the kitchen.

"I understand now." Ethan moved over to sit next to Ruth. "Tony and his family are really great people. It's clear how much they love you."

"I'm so glad you see it. I do love our parents, in spite of everything, but I've found such happiness here with the Russos."

"I've never seen you so at ease. It looks good on you. You know, Rachel and I are getting pretty serious, and this ..." he looked around, "this right here is the type of life I want for us too. I see today that it's not about the religion. It's about appreciating each other as a family."

"You're right. I've learned a lot about that recently, and that's what I want for Miriam too."

"You never have to worry about Miriam. Rachel and I are looking out for her. We'll always be there for her as if she's our own daughter. I promise you, her days will be filled with the same love and respect that you've come to know here."

"Thank you. I needed to hear that. Letting her go was the hardest thing I've ever had to do. I guess it's what needed to be done. The only thing that brings me comfort in this is that you are looking out for her. You know, every time I called the house Momma and Papa hung up as soon as they heard my voice. I used to call every day, then once a week, and now it's been once a month. I just can't keep this up anymore. I kept trying, hoping they would soften. But it's clear to me now that they won't."

"I'm afraid you may be right."

"But I still have you." Ruth smiled and put her hand on Ethan's.

"You will always have me." He squeezed her hand. "So, I have a little gossip." Ethan leaned in closer to Ruth. "Last week Naomi broke off her engagement to Isaac."

Ruth sat up straight. "Ethan. No! You're joking?"

"I am not joking." Ethan attempted to hide a smile but when he locked eyes with Ruth, they burst into laughter.

"Oh, this is terrible. Why are we laughing?" Ruth wiped her eyes with her napkin.

"Maybe because Isaac has always been the chosen one with our parents? You know he can do no wrong in their eyes." Ethan took a deep breath and shook his head as he tried to be serious.

"That is true. Not only was he the first-born son, but he became a doctor and joined Papa in his practice. How did they take it?"

"Not well. After all, Naomi is the Rabbi's daughter, and she did not hide the fact that she broke off the engagement because Isaac was too callous."

Ruth lifted her glass of water in a salute. "Good for her and good for Rabbi for supporting her. I wonder what Isaac will do for a bride now?"

"Actually, I overheard Papa telling Momma that if Isaac isn't good enough for Naomi, he will reach out to his people in Israel and find a suitable match."

Ruth closed her eyes. "Poor girl. She won't know what she will be in for."

"Ethan, I made up some Cannoli, can I interest you in some coffee as well?" Anna rushed in and placed a tray of coffee cups on the table, followed by Sal and Tony.

"I don't think I can eat another thing, but I would love a cup of coffee."

"Nonsense, there's always room for Cannoli." Anna started to fix a plate for him.

"I'll help you with that." Ruth stood and before she could take a step she buckled over in pain. "Ohhhh," she moaned.

"Ruthie, what's wrong? Are you ok?" Tony rushed to her.

"I think I'm in labor."

"Ok, ok, we practiced this," Tony paced. "Ok."

"Salvatore, go get the car. Ethan, there's a pad next to the phone with the hospital's phone number and Ruth's doctor's name. Call them and tell them Ruth's on her way. Tony, get a hold of yourself. Ruth's bag is packed and in your bedroom. Go get that and Ruth's coat."

All three men dashed away and reminded themselves of their task. "Come on honey, let's get you to the sofa. I was wondering how long you would wait before telling us you were in labor."

"How did you know?" Ruth looked at Anna in surprise.

"A mother knows."

FIFTEEN

APRIL, 1952
TONY

"GOD BLESS BABY Janet Marie!" Frank raised his wine glass in a toast. "I want to thank Tony and Ruth for the honor of being Janet's godfather. It's a responsibility I will not take lightly, and I'll model myself after you, Uncle Sal. If I can be half the godfather to Janet that you are to me, then I will be successful. To Janet Marie!"

"To Janet Marie!" All of the guests lifted their glasses in celebration.

As Tony took a drink of wine in honor of his daughter, he glanced around and thought about how he never dreamed he would feel this happy again. He'd been on cloud nine since the day Janet was born, and he had been even more motivated to make the restaurant a success for Ruth and Janet. Yet he still felt a bit unsettled. He wanted to make an honest woman out of Ruth and felt frustrated about the silence she received from both her family and Harvey's as well. It was celebrations like this that reminded Tony that he and Ruth were not legally bound to each other. But in their hearts, they were just as much a family as anyone else. He worried about the impact this could have on Janet in the future. Although both his mother and father reasoned that no one needed to know, he was still concerned.

Tony looked over at Ruth and Louisa engaged in a conversation. He hoped that Louisa was considerate of Ruth's feelings as they spoke to each other. While their relationship was much better since Christmas, Louisa still couldn't completely let go of her sarcasm. He breathed a sigh of relief when they both continued to smile as they parted ways to mingle with other guests.

"This has been a wonderful day. Janet has been doing so well being passed around from person to person with everyone wanting to hold her." Ruth smiled brightly as she approached Tony. "You don't think she'll catch anything do you? She's only a little more than a month old. Maybe I should go get her from your mother?"

It was remarkable to Tony that a mother's concern for her child could change their mood in an instant.

"Relax Ruthie, she'll be fine. This is our custom." He put his arm around her and got her to smile again. "Hey, I really do wanna tell you how much my family appreciated your agreeing to christen Janet. Look at my parents, they're in heaven."

"Your family has been so kind to me. Much kinder than my own family has been. I want our daughter to grow up with the same values, and embracing your religion seemed like a good start."

"I just wanna do this right. We should be married. If Pop wasn't so active in the Knights of Columbus and the church, I'm not sure Father O'Malley would've consented to this christening."

"I think your father's generous donation had a lot do with the Father's decision. But I know what you mean, there's nothing more I would like than to move on with our lives. I hate that neither Harvey nor his parents will answer my calls or letters."

"Hey, you two look entirely too serious. This is a celebration. What's going on?" Frank laughed as he moved toward them with one arm stretched out and the other around his girlfriend, Betty's, waist.

"Frank! That was a beautiful toast." Ruth smiled brightly at him. "We were just talking about Harvey."

"Oh, you shouldn't be thinking about that now. Come on Ruth, let's go dance. I'll teach you the Tarantella," Betty said, as she grabbed Ruth's hand and led her to the dance floor.

"You have perfect timing," Tony said as he offered Frank a fresh glass of wine.

"Actually, Betty noticed your expressions and thought we should lighten things up."

"Well, that Betty's a nice girl, definitely a keeper. I'm just getting fed up with this whole Harvey thing." Tony could feel his face getting flushed.

"Why don't you pay Harvey a visit. See if you can speak to him man-to-man." Frank raised his eyebrows.

Tony considered this for a moment. He imagined himself giving Harvey a piece of his mind many times, but never really thought of having a serious conversation with him. "You may be on to something. I suppose a conversation couldn't hurt. I'm gonna be out his way tomorrow. Let's keep this between us for now. Here comes Pop and I'd rather him not know."

"This is a great party, Uncle Sal."

"Nothing but the best for my new granddaughter." He looked over at Anna holding Janet and beamed with pride. "To our family, alla nostra famiglia!" Sal caught Anna's eye and raised his glass. "So, how are we on the restaurant? Are we all set for the grand opening Tuesday? Any loose ends I should know about?"

"We're good. We're ready. We worked out all those kinks we uncovered during the soft opening last week."

"Good, good. I've invited some very difficult and opinionated people for this opening. If we can impress them, we'll be a success. I also managed to get a couple reporters and their wives to commit to coming, just some guys I got to know through the years in the construction business."

"That's great thinking. I'm expecting a few last-minute deliveries on Monday, and I'm sure everything will be smooth."

Tony tuned out the rest of the conversation between Sal and Frank as he saw Ruth take Janet from Anna and started to slowly sway to the music with her daughter in her arms. His unsettled feelings agitated him and were getting harder to shake off. He knew he should feel lucky, but right now he resented the fact that his life, their lives, were being controlled by another man.

Who did this Harvey Goldberg think he was? His arrogant selfishness not only impacted Ruth and Tony, but now there was Janet to think about. Ruth was clearly a wonderful mother, but Tony could see that part of her spark was gone. This whole business took a toll on her. Tony tried things Ruth's way and gave it time, but now he knew nothing would change. Building the restaurant and preparing for the opening helped him bide his time but now he thought maybe Frank was right. Maybe he should take matters into his own hands and have a serious conversation with Harvey.

Tony tossed and turned throughout the night as he reconsidered whether he should really see Harvey or not. He wanted to do this right and not cause Ruth any unnecessary stress. He weighed the pros and cons and decided that the only con would be if their talk was unsuccessful. In that case, then nothing would change. He felt he owed it to both Ruth and Janet to at least try to convince Harvey to grant a divorce. He considered having Frank join him but decided that Harvey may get more defensive if they both confronted him. Approaching him in private was the way to go. He was obviously a hot head with a big ego and having an audience during this conversation wouldn't help. The last thing he really wanted was to have a heated altercation.

Tony decided to start his day earlier than usual and run his errands before he went to Harvey's office. But getting dressed in the dark was more challenging than he thought it would be, and he stubbed his toe on the nightstand and woke Ruth up in the process.

"You're up early, it's only 5 a.m. Everything ok?"

"Yeah, yeah, go back to sleep. I've got a lot to do today." He kissed her cheek and quickly slipped out of the bedroom. He knew she wouldn't like the idea of him going to see Harvey, and he wanted to leave the apartment before she could ask any more questions.

After his vendor stops, Tony decided to have lunch at the diner across the street from Harvey's accounting practice. The window booth he chose gave him a full view of the small office. Tony spent the rest of the afternoon drinking coffee as he watched and waited. He started to feel more confident in his plan as he noticed that in the two hours that he was sitting there, no one had come or gone, and Harvey's secretary had been keeping herself busy as she read magazines and powdered her nose. Harvey, himself, didn't appear too busy as he glanced out the window a number of times and straightened magazines on the table in the waiting area. Finally, he waved his secretary out of the office for the day and shook his head slowly with a defeated look on his face.

Tony quickly threw some money on the table to cover the check plus a little something extra for taking up a table for so long. As he approached the office, he could see Harvey seated at his desk with his face in his hands. Harvey looked up as the bell on the door rang. He jumped to his feet and hurried toward Tony with his hand stretched outright.

"Hello, I'm Harvey Goldberg, how can I help you today?"

"Hello Harvey, I'm Tony Russo." Tony said placing both hands together in front of him.

"Hmph, I should've known you'd come here. What do you want?" His face lost all signs of pleasantness and instantly turned stone cold.

"I thought maybe you and I could speak man-to-man, and maybe come up with an agreement."

"Agreement?" He snorted. "There's nothing I'll agree to with you. So, you can take your greasy self out of here."

"Look," Tony reasoned as he tried to control his temper. "I don't want no trouble here. The way I see it, you don't want Ruth in your life, so why not divorce her?"

"Why not divorce her?" Harvey mocked. "Tell me why I should?" He slammed his fist on his secretary's desk and leaned into Tony's face. "She's the one who left *me*! And she's the one who went around and got pregnant with a greasy low life! A divorce is just what she wants," he shouted, his face turning red.

"You beat her and disrespected her. She deserves better than that and I will do whatever it takes to give it to her," Tony spit back. "I'll tell you what …" He took a step back and pulled a checkbook out of his jacket pocket. "Let's end this here and now. What's your price?"

"My price? You think you can buy me?"

"It looks to me like your little accounting business isn't doing so well, is it? It's nearly Tax Day. Most accountants I know are working overtime for their clients. You haven't been busy all day. Seems like maybe you need this money."

"You've been watching me?" He started to look crazy.

"I have. So, what's it gonna take?"

Harvey took a step back and shook his head in disbelief.

"A million dollars. That's my price." He grinned.

"Ok, let's be reasonable, Harvey. I will give you ten thousand."

Harvey laughed. "Is that all she's worth to you? It looks like she's worth a lot more to me. I guess you just don't love her enough."

Suddenly the heat rose to Tony's face. He dropped the checkbook and slammed his right fist into Harvey's gut so hard he buckled and fell to the floor instantly. Tony began kicking him over and over in the stomach, chest, face, and any other part of his body he left exposed. Harvey couldn't move quick enough to protect himself, and Tony couldn't stop until Harvey laid perfectly still in a large puddle of blood.

Tony couldn't remember picking up the checkbook, returning to his car, or driving to Caruso's. But he found himself sitting at the bar with Frank as he downed three shots of whiskey.

"Tell me everything." Frank whispered seriously.

"That Harvey is scum. He wants a million dollars to divorce Ruth. I don't have that kind of money, so I offered him ten thousand."

"And?"

"He wouldn't take it. Started talking crap about my not loving Ruth enough. So, I lost it on him."

"What do you mean you lost it on him?"

"I beat him, beat him bad."

"Where? Did anyone see you?"

"In his office, I don't think anyone knew I was there. It was dark and there was no one around."

"Ok. I'll take care of it. Don't worry about a thing. Go home and get ready for the grand opening tomorrow. Whatever you do, don't tell anyone what happened." Frank pat Tony on the back and nodded at Gino the bartender.

SIXTEEN

APRIL, 1952
RUTH

ALL DAY RUTH and Anna primped and fussed over their hair and makeup to look beautiful for the restaurant's grand opening. Since the christening two days ago, Ruth had found peace in being a family with Tony spiritually, and she was not letting herself get caught up in the issue of legalities. She was going to try to discuss this with him last night, but he seemed very tired and went to bed earlier than usual. It's just as well, she reasoned, this was a time to celebrate and talk of her situation would only taint the mood.

As she applied her lipstick, the reality of leaving Janet for the first time hit her. She'd never been the type of mother that was overprotective, but she really didn't know the neighbor that Anna recommended to babysit.

"Are you sure Janet will be ok with Mrs. Scardino tonight? I hate to leave her."

"She'll be fine. Dorothea Scardino has raised six of her own children, takes care of three grandchildren daily, and babysits for most of the kids in the neighborhood. I trust her, and so can you. Relax honey, let's enjoy the evening," Anna said. "I'm so proud of Tony and Frankie. Did you see how handsome they looked when they left here with Sal earlier?"

"They did look very handsome. Have you noticed that Tony's been really quiet since he got home last night."

"Opening night jitters, I'm sure. Sal was the same way years ago when he opened up the dinner club. Oh, here's our ride. Time to go."

Ruth followed Anna down to the taxi and glanced over into Mrs. Scardino's window. Her heart melted as she saw Janet being rocked in her arms. "Tonight is going to be a great night, I just know it," she said as she slid into the car.

When they arrived, Ruth was overjoyed at the transformation of the restaurant. She hadn't seen it since before Janet was born and it was nothing but an old, dusty former luncheonette. Now it was a comfortably refined restaurant. The bright dining room contained a mixture of round and square tables of various sizes that would allow for groups of diners from two to ten at a time. Along the east wall were six cozy booths that contained burgundy leather banquettes, and all of the tables were dressed with ivory linens and small glass bud vases containing pink roses surrounded by baby's breath. Ruth was happy to see the beige damask and burgundy striped wallpaper that she picked out held brass candle-shaped sconces that matched the large chandeliers. She particularly loved the mahogany gold-upholstered chairs that matched the bar which stood in front of the mirrored west wall.

"Good evening, ladies."

"Lou! What are you doing here?" Ruth couldn't help but smile and giggle with joy.

"Tony came to Giovanni's and offered me the position of head Maître de. I couldn't turn my favorite customer down." He smiled at them.

"There's the girls." Sal cheered as they entered the dining room. "What do you think?"

Anna and Ruth quickly slipped off their coats and handed them to Lou while they surveyed the room.

"You've outdone yourselves." Anna whispered as she wiped a tear rolling down her cheek.

"Sal, those chandeliers! The shades match the table linens perfectly."

"Yes, you both made good choices. Wait until you see the chandelier we put up over the dance floor in the ballroom. The crystals shine so bright their reflection looks magical." Sal beamed as he led them through the dining room to the adjacent room.

Anna and Ruth were dazzled and thought the space appeared to be much bigger than they remembered. The burgundy and gold-marbled wallpaper along with the assortment of square tables arranged in a semi-circle surrounding an ample dance floor was inviting. Each table had the same tablecloths as the dining room and held a candle flickering in a small round candleholder. At the head of the room was a platform where the small orchestra and singer were rehearsing.

"Oh my goodness," Ruth exclaimed. "Everything is just perfect."

"I have to admit. It did turn out nice." Sal looked around with pride.

They were about to get their first glimpse of the kitchen and back office as Tony and Frank walked toward them whispering intensely to each other. Ruth was concerned because she couldn't quite make out Tony's expression as he nodded his head and Frank pat him on the back.

"Well, it's almost show time," Frank said nervously. "Before everyone arrives and everything gets crazy, I just want to thank you Uncle Sal and Aunt Anna for everything. You're giving me and Tony a big chance with this place and I think I can speak for both of us when I say how much we appreciate your confidence in us."

"Here, here," Tony chimed in.

Sal looked down and tried to hide his emotions. He took Frank into a bear hug kissing him on both cheeks before he did the same to Tony.

"Look the crowd is building outside." Anna said wiping her nose with her handkerchief.

"Let's do this." Tony flipped the closed sign over and said, "Welcome to Salvatore Bruno's Ristorante," as he opened the doors.

Everything picked up quickly as Tony and Frank got down to business. They orchestrated a beautiful symphony of service to everyone who filtered in. Sal, Anna, and Ruth worked the dining room as they greeted the friends and guests that had come out to offer their support. Just as the first wave of diners finished their coffee and dessert, they could hear the sweet melodies that enticed the patrons to the ballroom for after dinner drinks and dancing.

At the end of the night, while the staff was cleaning up, they all sat at a large round table and discussed the evening. Everyone agreed that Salvatore Bruno's was a huge success. Lou only confirmed this fact as he announced that they had a full reservation list for both Friday and Saturday evenings. They cheered and celebrated with a final night cap of champagne. When they headed to the door to call it a night, Ruth was taken by surprise when Ethan pulled up and jumped out of his car.

"Ethan! I was hoping you would come by tonight, but it's too late. We're closed now," she said as she tried to get him to meet her eyes, but he kept looking down.

"Something's happened."

"What is it?"

He was silent.

"Ethan, what happened?" Ruth said in desperation.

"Harvey's dead."

PART II
FAMILY

SEVENTEEN

APRIL, 1952

TONY

"FRANK, WHAT DID you do?" Tony demanded as he stormed into the restaurant Wednesday afternoon.

"I took care of it," Frank said as he sat at the bar and casually smoked a cigarette.

"What does that mean?"

"Don't worry about it."

"When I left Harvey, he was in rough shape, but I swear he was alive."

Frank turned to Tony and smiled. "Tony, all your worries are over. You and Ruth are free from that scumbag."

"My worries have just begun. The cops were at the apartment this morning asking Ruth and me all sorts of crazy questions. They know all about the marriage situation, and it looks like her family is pointing the finger at me!"

"You have nothing to worry about. You didn't kill him. He was shot, not beaten to death. Besides, you were hosting Salvatore Bruno's grand opening with me. At least a hundred or more people were with us throughout the night."

"How did you know how and when he was killed?"

"Again, don't worry about it," he said, as he crushed the cigarette in the ashtray.

But Tony was worried. Although Frank was right this freed them up to legally marry, he didn't like that it would be under these circumstances. He didn't like that the police were looking at him for it, and he really didn't like that Frank was obviously involved.

"I swear if I find out you're responsible for this man's death…"

"What? What'll you do? I was with you the whole night. Monday night I did go out to Harvey's office to check on things. By the time I got there, he was gone, and the office was locked up tight. Everything looked ok, so I left. End of story. Seriously, don't worry so much about this. Harvey was a smart-ass, violent guy whose business was failing. Who knows what kind of trouble he got himself into? Trust me. We need to focus on our success last night and not on Harvey Goldberg."

"Ok, ok." Tony shrugged and reluctantly gave in.

He left Frank sitting at the bar and headed to the back office. Frank made a lot of good points about Harvey, yet Tony couldn't help but think it's suspiciously convenient that Harvey was found dead the day after their run-in. Frank had done a lot of crazy things in his life, but Tony was sure that he wasn't a murderer. He's pretty confident that no one saw him on Monday, but he was concerned that Harvey could've told someone about their altercation. By the way the police were questioning him, Tony didn't think they knew it was him who had beaten Harvey, but he feared that someone could come forward at any time. Tony rubbed his eyes after he sat down in front of Sal who was at the desk reviewing the receipts from last night.

"How are you doing with all this, son?"

"I'll tell you, my nerves are shot. I didn't like leaving Ruth today, but honestly, I think I need the distraction of work."

"I can understand that. This Harvey getting killed. This is a big surprise."

"It really is. I don't know who's more in shock me or Ruth."

"I didn't like all those questions the police were asking you."

"Can you blame them? Ruth's family was quick to blame me."

"I'm sure they were but keep your head up. The police will find that this is a case of someone getting what they deserved, and you had nothing to do with it."

"I hope you're right."

"Why wouldn't I be right? Now, let's sit down with Frankie and get ready to meet with the staff. We need to review our service from last night."

EIGHTEEN

APRIL, 1952
RUTH

THE REALITY OF Harvey's death set in for Ruth when the police came to the apartment to question her and Tony so early in the morning yesterday. She wasn't surprised by their visit. The nature of her relationship with Harvey was no secret and the fact that she and Tony wanted to get married surely raised suspicion. They both answered all of the detective's questions fully and truthfully, but she sensed Tony's nervousness and found herself feeling a little defensive and protective when they were insinuating that he could've been involved. Ruth had to admit she was relieved that she was finally free of Harvey. This new sense of freedom made her feel guilty, and as she sat at the kitchen table with Anna, she decided not to share these feelings with anyone just yet.

"How are you doing, honey?" Anna asked as she handed Ruth a cup of tea.

"I just don't know what to think. I can't believe Harvey was killed, and all those questions the police were asking Tony."

"The police have to do their job. They'll realize Tony had nothing to do with it and then they can focus on finding the real killer." She reassuringly squeezed Ruth's hand.

"We are a success!" Sal announced as he bounded into the kitchen and waved newspapers in the air.

"Look, right here. We got rave reviews in both the Tribune and the Herald!"

Anna and Ruth jumped to their feet and grabbed the newspapers. There it was in black and white, spectacular highlights of Tuesday evening complete with pictures.

"Oh Sal, they got everything. I'm going to cut out this picture of you and the boys and frame it. And look here is one of Ruth and Louisa."

"I told you, there's nothing better for a restaurant than good press. I've got to head down there and show the boys. Wait til they see this."

"I haven't seen him this happy in many, many years. Not since Naples," Anna said as Sal rushed out.

"Surely, he's found happiness here in New York," Ruth offered.

Anna sighed, "He's been content. Don't get me wrong, we have a nice life here. We have great friends, our children have been good to us, and Sal has been successful. But he has demons that he can't shake from our life in Naples."

"What kind of demons?"

"Ah, nothing for you to worry about. When you get to be our age, you can't help but look back and think, 'what if?' But the past can't be changed. All you can do is look to the future."

"Amen to that," Ruth replied nodding her head.

"Look at the time, I'm going to be late for my hairdresser if I don't leave now. What are your plans for the day, Ruth?"

Ruth looked down as she answered, "Janet and I are going to meet up with Joan for lunch. I'm hoping to find out more about Harvey."

Anna pulled Ruth from the chair and gave her a big hug. "I'm sure this is hard for you. But chin up, better days are ahead."

"You know, I'm starting to feel that already."

Ruth saw Joan immediately when she entered the diner and was happy to see a cup of tea waiting for her.

"Let me see that baby! Hello Janet." Joan beamed as she took her from Ruth's arms. "Aren't you a sight for sore eyes today. This was just what I need, a little baby snuggle time with such a sweetie. Now, sit down, let me fill you in on what's going on. I took the liberty of ordering the soup and salad for you."

Ruth sat down and quickly rattled off questions, "First off, how's Miriam? Does she know? Is she upset?"

"Miriam's fine," Joan said reassuringly. "I spoke with Ethan just before coming here. He and your mother sat her down and told her Daddy died and he's in a beautiful place with God now. The good thing is she's young and wasn't close to Harvey. Ethan said she had a few questions but really took it well and wanted to have a tea party with her dolls after the conversation."

"Thank God. I really miss my little girl. I wish I could be there for her."

"I know you do. I assure you she's doing well. Ethan has really stepped up and is being a great uncle to her."

"I suppose that's the best I can hope for in light of everything. I just can't believe any of this. The police came to the apartment yesterday and were asking us all sorts of questions."

Joan nodded quickly. "I'm not surprised. Everyone's in shock, and no one knows what to think. When Ethan pulled up Tuesday night at the restaurant and told us Harvey was dead, Alan and I couldn't believe it. We went straight to my parents' house to pick up Paul and they filled us in on some of the details. Apparently, Harvey got home later than usual Monday night after work. His parents said he had been beaten but he wouldn't talk about it. They pressed him for details, but you know Harvey, when he doesn't want to talk, he won't."

"Beaten?" Ruth asked, surprised, and then quickly remembered seeing bruises on Tony's hand that night.

"Yup. But does that really surprise you? You know better than anyone how mean he was. Alan said Harvey has had a temper for as long as he can remember, and after we got married and Paul was born, Alan didn't want Harvey around our son because of it."

"I suppose it really shouldn't surprise me. But the police told us Harvey had been shot." Ruth tried to hide her concern from Joan. What if Tony really did have something to do with all of this?

"His mother told my mother that he went to work as usual Tuesday, but never came home. His father went down to the office and found him. He'd been shot once between his eyes while sitting at his desk."

"That poor man, to find his son like that." Ruth shook her head as she thought about how much David and Sarah loved him.

"Alan called his friend at the police station, and he said they were questioning everyone who might have a motive and the list is long. Harvey's temper was well known, and it looked like he was mixed up with some dangerous people."

"I never knew any of his business clients or associates. He kept that part of his life separate from me." Ruth considered that maybe Tony wasn't involved after all, and his bruises really were from unloading the meat deliveries like he said.

"Are you ok? You look pale."

"I'm fine," she said taking a deep breath. "This is all so upsetting. What about the funeral? Have they planned anything yet?"

"It's all set for tomorrow. But please tell me you're not going to show up. Nothing good will come of it."

"I know. But I feel like I need to pay my respects to his parents. No matter how terrible Harvey was, they were always kind, good people to me and Miriam."

"Well then you should tell them but do it in a letter. They've been through enough and I'm afraid that seeing you at the funeral might cause them more grief."

Ruth nodded her head. "Yes, of course."

"Now, on a happier note, we had such a great time at the grand opening. Thank you so much for inviting us. It was hard to choose what to order because it all sounded so good. But I was really glad I went with the Chicken Piccata, it was amazing. It wasn't as tart as some I've had, I loved the creaminess to the sauce. And Alan is still talking about his Ribeye. He said it was cooked to perfection." Joan laughed. "I had a hard time getting him to dance after dinner because he ate his whole steak, mashed potatoes, and part of my linguini."

"We decided to limit the menu choices to just a few classics to start. Most of them are Anna's recipes."

"Really? I remember you told me that Sal's friend had a son who was a chef. Were they able to hire him?"

"Yes, Roberto is the head chef and he helped to hire the entire kitchen staff. They're all from the neighborhood. It was very important to Sal to give people from our community a chance at employment."

"That's wonderful."

"It is. Some of them really needed the jobs but didn't have experience. So, Anna put on her apron and spent a lot of time down there in the kitchen with Roberto. They taught them all how to cook the family recipes. I have to say, everyone worked really hard to pull it all together. I'm relieved that it was a success."

"I have a gut feeling that this is going to be the beginning of good things for you, Ruth." Joan smiled.

"I hope you're right."

NINETEEN

JUNE, 1954
TONY

TONY AND RUTH fell into a comfortable life over the two years after Harvey was murdered. There was a lot of speculation about who killed him, and thanks to Al's friend at the police department, they learned Tony had been cleared. The police focused on a gambling ring that Harvey had gotten himself involved in but had not made any arrests. Tony suspected that Frank was somehow involved or knew more than he let on, but he put aside his thoughts and kept his focus on the restaurant and his family. Tony loved the life he and Ruth made together, and although the restaurant demanded a lot of his time, he made sure both Ruth and Janet got the best part of him. Every week he planned a special date for his girls and alternated between them so they could have special one-on-one time together. Although Janet was only two, she had a great time on their outings.

Tony wished he had the opportunity to spend the same type of quality time with Rena as she grew up and wondered if maybe he was trying to make up for it with Janet. To Tony's delight, Rena had been enchanted with Janet since the day she was born. He had to hide his emotions that first time they laid Janet in Rena's arms and Rena kissed her head. He got a lump in his throat every time she lovingly took Janet by the hand or sang with her. Tony noticed she was more like a protective big sister to Janet than she was to Sophia, and it was clear that Rena and Janet shared a strong bond. Maybe she sensed Janet's vulnerability compared to Sophia's willfulness or maybe it was Rena's innate twelve-year old sisterly instincts. He was trying to cultivate this closeness between them, but he had to approach it lightly with Louisa. She still got agitated and defensive easily, especially where Rena was concerned. But Tony and Ruth made great strides in spending more time with his daughter and included her, Bobby, and Sophia on some of their family outings. Louisa sometimes made a fuss, but ultimately gave in and allowed the kids to tag along with them. He would have liked to spend some alone time with Rena, but he hadn't quite figured out the best way for that to happen yet. He planned on trying to get Anna's help; Louisa was usually more agreeable when Anna was involved.

Tony and Ruth discussed marriage often after Harvey was killed. The time never seemed right, and they both felt that they shouldn't get married so soon after his death. The police never arrested anyone, and they certainly didn't want to raise any more suspicion back their way. But now Tony felt the time was right. It had been well over a year since they learned he wasn't a person of interest anymore. Ruth was now pregnant with their second child, and she insisted on working a few hostess shifts during the week to give her some much-needed time in the company of adults. Tony couldn't think of anything that should stand in their way of getting married.

He was ready to present Ruth with a ring and make a formal

proposal. They were going to enjoy a nice romantic evening at home while Sal and Anna took Janet and Louisa's kids to a special dinner at the restaurant. Sal made the arrangements with Lou to have the kids treated like little ladies and gentlemen being served Shirley Temple cocktails and spaghetti and meatballs. Anna got all of the kids new, fancy outfits for the dinner and had spent much of the day cooking all of Ruth's favorite foods. Tony checked his jacket pocket to make sure the engagement ring was there as he entered the kitchen.

"Mom, everything looks great. Thanks for doing this."

"Are you kidding? Your mother's been fussing all day over this meal."

"That's enough out of you Salvatore. Do you have the ring?" Anna asked as she flitted around the kitchen.

"Yeah, it's right here in my pocket." Tony said as he checked again.

"Ok, good. Now don't be nervous, just be your charming self." She kissed his cheek.

"I'm fine," he answered and felt his pocket once again. "You really should leave to meet Louisa and the kids at the restaurant. Ruth'll be home soon."

"Did she suspect anything when you asked her to work the lunch seating today instead of dinner?" Anna asked as she started taking flowers out of the vase and rearranged them for the second time.

"Actually, I asked her to cover lunch," Sal answered. "I told her Paula wanted to switch shifts today so she could take her son to a doctor's appointment. I figured it wouldn't sound suspicious coming from me." He gently pulled Anna away from the table. "Now Anna, those flowers are fine. Take off your apron and let's round up Janet so we don't get in the way of Tony's surprise."

"Yes, yes, ok." Anna nodded her head. "Janet let's get going. We're going to have a fancy dinner with your cousins," she sang as they entered the living room.

"Give Daddy a kiss goodbye." Sal lifted Janet and leaned her into Tony.

"Have fun sweetie," Tony said with a big hug. "Oh boy, you give the best hugs."

Tony felt his pocket a few more times while he paced through the apartment and waited for Ruth to come home. He felt lightheaded as he heard her coming through the door.

"Hey hon, oof, what a day. I didn't realize how busy the lunch seating was," Ruth said as she breezed through the door and dropped her pocketbook and keys on the side table.

"There's my girl." Tony gave her his usual greeting, but this time he took her into his arms and gave her a tighter hug and a longer kiss. Her body softened in his arms, and she returned the affection through her tender kiss.

"Well, maybe I should ask Sal to work the lunch seating more often. Where is everyone?" She slowly released their embrace.

"Mom and Pop took Janet and the kids to dinner. We have the apartment to ourselves for a change," Tony said as he took her hand and led her to the kitchen.

"Tony, look at this setup," Ruth said in delight as she surveyed the kitchen. "What's going on?"

"Mom thought it would be nice to make a romantic dinner for us."

"This is wonderful. Let's eat. I'm starving." Ruth immediately started placing food on their plates while Tony poured the wine.

"Oh, this is delicious. She really outdid herself."

"You know Mom, she puts her heart and soul into her meals, but I actually asked her to make tonight extra special," Tony said nervously. Ruth put her fork down and looked into his eyes with a look of concern.

"Ruthie, it's time we get married," he said as he pulled the ring box out of his pocket and opened it.

"I don't know what to say. I just don't know if we should now." Ruth started to shake her head. "Things are going great the way they are. Maybe we should leave well enough alone."

"Well enough alone?" Tony felt his face turn red. "How can you say things are great the way they are?"

"We're happy, the restaurant is doing well, Janet is thriving, and our family is expanding. If that's not great I don't know what is."

"Yeah, that's all true. But we aren't married. We're living in sin, and I won't have it."

"You *won't* have it?" Ruth accused. "It's not all *your* decision." She pushed back from the table and stood with such force her chair fell over.

"No! I will not allow another child of mine to be born out of wedlock!" Tony jumped to his feet and slammed his hand down on the table.

"Who are you to make demands?" She shouted.

"How will it be for our kids once they start school? Huh? Have you thought of that?"

"What do you mean? Our kids will be just fine. They have a mother and father who love them."

"The only problem is Mommy and Daddy aren't married, and Mommy has a different last name."

"Oh, don't be ridiculous."

"Now I'm being ridiculous? How is my wanting the best for us, our children ridiculous? I want us to be a real family. A true family bonded together through marriage and blessed by God."

"I thought we were a real family already, but I guess I was wrong!"

"I thought you loved me!" Tony tipped the table over and scattered the food, wine, and flowers across the kitchen. "But I guess *I* was wrong!"

Ruth took a step back, gasped, and ran into the bedroom slamming the door behind her.

"Shit!" Tony exclaimed as he stormed into the living room. He could hear Ruth crying in the bedroom and wondered how everything went so wrong. He never expected Ruth to say no. Getting married was the plan all along, wasn't it? He and Anna spent hours at the jewelry shop looking at ring after ring until he found the perfect one. To him, it was a symbol of how much he loved Ruth and was committed to her. He was so excited for her to see it, and it was all he could do not to show it to her when they came home with it last week. Ruth barely even looked at it. It was as if she didn't see him or his love. In fact, she didn't even hesitate with her answer. They've waited so long for this, and although their family and friends have embraced them as a family, Tony wanted the official union. He needed the official oath as a gift to his children.

Two hours passed quickly as Tony lamented how to move forward. When Sal and Anna came home with a sleeping Janet in tow, they found Tony seated on the sofa with his head in his hands and the mess in the kitchen.

"What happened here?" Sal asked as Anna let out a gasp.

"It didn't go like I thought it would. She wants to leave well enough alone. Whatever that means. I lost my temper."

"That temper of yours! You're just like your father," Anna accused. "Tell me, why do you both insist on flipping over tables when you get mad?" Sal and Tony lowered their heads in shame while Anna put Janet down to sleep and went to the bedroom to talk to Ruth.

"Let's have a drink." Sal said as he opened a bottle of Chianti and poured two glasses.

"I just don't understand her."

"Son, I don't know any man who fully understands their wife. But I will tell you when your mother was pregnant with both you and Louisa, she was irrational, moody, and emotional. Boy did we get into fights back then," he said as he shook his head and smiled at the memory.

"Do you think that's it? Ruth's only three months along."

"Could be part of it. The best thing you can do is talk to her. Let her talk about her feelings. Women like that. Took me over thirty years of marriage to figure that one out. Now let's go clean up before your mother comes out." Sal took the broom out of the closet and led the way into the kitchen.

TWENTY

JUNE, 1954

RUTH

"RUTH, CAN I come in?" Anna gently knocked on the door.

"Yes, please," Ruth managed to say between tears.

"Honey, what's happening?" Anna sat on the edge of the bed and started to gently stroke her hair.

"I just don't know what's wrong with me. Tony and I have discussed marriage so many times but when he showed me the ring, I felt suffocated and panicked."

"That sounds like fear. What are you scared of?"

"I can't figure it out. I've been trying all night," she said in between sniffles.

"Do you love Tony?" Anna asked bluntly.

"I do, with my whole heart."

"Does he make you happy?"

"Yes, he's wonderful to me and an incredible father to Janet."

"Do you want to grow old with him?"

"There's nothing I want more," Ruth whispered.

"So, why not get married?"

"I guess I'm afraid everything will change if we get married. I can't help but think about how awful my first marriage turned out, and I can't go through that again. And, I don't have to tell you, Tony has quite a temper."

"Oh honey, getting married is always a gamble. Every couple goes through good times and bad. You know that already. You and Tony have gone through a lot together, and it appears to me that you both came out stronger. I can understand your fear given your past, but Ruth, you have seen Tony at his worst. And by the way the kitchen looks, he was at his worst tonight. He loves you, and you love him. I know he'll never do anything to harm you or his children. That's not his way. Sure, he'll knock over some tables and maybe punch a wall, but I know Tony will never lay a hand on you. He's just like Sal in that way. In all of these years, I've had to replace a couple of casserole dishes, but I've never feared for my safety." Anna handed Ruth a clean tissue. "In reality, you're already committed to each other and living your life like a married couple so why not make it legal?" Anna raised her eyebrows.

Ruth sat up and realized Anna had a good point. She and Tony have weathered some pretty big storms together and they really were in a good place. She's always wanted to have a husband who loved and respected her, and she had that with Tony. Why would it change if they made it legal? Life was a cycle of change, nothing could or would ever stay the same. No matter how hard someone fought against it, they couldn't alter the inevitable. A person either grew and embraced the possibility of change or they became stagnant in fear of it. Ruth lived in fear for too long. Now she realized she was ready to take a chance on happiness and welcome life's everchanging possibilities by committing to a future with the man she loved.

"Thank you for everything. I'm going to go talk to him," Ruth said as she leaned in to kiss Anna's cheek.

"Can we talk?" She asked quietly as she entered the kitchen. Both Tony and Sal looked up from cleaning the aftermath of the fight.

"Here, give me that sponge, your father and I will finish up here," Anna said gently as Sal nodded his head in agreement.

Ruth led Tony into the bedroom and took his hands as they sat on the bed.

"I'm sorry, it's just that the thought of marriage scared me a little."

"Why are you scared to marry me?"

"I'm scared that our relationship will turn sour if we get married."

"What?"

"I'm not explaining myself well." She sighed and started over. "My marriage to Harvey was a living nightmare, and I don't want anything to ruin *our* life together."

"The way I see it, we have a great thing going here. Getting married'll only make it better, not worse. I'm not Harvey. Have I ever treated you the way he did?"

"No, you never have."

"So, what makes you think that'll change?"

"Well, you did flip over a table full of food."

"Oh, that, yeah, I was angry. I guess I got that from Pop. I can't promise you that I won't do that again, but I can promise you I will *never* physically hurt you or the kids."

"I have to ask you something serious, Tony, and you need to tell me the truth. Did you have anything to do with Harvey's murder?"

Tony's eyes widened and he released Ruth's hands. "What would make you think that?"

"The night of the grand opening you had bruises on your hand."

"Yeah and?"

"Harvey had been beaten the night before his murder. Did you have anything to do with that? I need you to tell me the truth. If we're going to be married, we can't have secrets from each other."

Tony rubbed his hands on his thighs and let out a large sigh. "Truthfully, yeah. I was the one who beat Harvey."

Ruth gasped, stood, and backed away from Tony. "Oh my God."

"Ruthie, hear me out. I went to see Harvey to try to talk man-to-man with him about giving you a divorce. Things got heated. But I swear he was alive when I left. You have to believe me. I had nothing to do with his being shot."

"Why didn't you tell me? All this time and you never told me."

"When it all first happened, I thought it was best that you didn't know about the argument. The police were asking all sorts of questions, and I figured the less you knew the better it would be. I didn't wanna put that burden on you."

"How am I supposed to believe that you didn't kill him?"

"First of all, I don't own a gun and I never have. Second, if I wanted to kill Harvey, I could've done it with my bare hands. But I didn't. I made my point and walked away. I'm not gonna apologize for pounding him, he had it coming. But I do apologize for not confiding in you about it. I was only trying to protect you."

Ruth closed her eyes for a few moments and placed her hand on her growing stomach. "Your mother said that I've seen the worst that I can expect from you. Is that true?"

"Yeah," he whispered.

"You have to get a handle on your temper. You can't keep knocking over tables or beating people when you get angry."

"You have my word. I'll try my best." He smiled and kissed her tenderly. "So, what do you say, wanna finally get hitched?"

Ruth took a moment to think. She hated Tony's temper and considered it his biggest flaw. Yet through the years and all of the challenges they faced, his temper never compared to Harvey's wrath. Tony had never threatened or been cruel to anyone he loved, and he was the most compassionate and understanding man she's ever known.

"Ok, Tony, Ok." Ruth giggled with relief.

Tony pulled the ring out of his pocket, got down on his knee, and said, "I make a promise to you today that I will love you and be loyal to you for all of my days."

Ruth smiled as Tony slid the ring on her finger. She slowly looked down and gasped. "This is beautiful. Can we afford it?"

"Don't worry, Frank knows a guy that helped me out. Look here, there are smaller stones on each side of the big one. I thought every time you look at it you would see a reminder of how me and the kids are always beside you."

"It's perfect." She wrapped her arms around him and wondered how she could've ever hesitated to marry this man. He grabbed her by the hand, pulled her into the kitchen, and shouted, "She said yes!"

"Oh, thank God." Anna ran over and embraced them both at once. "I'm so happy."

"Thank you, Anna."

"Oh no. This I don't like anymore." Sal shook his head. "Ruth, you're a daughter to us. You call us Mom and Pop from now on."

"I would be honored," Ruth said embracing Sal.

"Let's start planning, any thoughts on what kind of wedding you would like?" Anna took out a notepad and pen and started writing.

"Actually, Tony, if it's ok with you I would like something small. Maybe at the restaurant?"

"That's a wonderful idea," Anna looked to Tony.

Tony nodded in agreement, "I love it."

TWENTY-ONE

JUNE, 1954
TONY

"GOOD MORNING, FRANK." Tony said as he entered the restaurant. "Is there any coffee?"

"Wow, you look tired, long night?" Frank poured two cups of coffee.

"Actually, it was a long night. Ruth and I were up for hours planning our wedding with my parents."

"Wedding? Well, it's about time. Congratulations. I mean that. I'm happy for you." Frank held up his cup in a salute.

"Thanks. I wanted to ask if you'd be my best man? We're not gonna have anything fancy, just close friends and family here at Salvatore Bruno's. We're looking at Sunday, August 19."

Frank put down his coffee cup and placed his hands on Tony's shoulders, "Of course, anything for you. You know, Tony? Maybe it's time for me to settle down with Betty too."

"Well, I'll tell you, Betty'll make a great wife, I'm sure. But it's a big commitment, both emotionally and financially. Are you ready for that?"

"Yeah, I think I'm up for it." Frank shrugged.

"You'll have to lighten up on the gambling that you're so fond of." Tony raised his eyebrows and looked him straight in the eyes.

"That's why I think it's time for me to get married. If I have to take care of a wife and maybe some kids, that'll be a good incentive to stop." Frank lit a cigarette and said softly, "I need to do something."

"Are you in trouble?"

"No, not really, but I did lose pretty big on game two of the Yankee's double header Friday night."

"How much?"

"A couple G's."

"Are you crazy?"

"I was feeling a little too lucky after the Yanks took down the Sox nine to six in game one, so I called my bookie. I was sure they'd pull it off again in game two," he said casually and shook his head.

"Do you have the money to cover it?"

"Yeah, it'll wipe me out, but I got it. That's why I gotta stop. I'm on a losing streak."

Tony took a deep breath. "Look, Frank, I've never been one to offer advice, but you really gotta get it together. Marry Betty if you love her and not for any other reason. But this gambling of yours is getting dangerous. You're gonna wipe yourself out. And then what? Don't think you can turn to the restaurant to cover your losses. Business is good, but we can't take any chances."

"No, it won't come to that."

"It better not," Tony warned. "Ok, I gotta go. I'm headed to Louisa's to tell her about the wedding."

Frank rolled his eyes. "Good luck with that. How do you think she'll take it?"

"Not sure. She's come around where Ruth's concerned. But you never know."

"Ha ha, let me know how that goes," Frank called out as Tony left the restaurant.

Tony searched for a parking spot near Louisa's apartment just off Mulberry Street in Lower Manhattan. It was never easy getting out there to visit and traffic was especially bad. Louisa sounded suspicious when Tony called to tell her he was going to stop by for lunch. He used to go to the apartment for dinner or an occasional lunch back when he had more spare time and was working at the factory. Now, he only went into the city when they'd made plans for the kids to get together. He appreciated that Louisa put in an effort to be civil with Ruth, but he still sensed an uneasiness from her whenever the two of them were together. He hoped that this turned out be a pleasant visit and she didn't get moody over the idea of the wedding.

"You're late as usual," Louisa accused as she opened the door before Tony got a chance to knock.

"Sorry, there was lots of congestion on the bridge. Here's some sausage and peppers Mom sent over for dinner tonight." He handed her the dish and kissed her cheek as he entered the apartment. Louisa's place was one of the nicest around. Bob's father was friends with the landlord and secured a great deal for the modern three bedroom back when Louisa was pregnant with Bobby. Bob's family was always so good to them, and Tony could see where Bob got his calm and generous demeanor. But he often wondered what attracted Bob to Louisa in the first place. Maybe it was a case of opposites attracting because there weren't any two people more opposite than them.

"Oh great, Bob loves Mom's sausage and peppers." Tony was relieved when Louisa smiled and led him into the kitchen. He felt optimistic that this could be a good day with her.

"I made up some sandwiches and got some salads from the deli. So, what's this visit all about?"

"I've got some good news."

"I could use some good news about now. What is it?"

"What's going on that you need good news?"

"It's not easy raising three kids you know, and Bob's never home what with the deli and all," she said sounding defeated.

"I know it's hard. Don't forget I keep long hours at the restaurant too."

"Yes, but you have Mom and Pop helping you. Who do I have?"

"We thought things were going good for you. We didn't know you're struggling."

"We're not struggling," she said exasperated. "Just forget it, what's your good news?"

"Ruth and I set a date and we're gonna get married in August."

"Why?"

"What do you mean, why?"

"I mean, why now? Why after all this time are you going to marry her?"

"You know very well we've wanted to get married all along but couldn't. Things are good now so we wanna make it official."

"Hmph, ok, so now you'll be married with two kids. Where are you going to live? You certainly can't keep staying with Mom and Pop."

"We've been talking about that. I wanna maybe find a bigger place for all of us to live."

"Have you thought any of this through? Do you have the money for a bigger place?"

"Actually, between Pop and me, I think we could swing it."

"So there you go, you're still depending on our parents for your own comfort."

"My own comfort? Oh, please. There's nothing comfortable about this at all. Yeah, ok, Mom and Pop are a great help to Ruth and me, but if you needed help you know they'd be there for you."

Before Louisa could respond Rena walked into the kitchen with her head down.

"Hey, there she is. How are ya kiddo?"

"Hi Uncle Tony, I'm fine," she said quietly sitting down at the table.

"Did you do everything I told you to do today, Rena?" Louisa's voice was flat.

"Yes."

"Well, I hope so. I better not go into that bathroom and find that it isn't cleaned the way I like it, and look at me when I'm talking to you," Louisa said as she reached over and placed her hand under Rena's chin and pushed her head up.

"So, did you clean it properly?"

"Yes, it's cleaned properly." Rena shook her head away from Louisa's hand and looked down again.

"Rena, you must be excited for the school carnival coming up." Tony attempted to lighten the mood.

"I'm not going," Rena whispered.

"Why not?"

"I'll tell you why not," Louisa answered. "She fell behind on her studies. Her grades went from mostly A's last year to some B's this year."

"Well B's aren't so bad. Surely going to a carnival wouldn't be so terrible." Rena looked at Tony, smiled, and turned her head hopefully to Louisa.

"Rena has to earn the right to enjoy the fun stuff. When she brings up her grades and does her chores to my satisfaction, she can participate in social activities. She knows the rules."

Tony stared at Louisa for a moment shocked at what he just heard and took a deep breath. He wondered if he should continue the conversation but decided to let it go for now. He didn't want to make things worse for Rena. It was moments like this that Tony felt exceptionally guilty. Rena's sad and defeated expression broke his heart, and he was at a loss on how to help her. He was the one who agreed years ago to allow Louisa and Bob to raise her as their own and now he hated how hard Louisa was on her.

"Maybe Ruth and I can help you with some of your studies over the summer. What do you think, kiddo?"

Louisa sighed and rolled her eyes as Rena said, "I would like that, Uncle Tony."

"Speaking of Ruth," Tony said. "She and I are gonna get married in August. Ruth really wants you to be a part of the ceremony. Maybe a bridesmaid? Would you like that?"

Rena shrugged. "I guess so. What would I have to do?"

"Well, it's gonna be a small ceremony at the restaurant. You will stand up front with us while the justice of the peace marries us. You will be an official witness to the marriage. It's not a hard job, but it's a very important one."

"Well, we'll have to see," Louisa interjected.

"No, I'm insisting on this. If Rena would like to be a part of our day, then she will." Tony stood and tapped his pointer finger on the table. He stared at Louisa until she backed down.

"Ok, fine. Now Rena say goodbye to Uncle Tony and go clean

your room."

Rena raised her arms up and hugged Tony. "Bye Uncle Tony. I love you," she said as she hugged him tightly.

"I love you, kiddo. We'll see you real soon." Tony kissed her forehead, waited for her to be out of earshot and said, "Do you think you're being a little too hard on her?"

"Don't you tell me how to raise her. You haven't been in it day to day like me. You don't know. You don't have the right to be judgmental. You just don't know. It's hard keeping up with three kids and a husband who's never around."

Tony raised his hands up in defense. "Okay, but I mean it about the wedding. We insist she be a part of it."

"Ok, fine, she can be in it."

TWENTY-TWO

JUNE, 1954
RUTH

THE LAST TIME Ruth had seen Ethan was in March. He had gotten engaged to Rachel and she and Tony took them out to dinner to celebrate. Ruth had just found out she was pregnant, and they agreed not to announce her pregnancy to keep the celebration focused on Ethan and Rachel. But, during dinner Ethan noticed Ruth wasn't eating much and they wound up sharing their good news after all. Since that night Ruth and Ethan had tried to find a good time to see each other but between her morning sickness and Ethan's new responsibilities at work, it's been hard to find the free time. They finally settled on a quick visit during his lunch hour at the park by his office. After finding a bench near the playground, Ruth saw Ethan stride toward her, and barely recognized him as he approached. He appeared taller, broader, and more confident than she had ever seen him. She remembered Ethan as a child. He was always so different than their older brother, Isaac. Ethan was more sensitive and affectionate. When Isaac would push him around or bully him into doing chores Isaac didn't want to do, Ethan wouldn't always stand up for himself in the moment. That's not to say he was a pushover. Ruth remembered many times when Ethan won a battle or had the last laugh, but it wouldn't be through fear or intimidation. Ethan quietly and strategically planned his defense and stayed his course until he was triumphant. Ruth always admired his calm demeanor, but she thought he was misunderstood as a result of it.

"Hey there," he said as they hugged.

"You look fantastic."

"Things are really going well for me. I've gotten a promotion at the insurance agency and Rachel has agreed to marry me. It doesn't get better than this."

"You deserve this happiness, baby brother, you really do." Ruth loved Rachel like a sister. She hoped their marriage worked out well for them, and she thought they stood a good chance together just so long as Ethan and Ruth's parents didn't try to make demands on them. Rachel's family was not as conservative as their parents were, and Ethan was growing to appreciate their point of view over his strict upbringing.

"Thanks. Before I forget, here's some of the latest pictures of Miriam."

"Oh." Ruth felt a large lump in her throat as she looked through the pictures. "She's gotten so big, so mature looking. Ethan, is there any way I can see her? I don't want to put you in a difficult position, but I just miss her so much."

"I'm sorry. You know it's not a good idea. Miriam is at that age where she's a talker. At seven years old, she can't help herself, and I'm afraid she'll slip and tell. You know what happened the last time you saw her. She told Mom everything. It was all I could do to convince

Mom that we ran into each other by accident, and I assured her that we would ignore you if we ever saw you again." Ethan put her hands in his. "I know it's hard but it's the only way. Dad threatened to send Miriam to Israel to live with his relatives if he heard you had contact with her again."

"Oh, he wouldn't do that." She shook her head in disbelief.

"You don't know him anymore. He's changed. He's hardened, shows no emotion now except anger. I have no doubt that he would send Miriam away, and if that happens, none of us will ever see her again. At least now, I'm able to be there for her and make sure she's ok."

Ruth looked out over the playground and wondered if a day would come where all of her children could get to know each other. She often daydreamed about Miriam and Janet doing things together like most sisters do, and now that she's pregnant again she felt Miriam's absence just as strong as she did three years ago. She nodded her head in agreement. "Thank you for all you're doing. I really do appreciate it."

"I just want both of you to find some happiness under the circumstances."

"I'll never be fully happy without Miriam, but this helps." She said and rubbed her finger on the pictures. "So, Tony and I decided to go ahead and officially get married," Ruth said to change the subject. When she started to feel that familiar weight of loss come upon her, Ruth found that blocking all thoughts of Miriam out of her mind was the only thing that helped her cope.

"You did! Mazel Tov."

"Thanks." Ruth smiled widely. "Do you think you and Rachel can come? It's going to be on Sunday, August 19th at the restaurant. Nothing fancy, just close friends and family."

"Yes, of course we'll be there. We wouldn't miss it."

"Good," she took his hand. "And while you're there what do you think of walking me down the aisle?"

Ethan's mouth opened slightly, and Ruth couldn't quite read his reaction.

"It would be my honor," he whispered and kissed her hand.

"You know, you, Rachel, and even Joan are all I have left of my family."

"I know, and it breaks my heart. I wish things could be different. Let me ask you something, was it all worth it?"

"I'm not going to lie. There are some days that I just don't think I'm going to make it through the dark sadness. But I do. I smile and feel happy as I watch Janet laughing and playing with Tony. I feel peace in Anna's warm touch as she hugs me every morning when I get up and every night before I go to bed. And I find comfort in Sal's wink when he takes the first bite of a dish I've prepared. I've found a type of love and acceptance in this new family that I've never known before, and I know I can't live without."

"Good. If anyone deserves love and peace, it's you. I hated Harvey for all he's done to you, and I never thought it was right the way the family wouldn't help you from the beginning. I know it's hard to let go of our ways and customs, but I've already told Rachel that I will not stand for any child of mine to be treated the way you've been, and I'm not afraid to be ostracized by the community."

"Be careful, sometimes that's easier said than done." Ruth feared how her parents would react to Ethan's independent thinking. Being the baby of the family, he was indulged more than both Isaac and Ruth, but she knew there's a limit to her parents' level of tolerance even where Ethan was concerned.

"Rachel understands and agrees. We both feel that the culture that you and I were raised in is too harsh. When we get married, we're going to live in Rachel's less orthodox neighborhood."

"Really? Good for you. I'm proud of you. That's a big step. But tread lightly with the family, Ethan. I'd hate to see you shunned like me. It's one thing to think it won't be hard, but trust and believe me, it's not easy."

"You're an inspiration. You don't know it, but you've given me the confidence to make decisions based on my own happiness."

"I don't want to be the cause of trouble between you and the family."

"You're not. And I *am* treading lightly. I've started dropping hints about my plans and Papa just silently nods. Maybe he's starting to realize he can't control everyone. I'm just sorry that things are so bad for you."

"Don't be sorry. I'm glad my experience has made you and I both strong. That's one good thing that came out of it all."

They sat in silence together for a few moments before Ethan said, "I'm sorry I can't visit with you longer, but I really do have to get back to work. Call me at the office and let me know the details of the wedding."

"I will. Give my love to Rachel." Ruth watched Ethan as he walked away thinking how lucky she was to have such an amazing brother.

TWENTY-THREE

AUGUST, 1954
TONY

THE NEXT TWO months flew by in a whirlwind of wedding planning. Anna took control of organizing the whole event following each of Ruth's wishes and made some suggestions of her own. It was an easy task for Anna. She enjoyed entertaining and putting together parties, and this wedding was an extra special event for her. She couldn't love Ruth more if she was her own daughter. She thanked God every day for answering her prayers by bringing love and happiness into Tony's life again. Pouring over each detail and wanting everything to be more than perfect was Anna's way of showing her love.

Tony had been marking off the calendar each day in anticipation for this one. He would've been happy getting married in the courthouse, but he was glad he didn't push the idea. He noticed the excitement that had gone into planning their wedding had made Ruth blossom, and he had never seen her so full of life. He really got a kick out of watching Ruth and Anna as they sat at the table with their heads together. They would excitedly talk about every little detail essential for the wedding and made meticulous notes about flower arrangements, centerpieces, and color schemes. During these times he and Sal would be happily banished from the kitchen and charged with looking after Janet. Now that the big day was here, Tony found himself more nervous than he ever thought he would be. Ruth and Anna made him spend the night at Frank's apartment for fear of having bad luck at seeing the bride before the wedding. Tony was glad they did. He appreciated the time he got to spend with Frank as they sat up long into the night and reminisced about their younger days and made big plans for the future. But nothing, not even Frank's sense of humor could calm Tony's nerves.

They closed Salvatore Bruno's for the wedding, and Anna gave Lou strict instructions and diagrams on how the entire place should be set up for the ceremony and reception. He supervised all of the arrangements and if any rose or carnation was out of place, he knew he would suffer Anna's wrath. When Anna arrived at the restaurant, he was relieved after she gave him a smile and a nod in spite of straightening the candelabra centerpieces on each table.

Tony stood under a flower arch made of white hydrangeas and pink carnations that Anna had made special for the ceremony. He wiped his sweaty hands on his black tuxedo pants when Frank whispered, "This is it." He took a deep breath and turned to see Ruth walk down the aisle. She was radiant in her champagne colored, A-line, satin dress with lace overlay. She held a full bouquet of pink roses and green ivy in front of her stomach, and no one would have noticed her growing belly. At the very moment when their eyes met, Tony's body tingled. As Ruth slowly glided toward him on Ethan's arm, she smiled brightly. He couldn't help but think about all they've gone through to get to this day. Ten years ago, he never would've thought his life would take the turns it had, and he knew how lucky he was to be where he was now. He shook Ethan's hand and took Ruth's in his own and noticed a small tear that streamed down her cheek. He softly swept the tear with his thumb and Judge O'Connor began the ceremony.

"Dearly beloved, we are gathered together here today to unite Anthony Arthur and Ruth Sarah in marriage. This contract is not to be entered into lightly, but thoughtfully and seriously with a deep realization of its obligations and responsibilities." Tony looked around and beamed as Anna wiped her eyes with a handkerchief, Sal lovingly patted her shoulder, and Louisa tried to take away a yo-yo that Bobby somehow smuggled in.

"Do you, Anthony, take this woman to be your lawfully wedded wife to have and to hold from this day forward, for better, for worse, for richer, for poorer, in sickness and in health, to love and to cherish, till death do you part?"

"I do," he said proudly and firmly which made Ruth chuckle.

"Do you Ruth, take this man to be your lawfully wedded husband to have and to hold from this day forward, for better, for worse, for richer, for poorer, in sickness and in health, to love and to cherish, till death do you part?"

Ruth squeezed his hands and tenderly replied, "I do."

"If there is anyone present who may show just and lawful cause why this couple may not be legally wed, let them speak now or forever hold their peace."

Both Ruth and Tony rolled their eyes when Frank sternly scanned the room and then nodded at the judge.

"By the authority vested in me by the State of New York, I now pronounce you both husband and wife. You may kiss your bride."

"Thank you, Judge."

Tony leaned in and lovingly kissed Ruth just before he dipped her, kissed her again, and raised their clasped hands in the air. With a roar of laughter and cheers, everyone rushed forward and exclaimed their congratulations.

After dinner, Tony took Ruth into his arms to dance their first dance together. Their wedding song was the only thing that Tony insisted he choose himself, and as the band crooned Nat King Cole's hit, "Unforgettable," Tony sang the words softly into Ruth's ear.

They were uplifted by the applause of the guests, and after he twirled Ruth, he said "Ruthie, you look stunning."

"Aw." She softly kissed his cheek. "I was worried about picking out a flattering dress being five months pregnant now."

"It's perfect. I mean it, Mrs. Russo."

"Now, I like the sound of that." She glowed as she heard her married name for the first time.

"So do I."

Sal interrupted their blissful moment as he spoke into the microphone with Anna by his side.

"Can I ask everyone to please take a seat and grab a drink," he said nervously. "At this time, we want to offer our congratulations to our son, Anthony, and our new daughter, Ruth, on their marriage. This day was a long time coming, and we just wanted to say how proud we are of both of you." Sal raised his glass of champagne, "May your lives improve with every passing year and be filled with health, wealth, and happiness. To our family, alla nostra famiglia."

Tony and Ruth were caught up in the moment and lingered over a kiss before they touched their glasses together and whispered, "alla nostra famiglia." When they looked up, they saw Sal, Anna, and Frank circled around Betty.

"What's going on?" Tony asked as he and Ruth joined them hand in hand.

"We got engaged," Betty beamed. "Frank just asked me."

"Really? You had to do it today?" Tony joked.

"I thought what better time than at a happy family gathering." Frank shrugged.

"Well, I think it's wonderful." Ruth smiled. "Congratulations." She playfully jabbed Tony in the side.

"Yes, congratulations! I'm happy for you both." Tony gave Frank a bear hug as Ruth admired Betty's ring.

"Oh, I love this song. Come on everyone," Anna exclaimed.

Tony noticed Rena was sitting alone at a table and grabbed her hand on his way to join everyone on the dance floor. He couldn't believe how mature she looked in her rose-colored gown and her hair all pinned up. They all formed a circle while the band played Dean Martin's, "That's Amore." Together they sang loudly and smiled brightly and swayed to the music. Tony closed his eyes as he took in the moment that he would remember for the rest of his life.

The next morning, Tony wondered if leaving for their honeymoon in the Poconos the day after their wedding was such a good idea after all. Ruth was very tired, and he was very hungover.

"Well good morning, you two. I'm making a nice breakfast before you leave."

"Thanks, Mom. But, I'm not very hungry."

"After all you drank, you'll need a solid meal." Sal winked and filled two cups of coffee.

"Here, let me help." Ruth offered.

"No, now you just sit down. You are officially on your honeymoon, and I won't have you cooking or cleaning. Not today."

"Well, alright. You know, Tony and I want to thank you both for everything you've done for the wedding. It was an amazing day. One of the happiest days of my life."

"Yes," Tony added. "You both really went above and beyond."

"That's all your mother. No one can plan a party like she can," Sal said proudly.

"It's nothing." Anna waved her hand. "All done from love. But I will say, everyone seemed to have a great time."

"Everyone except Lou," Sal laughed. "You had him on his toes the whole night. I don't think he's ever worked so hard, and he's one of the best."

"Oh please, I just wanted him to pay attention to the fine details, that's all. Ruth, it was so good to spend some time with Ethan and Rachel. Such a nice girl she is."

"She is a nice girl. I think she's really good for him. They make a great couple."

"I like Ethan, he's a good man." Sal nodded. "So now Frankie's getting married, huh?" Sal raised his eyebrows.

"Did you see Betty's engagement ring? Frank must've paid a fortune," Anna said.

"Yeah, I saw it," Sal said. "Where do you think he got that kind of money?"

"I dunno, Pop." Tony shook his head and thought about his conversation with Frank a few months ago. He wondered if Frank did the right thing and saved the money or if he won big on a bet.

"He couldn't have saved that much money. I think he's still betting on the horses among other things." Sal said as if he read Tony's mind.

"Well, maybe marriage'll be good for him, settle him down,"

Tony suggested.

"We'll see. I'm going to have a little talk with him. The gambling needs to stop. Why don't you start to keep a closer eye on things when you get back. Just to be sure," Sal said.

"Okay." Tony took a bite of toast. He was glad Sal was going to talk to Frank about gambling. Maybe Frank would take it more seriously coming from Sal. Besides, right now Tony was more concerned about his daughter than he was about Frank. "Hey, Mom, have you noticed anything off about Rena?"

"What do you mean?" Anna placed platters of eggs, bacon, and pancakes on the table.

"Every time I see her lately, she seems to be very quiet, withdrawn almost. She doesn't seem happy."

"I haven't really noticed these past few weeks, my mind's been on the wedding and all."

"Actually, I've noticed she hasn't been eating much during our Sunday dinners," Ruth added.

"I'm a little worried about her. I think Louisa's being really tough on her," Tony said.

"I'm sure it's nothing, but your father and I will go in and pay a visit sometime soon and see for ourselves."

"We will? Why can't they come here? You know I hate driving over there. You can never find parking."

"We will!" Anna insisted. "Now don't worry about a thing you two go ahead and enjoy your honeymoon."

TWENTY-FOUR

OCTOBER, 1954
RUTH

RUTH AND TONY were home from their honeymoon for about a week when she started to cramp. Anna took her to the doctor who didn't seem to be worried and said she needed to get rest and gain more weight. His advice seemed to have worked because over a month later she had been starting to feel better and had gotten a healthy glow. But now something felt wrong. As Ruth rolled over and looked at the clock, she saw that it was two in the morning and the cramping had come back. "Ok, ok, it's going to be ok," she said to herself as she tried to make her way to the bathroom. But fear hit suddenly as she noticed blood. She rushed back to the bedroom, shook Tony forcefully and cried, "Tony wake up. TONY!"

"Ruthie, what is it?" He bolted up.

"Something's wrong. We've got to go to the hospital." Ruth tried to contain her panic as Tony rushed around the apartment and woke Sal and Anna. Ruth's felt some concern about this pregnancy almost from the beginning. The doctor didn't seem worried, but Ruth felt things were different this time. She's had all-day morning sickness, and this baby seemed to be much smaller than both Miriam and Janet.

As Sal and Anna helped Ruth down to the car, Ruth whispered, "I'm scared."

"I know you are honey, but you be strong and think positive thoughts. You and the baby are Russos and Russos are fighters." Anna's confidence was the very thing that Ruth needed.

As he helped Ruth into the car, all Sal could do was kiss her cheek. He wanted to be strong for them, but his fear was paralyzing. As he stood at the curb his eyes watered as they pulled away. He silently prayed, "Dear God, please protect them."

Ruth tried to remain calm while Tony navigated the empty streets to the hospital. She remembered a conversation they had on the way back from their honeymoon.

"I wonder if I'm carrying a boy this time?"

"A *boy*? Wouldn't that be something. What makes you think it's a boy?"

"I don't know. All around this pregnancy is different."

"I suppose you could be right," Tony said beaming. "Anthony, Jr., imagine that."

From the start, Ruth convinced herself that she was carrying a boy to ease her anxiety. To her relief, Anna's friends from the neighborhood predicted a male baby based on how she was carrying and her sickness. They even confirmed this by holding Ruth's wedding ring tied to a string over her belly. Ruth laughed with delight when it started rocking in a back-and-forth motion which signified a baby boy.

Tony grabbed her hand. "We're here." She had never seen him

look so scared before, his face was white, and his hand was sweaty.

Everything happened so quickly, and Ruth reached out her hand and cried, "Tony ..." as they wheeled her into an examining room,

"I know, honey, I'm right here. These doctors are good. They'll make everything all right."

"Mr. Russo," a nurse approached Tony, "we're going to have to ask you to wait in the waiting room, now. We will keep you updated."

"Oh, ok," Tony said confused. "Ruthie, you hang in there. I, I won't be far away, honey." He leaned over and kissed her forehead and was pushed out of the room by the nurse. All at once Ruth couldn't breathe. She saw black spots before her eyes and reached out for Tony once more just before she lost consciousness.

TWENTY-FIVE

DECEMBER, 1954
TONY

"TONY, ARE YOU sure you don't want me to drive you?" Sal asked as he handed Tony the car keys.

"No, I got this."

"Everything's all set for when you come back. We'll have a light dinner today, and a fine Christmas celebration tomorrow with just the family," Anna said as she put a scarf around his neck and handed him a tray of cookies.

"That'll be perfect."

"Now get going, Janet's waited long enough to see her mother and meet her baby sister, Nancy."

Nancy, their miracle baby. It was pretty scary there for a while and they weren't sure she was going to make it. Ruth was admitted to the hospital on that crazy night in October when she started bleeding. The doctors were worried about the placenta and a premature birth, so they kept her confined to a bed and monitored her and the baby in an effort to prolong the pregnancy. There could've been a chance that the baby's lungs and other organs wouldn't have been developed fully if she were born so early. Ruth held out as long as she could, but Nancy was eager to come into the world and decided that her time in the womb was long enough. She was born on November 23 and weighed almost four pounds. Ruth had lost a lot of blood during the delivery, so it was decided to keep them both in the hospital until they improved. Nancy spent most of that time in an incubator, and Ruth tried to spend as much time as she could at her side. Everyone was thrilled when they found out that Nancy's lungs were strong, and they were being discharged just in time for Christmas.

On his way to the hospital, Tony thought about how grateful he was to have his wife and daughter home and healthy for the holiday. He didn't even mind navigating the crowded department store earlier in the week so that he could buy gifts for everyone. Ruth always took care of the Christmas shopping and actually enjoyed the hustle and bustle of the season. Everyone knew that Tony would rather do just about anything but spend hours shopping in a department store filled with people pushing and shoving just to get their hands on the latest bargain. But this year, he was happy to do it. Anna helped wrap the gifts while Sal took Janet to see Santa. Tony and Ruth were both disappointed that they couldn't bring her themselves, but they knew how much both Sal and Janet enjoyed it.

Tony greeted the hospital receptionist and while he waited for the elevator, he stole a cookie from the tray Anna made for the nurses. Each year her cookies were one of the highlights of Christmas, and this year she insisted on making extra for the nurses at the fourth-floor nurses' station. They all appreciated how attentive and caring they were and seemed to take a genuine interest in getting to know the whole family. They were always so kind and even looked the other way when Sal snuck Janet in to see Ruth. Tony made the rounds and thanked each nurse personally for taking good care of his Ruthie and their baby, Nancy. When he was finished, he paused for just a moment outside of Ruth's room. He had bottled up all of his stress over the past few months, and once the doctor said his girls could come home, the tension started to release itself. He found that his right eye started twitching, he had a mild but constant headache, and he had become more sensitive emotionally. He took a deep breath, wiped his tear-filled eyes and breezed into the room.

"Hey, beautiful, are you ready to go home and meet your family?" Tony gingerly lifted Nancy and cradled her in his arms.

"Yes, Daddy, we're both ready." Ruth smiled and wrapped her arms around his waist. "I can't wait to get out of here."

"Well then let's go. Mom is making dinner while Pop is helping Janet make a welcome home banner. I don't know who's more excited to have you home out of the three of them."

It took them close to a half hour to gather their things and say their goodbyes to the nurses. Tony drove slowly and he put his arm out across Ruth and the baby each time they came to an intersection.

"So, tell me about the new rental house." Ruth hoped the conversation would relax Tony some.

Tony chuckled, "That's right, you were pretty out of it when it all came to be."

"All I remember is that your father had a friend who had a house to rent but it needed some work."

"Yes, Pop made a deal with his good friend, Vic Dionota, to rent one of his properties in the neighborhood. It's only a few blocks from where we are now."

"It's perfect timing. I don't know how all six of would manage in the apartment."

"The timing really is perfect. Vic had to evict the tenant from the house for lack of payment. When he saw the condition of the place, he knew he didn't have the time to work on it himself, so he offered it to Pop. They made an agreement that we would fix it up in exchange for a break on the rent."

"That was so very kind."

"Originally Vic wanted to sell the house to us, but it really is best to rent it first and make sure we all really like it there."

"I can't wait to see it."

"I think it'll work well for us. Pop just loves it. Not only does it have four bedrooms, but it has a finished basement. Pop thinks he can build a bedroom and living area down there for him and Mom and give us all some privacy. I really love the yard. There's enough room to put up a swing set for the kids, a vegetable garden for Mom, and a patio area that we can all enjoy."

"How's your mother feeling about this?"

"Mom's struggling with the idea of moving out of the only home we've had in New York. It's hard for her because the old apartment has a lot of memories. But Pop's been going over there every chance he gets. He's trying to spruce it up nice for everyone and has done most of the painting and repairs. He's now putting in modern cabinets and appliances."

"A brand-new kitchen? Now I'm really excited."

"Yeah, once Mom heard about that she started warming up to the idea of moving. Of course, she's happy we'll all be together in a bigger place, but I think the kitchen is what's really winning her over." Tony was quiet for a few moments, then added. "I'm starting to wonder if Louisa has anything to do with Mom's resistance."

"Why do you say that?"

"It's nothing specific, it just seems that after Mom speaks with

Louisa, she is quieter than usual. Sometimes she even gets extra snappy with Pop."

"I remember you had said a while ago that Louisa wasn't keen on the idea of us getting a bigger place with your parents. But if it's what they want, I would think Louisa would be okay with it."

"The problem is Louisa thinks Mom and Pop help us financially more than they do her."

"That's ridiculous. We pay your parents every month for rent and utilities, not to mention food. I can't tell you how many coupons I clip and things we do without so that we can save enough money for a new place."

"I know, honey, I know. Don't get yourself upset. Besides, Louisa is gonna think what she wants regardless of what anyone says or does. We'll move into the house soon enough, and Mom'll be just as happy as she was living in the apartment. Even happier." Tony smiled at Ruth as he pulled up in front of their building.

"We'll be sure to make lots of happy memories in the new house." Ruth nodded and kissed Nancy gently on her forehead.

TWENTY-SIX

DECEMBER, 1954
RUTH

"HERE THEY ARE!" Sal announced as Ruth carried Nancy through the door. "Janet, come. Come meet your baby sister." Each time a new grandchild was carried through their door, Sal's heart grew with an abundance of pride. Today, it was greater than ever. All of his other grandchildren were full-term, healthy babies weighing in at close to six pounds or more. Nancy's premature birth really shook him, but he had to hide it and be the strong one. Especially for Janet. She needed him throughout the whole ordeal and truth be told, he needed her just as much. Sal took it upon himself to look after Janet so that the weight of missing her mother wouldn't be so heavy. In turn Janet's innocent laughter and enormous hugs gave him strength. He took Nancy from Ruth's arms and was astounded at how incredibly tiny and delicate she was. Getting choked up, he just stared into her angelic face and silently said a prayer of thanks. Fearful that he might accidentally hurt her, he delicately handed her over to Tony and led Janet to the sofa so she could sit next to her father.

"Here pumpkin, sit here next to Daddy and Nancy." Sal pulled out his handkerchief and wiped his eyes as he turned and walked into the kitchen.

Ruth sat on the other side of Janet, grabbed her face, and showered her with kisses all over her cheeks, forehead, and nose. "Oh, how I missed you." Janet giggled and hugged Ruth tightly. "Did you miss Mommy?" Ruth asked.

"We all missed you, Ruth," Anna said as Janet nodded her head. "It's so good to have you and the baby home. I've decided this year we're going to have a simple Christmas and not the usual open house feast we usually host."

"Oh, no. You didn't have to do that on account of us. I know how much you love your Christmas celebrations."

"I love celebrating Christmas. It's a time for me to express how grateful I am for having the people I love in my life. This year, I'm most grateful for my family. I want us to spend the time celebrating each other. I'll have a nice open house party for the neighborhood sometime after New Year."

"Thank you," Ruth said. "That sounds wonderful."

"It will be." Anna smiled. "I've invited Ethan and Rachel to join us tomorrow."

"You did?"

"Of course, honey. They're family."

Ruth enjoyed every bit of the holiday more than usual. She didn't realize how much she missed spending a holiday with her brother, and although this was Ethan and Rachel's first time celebrating Christmas, they took it in stride. For Ruth, her favorite part of day was watching the kids' excitement over the magic of Santa Claus.

Tony took great care to surprise Janet on Christmas morning with a pile of gifts especially picked out for her and Nancy by Santa. They all got a kick out of watching Janet bring each of Nancy's gifts over to her. Ruth noticed everyone seemed to be more relaxed and festive this year, but she still took great care in her conversations with Louisa. She didn't have the energy for Louisa's negativity and thought it best to stick to simple topics. Nancy was a nice, safe topic, and Louisa was very loving to her brand-new niece. By the end of the night, she became a bit of a baby hog and wouldn't let anyone near her.

Anna passed out the last of the eggnog, as Ruth slumped onto the sofa. "I thought she'd never fall asleep. Janet never wants to miss a thing and wills herself to stay awake. Thank goodness Nancy was able to sleep most of the time what with everyone passing her around like a hot potato."

"I remember those days. It was all I could do to get Tony to go to sleep whenever we had company. He was the social one, and always had a way of convincing us to let him stay up until all hours." Anna laughed.

"Sophia and Bobby are the same way with Louisa. Looks like it drives her crazy." Sal put his glass down and leaned in seriously toward Tony. "I've noticed what you were saying about Rena. She didn't have her usual Christmas spark tonight."

Tony nodded his head. "I was thinking she'd be more excited to meet Nancy. Do you remember how captivated she was with Janet? She barely looked Nancy's way."

"Oh honey, I wouldn't read too much into that. She's heard a lot of talk about how fragile Nancy was and she's probably a little intimidated because she's so small. Maybe she's going through a phase. I know Louisa was very moody when she was turning thirteen."

"I hope that's all it is."

"It's been such a difficult time for us lately. Now that Ruth and Nancy are healthy and at home, your father and I will go over there after the New Year like we promised. By the way, did I hear Frankie and Betty ask her to be a part of their wedding?"

"Yes." Ruth nodded her head. "Betty said that they asked Louisa if all the kids could be in the wedding."

"How big is this wedding going to be?" Sal asked.

"All I know is they are having a church service and reception over at that new fancy place, Esposito's."

"Esposito's?" Sal leaned in. "Isn't that Carmine Esposito's place?"

"I don't think Carmine owns it; I think his nephew does. Frank said Betty fell in love with the place and he couldn't talk her out of it." Tony shrugged his shoulders.

"I don't like it," Sal grumbled.

"It really is a lovely place," Ruth offered. "In May their gardens will be beautiful."

"I'm sure Betty will make a beautiful bride also," Anna added. "Salvatore, so what if the reception is in a fancy reception hall. If they're happy, then we will be too."

"I don't mind where they have the reception, I'm just concerned about Frankie's connection to Carmine. It seems to be too much of a coincidence for me."

"Pop, I haven't seen any funny business going on with Frank," Tony said. "I know Betty does like nice things, and Esposito's is a very nice place."

"Yeah, ok. Good." Sal sighed and leaned back in his chair.

"Ruth, I was so happy that Ethan and Rachel were here today," Anna said changing the subject.

"They really seemed to enjoy themselves, and it was so great to spend a holiday together again. They knew how I felt about not being able to be at their wedding, so they gave me a home movie from that day as a gift. They even wrapped it up in Christmas paper."

"You know, I've been telling Sal that we need to get one of those film recording cameras. Mrs. Scardino's son-in-law has one and they love it. Maybe you can borrow her projector to view it."

"That's a great idea, I'll speak with her next week." Ruth yawned. "It's been a long couple of days, and I'm exhausted, so I'm going to say goodnight."

Ruth hugged and kissed Anna and Sal and overcome with emotion said, "I love you both so much."

TWENTY-SEVEN

JANUARY, 1955
TONY

A FEW DAYS after the start of the New Year, Tony borrowed the film projector from Mrs. Scardino. He knew Ruth was feeling both excited and anxious about seeing Ethan's wedding and decided that they should watch it together. He was hoping for the moral support of his parents, but they arranged to go have dinner at Louisa's on the only night he was free to watch the film. Tony knew it would be tough for Ruth to see her family on the screen, especially her daughter, but at the same time, he was also glad his parents were going to check in on Rena.

"Hey, Pop, can you help with this?" Tony asked as he tried to get the projector through the door.

"Easy, easy with it," Anna navigated. "I'll never hear the end of it from Mrs. Scardino if something happens to that thing."

"It was nice of her to let us borrow it. I only wish that you could watch the wedding with us. What time are you supposed to be at

Louisa's?" Ruth asked.

"Dinner's at seven," Sal mumbled as he attempted to load the film reel.

"Why so late?"

Anna placed her hand on Sal's shoulder and said, "Bob has to stay late at the deli, and I don't want to wait any longer to talk to Louisa about Rena. She flinched when I touched her arm on New Year's. She said I startled her, but I'm not so sure."

"Why didn't you tell me?" Tony looked up concerned.

"I knew you'd be upset, and I want to talk to Louisa before we jump to conclusions."

It was too late. Tony already jumped to conclusions. He didn't like the big change in Rena's personality over the past few years. Everyone's been chalking it up to pre-teen angst, but as her father, he felt strongly that it was something more serious. He might not have been with her on a daily basis, but Tony knew his daughter. She was a part of him, and he knew in his gut something was not right.

"I think we should get going," Sal said as he looked at his watch.

"Ok, ok." Anna hugged Ruth. "Ruth, honey, I'm sorry I can't be here with you to watch the film." She leaned in and whispered to Tony, "Be prepared, it's going to be difficult for Ruth to see Miriam on that film."

"I got it, Mom. Don't worry."

Sal winked at Ruth, pat Tony on the shoulder and then said as he and Anna walked out the door, "Why so many bags? Bob owns a deli and we're not moving in."

Tony and Ruth chuckled as Sal and Anna fussed with each other as they made their way out to the car.

Tony woke up, startled to hear someone pounding on the apartment door at one o'clock in the morning. He rushed to answer it before they woke everyone else up.

"Joan, Alan, what are you doing here? What time is it?" Tony said confused as he tried to process why Ruth's best friend and her husband were standing at the door.

"What's going on?" Ruth said as she tied her robe closed.

Alan spoke first, "Can we come in? This is my friend, Officer Donohue."

"Please, call me Jack," he said as he extended his hand.

"What's wrong?" Ruth reached out for Joan's hand.

Jack removed his hat, looked down, and said, "There's no easy way to tell you this." He then looked directly into Tony's eyes.

"A call came into my precinct from the New York City police. There's been an accident involving your parents tonight. I recognized their names and knew that Alan and Joan were good friends of yours so I asked if we could all personally come out to see you."

The silence in the room was deafening as Jack paused to take a deep breath.

"I'm sorry to tell you this, but your parents have been killed."

Tony stared at him in disbelief, and could hear Ruth say, "I don't understand, there must be some kind of mistake. They're here! They're here! They're sleeping in their bed."

He shifted his eyes to Ruth as her panicked voice got louder and she rushed over and opened their bedroom door.

"Oh my God! *Tony.*" She sobbed and fell to her knees as she found the room empty.

Tony was stuck. He couldn't comfort his wife. He couldn't speak, he couldn't move, he couldn't even think. In that moment, Tony could not comprehend what was happening. He just stared as

Joan rushed over to Ruth, sat on the floor next to her, and embraced her as Ruth wailed and rocked back and forth.

"What's happening?" Tony thought to himself. He had a strange feeling of being disconnected from reality. He knew in his mind that he was there in the living room, but his consciousness was foggy, almost as if he was in another realm looking at himself.

Tony shook his head to try to end the nightmare.

A loud ringing blared through his ears, and he could barely hear Jack say, "I'm so terribly sorry."

He backed away from Alan who tried to place his hand on Tony's shoulder. He turned and punched the wall so hard it rattled the lamp on the side table. He looked down at his bleeding knuckles and felt no pain. He just stared at the blood as it dripped from his hand onto the floor and formed a small pool.

He mumbled, "Mom will be upset when she sees this stain on the rug." Jack led Tony to the sofa as Alan gathered ice from the kitchen for his hand.

Faintly, in the distance Tony heard a small voice, "Mommy?"

But Tony was still stuck. His existence still felt murky and all he could do was observe as Joan jumped to her feet and raced over to Janet.

"Hi honey, everything's ok. Mommy and Daddy aren't feeling very good right now. Let's see if we can get you back to sleep."

He noticed Ruth gathered herself together just enough to say, "We're ok sweetheart. How would you and Nancy like to spend some time downstairs with Mrs. Scardino?"

Was it Joan who said she would gather their things and asked Alan to take the kids downstairs? Tony couldn't tell anymore who was speaking or what was being said. He just sat on the sofa trying to make sense of everything. He felt something in his hand. He looked down and saw he was gripping a glass of whiskey. He turned his head and saw that Alan was sitting next to him encouraging him to drink it. A few shots of the deep brown liquid did the trick and brought Tony back to reality. After he splashed cold water on his face, Tony felt he was ready to hear everything Jack had to say. He and Ruth sat on the edge of the sofa together, held hands and tried to process where to begin.

"What exactly happened?" Tony asked.

"According to an eyewitness who was walking his dog, at a little after eleven your parents were walking across Mulberry Street by Grand. A car travelling at a very high speed veered over and hit them."

"Who was it? Who was the driver?" Tony felt his face getting red.

"We don't know. The car didn't stop, and the eyewitness said it all happened so quickly. He couldn't make out the license plate, but he did say the car was an older black Lincoln."

"Who's this eyewitness? Can we speak with him?" Ruth asked.

"Unfortunately, we can't let you do that. If you have any specific questions, you can let me know and I'll work with the New York City police directly."

"So, what happens next?" Tony asked as he shook his head.

"The police will talk with you and your sister and continue their investigation. They will try to find other witnesses and are looking for the black car. But there's one more thing." Jack leaned in and put his hand on Tony's arm. "The police will need you to formally identify their bodies."

Tony nodded, and whispered "Ok," as Ruth started to sob.

———

The following week was just as dark and depressing as a storm cloud hovering in the sky refusing to leave. Tony numbly walked around in a haze of sadness and shock. Nothing could've prepared him for the grueling task of identifying his parents' bodies, and he didn't remember much from that day. In fact, he didn't remember much of anything since he and Ruth were told about the accident. The police had no luck in finding the driver or any other witnesses and felt it was likely a drunk driver. Ruth had been the strong one for everyone, just as Anna had always been. It was as if Anna's spirit was guiding her and helped her to be the new backbone of the family. Ruth didn't waste any time seeing to all of the arrangements for the funeral, making sure each and every detail was a tribute to Sal and Anna. They both took a lot of pride in the restaurant and thought of it as a member of the family. She couldn't think of a better place to honor them after the funeral than to have the reception there. Lou worked with Ruth and managed every aspect of the gathering and made sure everything would have met Anna's standards. The entire staff wore black bands on their sleeves, and when the family arrived, they formed a line to greet them and express their condolences. They all shared stories on how Anna and Sal had impacted their lives and how grateful they were to have had the opportunity to know them.

Tony looked around at the crowd that was gathered at the restaurant and realized just how many lives Sal and Anna both touched and how much people truly loved them. He let out a deep sigh as he tried to release the overbearing feeling of loss just as Frank walked over with two glasses and a bottle of Sambuca.

"A toast to a one-of-a-kind couple," Frank's voice cracked.

"They loved you like a son, Frank, they really did."

"I know," he said looking down. "I just wish I could've made Uncle Sal proud."

"He *was* proud. He just worried about you is all. Always wanted the best for you."

"He really did look out for me. I hope I can do right by him." Frank filled both glasses.

"You and me both. By the way did I see Carmine Esposito at the cemetery earlier?"

"Yeah, yeah he was there."

"I didn't think he knew Pop." Tony frowned.

"They didn't know each other personally, but Carmine knew he was my uncle, so he came to pay his respects to me."

Before Tony could continue the conversation, Ruth joined them waving a glass. "You have any of that Sambuca for me?"

"Here," Frank poured some in her glass. "You did a fine job organizing everything. The service was touching."

"Thanks," she sighed. "Saying goodbye to them is one of the hardest things I've ever had to do. They were my parents too, you know."

"I know, honey, I think we're all gonna be lost without them."

"I know I will be." Frank nodded his head.

"No matter what we do, we have to keep their memory alive," Ruth insisted.

"We will. Here's to the best parents ever, To our family, alla nostra famiglia!" They raised their glasses and emptied them quickly.

After a few silent moments, Ruth said, "I should probably keep making my rounds to thank everyone."

"Yeah, me too," Frank sniffled. Tony watched Ruth as she made her way across the room lovingly greeting people and Frank joined Alan and Ethan at the bar.

"Tony, there are no words." Sal's friend, Vic Dionota and his wife Mary approached with their arms outstretched.

"I just spoke with Anna the day it happened." Mary shook her head and wiped her tears, "We were on the phone for an hour talking, gossiping mostly. I miss her already."

"I know, Mary. So do I."

"Listen, your father put a lot of time and effort into that house. He wanted it to be just right for all of you. It's finished and all yours when you're ready."

"Thank you so much, but I'm not sure I can swing it without Pop's help."

"Nonsense, you move your family in. Don't you worry about a thing. You rent it for now at what you're paying on your current apartment. Then, when you're ready, we'll talk about using the total you paid in rent as a down payment for purchasing it under market value. I'll float you a loan for the rest if needed."

"I, I can't let you do that." Tony shook his head.

"Listen to me, Sal and me we was like brothers. We took care of each other through the years. I don't know what I'm gonna do without him. But I do know that I will look out for you and your family as long as I'm still drawing breath."

"That means so much, are you sure?"

"I insist. Come by when you can, and we will draw up the papers to make it all legal and binding."

"How can I thank you?"

"I'll tell you how," Mary answered. "Come visit us regularly. We've got lots of great stories to share with your kids about your parents and even you when you were growing up."

"It's a deal," Tony said as he hugged them both.

"What's a deal?" Louisa asked as she greeted Vic and Mary.

"Tony here just agreed to move his family into one of my houses your father was fixing up for them."

"Really? How nice," Louisa scoffed and stormed away shaking her head.

"Did I say something wrong?"

"No, it's not you. Louisa's just grieving." Tony said trying to convince himself as much as Vic.

TWENTY-EIGHT

JANUARY, 1955
RUTH

RUTH FOUND HERSELF sobbing uncontrollably as she sat on Anna and Sal's bed clutching Sal's flannel work shirt. It had been only two weeks since the funeral, and she had not been able to enter their room. After Tony left for the restaurant and the breakfast dishes were done, she dropped the girls off at Mrs. Scardino's and forced herself to face the grueling task of sorting through Anna and Sal's things. There had been a fire in an apartment building a few blocks over and the neighborhood was collecting donations for the families who lost their homes. Tony and Louisa agreed that Anna and Sal would've done all they could to help those poor families and donating some of their things was a good way to honor them. But Ruth's emotions were still very raw. She was doing fine up until she came across the shirt hanging on the closet doorknob. Sal must've put it there when he changed his clothes to go over to Louisa's for dinner that terrible night. She could feel his presence in the room when she lifted it and breathed in his familiar musky scent combined with the Old Spice Cologne he slathered on every day.

In the almost five years that Ruth had lived with Sal and Anna they had become more like parents to her than her own mother and father. Ruth had come to believe that the words mother and father were just titles. Terms used to reference the biological beings that had given Ruth life. But Mom and Pop ... those were the most special words. They were expressions of devotion and appreciation for the two most wonderful people who gave her their never-ending love and support. Ruth never understood the value of a warm touch or a wink until she became part of the Russo family, and losing Anna and Sal left a hole in her heart far greater than being rejected by her own parents. They taught her so much about loyalty, compassion, and faith and she knew she became a better person through their example.

She was raised to believe that a woman's role in life was to passively blend into the background of their husband's world. Marriage and children were the ultimate goal, and they devoted their lives into building up their husband's confidence, anticipating all of his needs, and insuring his life at home was happy and comfortable. If a woman questioned, challenged, or contradicted their role they were often shunned and rejected. Anna and Sal taught Ruth so much about acceptance, and because of them, she evolved from being the woman who was a disobedient failure to Harvey to being the confident, self-respecting woman she was. Like Anna, Ruth enjoyed being a housewife and mother and took great pride in her family and life choices. But she was determined to empower her children to make their own choices rather than conform to the oppressive ideas of who they should be.

Ruth lovingly folded the shirt and placed it in a box along with

Sal's favorite tie, a bottle of Anna's favorite Youth Dew Cologne, her crystal rosary beads, and her favorite brooch. These were just small remembrances that they could lean on to keep Anna and Sal close. Ruth kissed the box of mementos and gently placed it on the shelf of her closet next to the box of Tony's keepsakes in honor of Carmella. She placed her hands on both boxes and whispered a promise to honor all of them and keep their spirits and memories alive. She vowed to live by their examples, and to instill their values to Rena, Janet, and Nancy just as they would have.

Ruth smiled at the boxes and as she made her way back to the task of sorting the donations, Joan had called to check in.

"Hey, sweetheart. How are you and Tony doing?"

"I'll tell you, it hasn't been easy for any of us. Some days it's so hard to breath. We get so overcome with emotions."

"I can't even imagine. They were a wonderful couple."

"They really were. And poor Janet doesn't understand. She keeps asking when they are going to be back from their vacation with the angels." Ruth's voice cracked and she willed herself not to cry.

"Oh, Ruth. Oh no."

"I guess it's going to take some time for all of us."

"Yes. In time things will get easier, I'm sure. What's happening with your move to the new place?"

"Tony is really having a hard time. I don't think he is ready to move yet, and every time I bring it up, he gets very short-tempered. So, I called Vic and explained that I'm not sure we will be able to move in after all, and he assured me that we can move whenever the time is right. He even said not to worry about rent or anything, the place is ours when we're ready."

"Wow. That's very generous of him."

"He and Sal were very close. They always looked out for each other, and he and his wife are like family. He understands how hard this is on us. Actually, they've offered to take the girls for an overnight visit to give Tony and me some time together."

"That's not a bad idea at all."

"We think we may take them up on it next weekend or the weekend after," Ruth said and then remembered she had never talked to Joan about the wedding. "We never did get a chance to talk about Ethan's wedding. I saw the film, Rachel was just beautiful."

"She was a beautiful bride. In fact, it was a lovely wedding. I just wish you could've been there."

"You know, after seeing the film, I was glad I wasn't. Don't get me wrong, I would've loved to share in celebrating my brother's happiness, but seeing Miriam on the film was hard enough. I don't think I could've handled it seeing her for the first time in person after all this time at a public event."

"That's a good point. I know in my heart you will reunite with her, but it would be best to do it under different circumstances."

"Especially without my parents there to interfere. They looked so miserable in the film."

"Yeah. I'm sorry to say that your parents have become, how should I put it …. bitter and judgmental. Even my parents have noticed they are perpetually dissatisfied at everything and nothing seems to be good enough for them."

"They never really were happy people. I've come to realize that as parents, they were always somewhat cold and distant. I tried so hard to please them and I just never could. Ethan had it easier than I did, but Isaac was always the one they favored."

Joan chuckled. "So much so that they arranged for his marriage with Ellie."

"Oh yes, Isaac's wife." Ruth chuckled. "Ethan said she was a quiet girl, on the plain side, and she looked so meek and scared from what I could tell on the film."

"You pegged her right. She is the perfect match for Isaac, very submissive and doesn't speak unless she is spoken to. Especially around him."

"I pray for her, you know. Being married to my brother will not be easy, and I'm sure she didn't know what she was getting into when she married him. Ethan told me at the funeral that she's pregnant."

"That sounds about right. I'm sure Isaac felt like he had to prove his manhood after his breakup with Naomi."

"Yes, I'm sure his ego took a big hit after that." Ruth was startled to hear loud knocking on the door and wondered who would be coming by at two in the afternoon. "Listen Joan, I've got to go, someone's at the door." She rushed to the door as the knocking had gotten even more persistent.

"Louisa?" Ruth was surprised to see her standing at the door with various empty boxes.

"Hello, Ruth," Louisa said as she pushed passed Ruth and almost hit her in the face with a box. "I came for my parent's things before you pack them up."

"Oh, ok," Ruth said confused. "I wasn't expecting you."

"I didn't know I needed your approval."

"Of course not, it's not that. It's just that I didn't even know myself that I was going to start sorting until today."

"Tony told me your plan when he called to check in on Rena this morning. I decided it was best that I come and collect their valuables before you gave them away."

"Gave them away? I would never do such a thing." Ruth was offended.

Louisa marched into her parent's bedroom and swiftly packed all of their personal things. Ruth was relieved that she put aside the few personal mementos earlier that morning.

"How is Rena doing?" Ruth asked softly and gently hoping to relax Louisa a bit.

"Rena is just fine. She's always been fine." Louisa glared at Ruth as she put Sal's cuff links in the last box.

"Louisa," Ruth again spoke gently. "Tony wanted to wear the cuff links in memory of your father."

"Well, you tell Tony that as the eldest, I am entitled to all of their things. If he wants them, he's going to have to come to me himself."

Ruth was speechless as Louisa carried the boxes to the door.

"You know, they were my parents *too*. I might not have shown it, but I loved them just as much as Tony did." She took a deep breath. "I don't know if they knew that."

"Oh, Louisa," Ruth said gently and reached out to embrace her, but Louisa turned away swiftly and slammed the door in her face. Louisa's painful sobs echoed throughout the building.

TWENTY-NINE

MARCH, 1955
TONY

THE TWO MONTHS since Anna and Sal's death had been a struggle for the family as they tried to navigate a life without them. Tony was introspective and angry most of the time and Ruth put on a smile each morning to mask her sadness and tried to maintain some normalcy for the kids. It was difficult for them to gather themselves emotionally, pack, and move their things into the new house. Even though they only moved a few blocks away, Tony had a hard time saying goodbye to the apartment and the neighbors living in the building. It was like he was saying goodbye to his parents all over again. He realized that moving to the house was a new beginning that he needed. He was having a hard time shaking the paralyzing sadness that was smothering him all day and night. The silence in the apartment without his parents rang through his ears so much he could barely function, and he hoped the move would help him find some peace. Packing was especially tough for him. Each apron, coffee cup, and wine glass held memories that Tony wasn't ready to let go of, so he packed it all.

"Is that the last of it?" Tony asked Frank as he carried a box into the new house.

"Yup, that's it. Boy do you have a lot of stuff." Frank wiped his sweaty brow with his handkerchief.

"So will we after we're married," Betty said as she unwrapped a pair of glass candlesticks. "I'm just glad that the landlord agreed to let us have the Russos' apartment."

"Hah, yeah, let us have it. I have to repaint the whole thing and make the repairs we want at my own expense. Not to mention the rent increase he's charging us."

"I'm really glad you're moving into the apartment. Mom and Pop would've liked that," Tony said.

"Yeah, I love that place. There's been so many happy memories there. You don't mind that we want to change it up a bit, do you?"

"No. Make it your own. Besides, I seem to remember agreeing to pay for half of the painting and repair expenses." Tony said lifting his eyebrows.

"Tell me this, how'd you ever get Tony to agree to do half of the work also?" Ruth chuckled.

"Oh, I owe that to the whiskey I kept giving him." Frank pat Tony on the back and they smiled, but their cheerfulness turned to concern as the doorbell rang repeatedly.

"Tony!" Louisa yelled, "Let me in."

"Louisa?" Tony opened the door and Louisa dragged Rena in by her arm. He had never seen Louisa look so crazed.

"Here! Here you go. You think I'm not raising her right? You think I'm too hard on her? Well, she's all yours, isn't she? You raise her! You've got plenty of room in this house. Especially since Mom and Pop are gone." Louisa threw a suitcase across the room and pushed Rena in the back so hard she fell to the ground sobbing.

"What the hell? Louisa!" Tony screamed.

Ruth rushed over and helped Rena up, pushed her hair out of her face and kissed her cheek. "It's ok," she said. "It's going to be ok."

"Well, aren't you the sweet little mother?" Louisa hissed.

"Tony," Ruth said looking at him pleadingly.

"What's this all about?" Tony demanded.

"It's all your fault! Mom and Pop would still be here if it weren't for you." She tried to shove Tony in the chest. "If you didn't convince them to come to my house and question me about how I'm treating Rena, they never would've been hit crossing the street. You took them away from me. Just like you took all of that savings they had. You took it for your restaurant. You want it all? You can have it. Now it's time for you to take your daughter too!"

"Now calm down," Tony slammed the door. "I didn't take Mom and Pop from you, it was an *accident*. They were at the wrong place at the wrong time. Yeah, they were there to talk to you about Rena, but they had their own concerns too. We're all worried about Rena, for God's sake."

"Wait a minute," Rena sobbed. "What do you mean it's time for you to take *your* daughter?"

"Oh that's right, sweetheart," Louisa said sarcastically. "Your Uncle Tony, here. He's not your uncle. He's your father."

"Louisa! Stop!" Tony shouted.

"He gave you up when you were three years old. So, that saint of an uncle you've been idolizing your whole life, he's been lying to you. He's no saint."

Rena turned to Tony, "Is that true?"

"Rena, I ..." Tony was speechless. This was not how he wanted his daughter to find out the truth. He envisioned sitting down together and having a heart-to-heart conversation when she was a little older and could understand the truth better.

"Oh my God," Rena cried looking back and forth between Tony and Louisa.

"Well, there's no need to be concerned on how I'm raising her anymore. I don't want her, she's all yours. I'm giving her back. You think it's easy raising three kids? You'll see."

"Now that's enough. What has gotten into you? Have you gone mad?" Tony boomed.

"No, this is something I should've done years ago. It's just too much raising your child when I have two of my own to raise."

Frank interjected, calmly, "Rena, come on let's get you out of here. Let's get you away from this craziness."

"Thank you, Frank," Ruth said relieved. "Rena, why don't you go upstairs with Uncle Frank and Aunt Betty while we sort this all out. I'll be up in a bit." She hugged Rena and nodded at Betty.

"Hmph," Louisa snorted. "Maybe little Miss Jewish Princess will be better at it than I am."

"Excuse me?" Ruth bellowed.

"I've had enough. You will *not* come into *my* home and disrespect *my* wife that way."

"Oh, that's right, your home! It wouldn't be your home if it weren't for Pop. He did all the work to fix this place up, and probably used the rest of that savings to pay for it too. That's right Tony. I know all about that secret savings. I know all about Pop giving it to you to open that restaurant of yours." Louisa smirked.

"How do you know about that?" Tony's eyes narrowed as he glared at her.

"Oh, I know things, you couldn't keep that a secret forever. Especially not with Frank involved."

"What are you saying?"

"I'm saying Frank got drunk at a poker game he was at last night with Bob, he told Bob all about Pop's money and how he gave it to you."

"He didn't *give* it to me, he *invested* it in a business!"

"Invested, huh? So I suppose half of that money should be mine. That's my inheritance." Louisa put her hands on her hips, "I want my money!" she demanded.

"I can't just give you half of the money, you know that. It's tied up in the restaurant."

"Well, then, I guess I own a share of the restaurant, I'll take that, but I'm not taking Rena." Louisa laughed and headed toward the door. "Good luck with her," she said and slammed the door.

"I'm not gonna let her get away with this." Tony clenched his fists and started to follow her.

Ruth swiftly put herself in front of him and said, "Tony, wait. Let her go."

"Ruth, don't get in my way."

Ruth cupped his face in her hands, "Let her go. There's something wrong with her, she's not herself." He let out a deep breath. "Rena's more important right now. You need to go to her."

Tony needed a few minutes to calm down after Louisa left. He just couldn't fathom what had gotten into her. Why would she do this to Rena? He paced around the living room as he tried to think of what to say to his daughter. How could he possibly undo the damage that Louisa had done here tonight? If Ruth hadn't stopped him, he feared he could've said something to Louisa that he would've regretted. He'd never felt so angry in his life. Once again, his sister thought only of herself and didn't consider the impact her words and actions had on other people. It wasn't only the personal betrayal that infuriated him, but it was her lack of empathy that he couldn't wrap his head around. Tony would get over the betrayal, but would Rena be able to get over learning the truth the way she did?

"What the hell just happened here?" Frank asked as he and Betty gathered their coats.

"I wish I knew. You can be sure I'm gonna find out what caused Louisa to lose it the way she did," Tony sighed, "How's Rena?"

"Confused. Shook up. Ruth's with her trying to get her to talk. Listen, do you want us to take the girls tonight or anything while you see to Rena?"

"No. Thanks though. I don't wanna rouse them. It may scare them unnecessarily."

"If you need anything, just let us know. Please tell Ruth, I'll call her tomorrow." Betty kissed Tony's cheek and Frank pat him on the back as they left.

Tony carried a glass of chocolate milk up to Rena hoping it would help make her feel better. He stood in the bedroom doorway and watched as Ruth rocked Rena in her arms. He was incredibly grateful for Ruth's compassion, but he also wished Carmella could somehow guide him through one of the most difficult conversations he has ever had to have with their daughter.

Silently he said, "Carm, if you can hear me, please help. It's time for Rena to hear the truth. Please give me the right words to say, and please help her to understand."

Ruth looked over at Tony, kissed Rena on the head and quietly slipped out of the room.

"Hey, I brought you a glass of chocolate milk. I know it's your favorite."

"Thanks." Rena and put it on the nightstand.

Tony put two pillows on the floor and motioned for Rena to join him. They sat for a few minutes with their backs against the bed in silence.

He finally said, "I'm so sorry for everything that happened tonight."

Rena nodded.

"I know it had to be a shock to find out I'm your father."

Rena nodded again.

"I had planned to tell you, myself. All these years, I've wanted to tell you but thought it would be better when you were older and could understand better."

"I'm not dumb," she said flatly.

"No, no you're not dumb. I guess I was the dumb one. All I ever wanted to do was protect you."

Rena was silent.

"When your mother ..." Tony started.

"You mean Aunt Carmella?"

"Yes, Aunt Carmella. When she got sick, you were so young. I couldn't take care of both of you, and it was clear she wasn't gonna get any better. She didn't want you to see her that way, didn't want you to have any memory of her being sick. So, we all thought the best thing was for you to go stay with Louisa and Bob."

Rena was silent.

Tony struggled to continue. "My life crumbled when your mother died. Nonna and Pop-Pop had to take care of me. By the time I started to get better, you had become so attached to Louisa and Bob. You thought *they* were your parents."

Rena silently turned to Tony and stared at him.

"I wasn't in a position where I thought I could take care of you like they could, and I wanted you to have a happy childhood with two parents. Louisa wanted so much to be your mother."

Rena frowned at Tony and looked straight ahead.

"We all thought you would be happiest with them. I'm sorry, Rena. We should've told you from the beginning."

Rena nodded.

"But I wanna make things right from now on. I wanna be the father I never was."

Rena was silent.

"I know you had it hard over at Louisa's. I, I should've done more to help you."

Rena was silent.

"From now on though, I vow I will protect you against anyone or anything that intends to do any harm to you. I should've done better. I will always regret that. But please know, I love you."

Rena nodded.

"So what do you say? Can we try to make a fresh start?"

"Ok," she said quietly.

"Tomorrow we'll decorate the bedroom any way you want and make it yours. We'll get you new furniture and everything. How does that sound?"

"Good."

Tony kissed Rena on the head, "Do you have any questions for me or anything you wanna say?"

"Just one question, what do I call you?"

Stunned, Tony didn't know how to answer. His heart wanted her to call him Dad, but he knew she was probably not ready for that. In her eyes and in her heart, Bob has been Dad all of her life. And if Tony were going to be completely honest with himself, Bob was more of a Dad to her than he was. He was the first one to kiss the boo-boos, see the report cards, and help her with her homework. Tony was just the fun uncle who tried to be there as much as he could.

"Well, you can call me whatever you're comfortable with."

"I'll call you Tony for now."

"Of course," Tony said trying not to let her see how heartbroken he really was.

PART III
TRUTH

THIRTY

APRIL, 1959
TONY

TONY WALKED SLOWLY, hesitantly toward his parents' grave. In the four years since their death, he hadn't had the courage to go out to the cemetery and visit. Ruth made regular visits for each holiday and change of season, and she found comfort in looking after their grave. She's been after Tony for years to come out suggesting it will "do him some good." But he always used the excuse of being too busy with work. Tony had avoided facing their gravesite in an effort to suppress the sorrow he had battled all these years. He didn't know what changed, but when he woke up, he felt ready to spend time with them. A bubble formed in his throat as he placed fresh flowers in the vase next to their headstone. He ran his hand over their names carved in the marble and took in every detail of their memorial. A calmness came over him and he felt lighter than he had in five years. A gentle smile lit his face, and he found he was ready to let his parents' memory hold him close as he spoke to them.

"Hey Mom, Pop. I'm real sorry this is my first visit. I, I just couldn't come before is all. I just couldn't face the fact that you were gone." Tears welled up in his eyes. "There's so much I wanna say to you both. Not a day has passed that I haven't thought of you and started to say something to you only to realize that I couldn't." The tears started flowing freely down Tony's face and he finally allowed himself to release the emotions that had been built up. He knelt with his head down and sobbed quietly for what felt like an hour but was just mere moments. Comforted by a soft breeze, Tony gathered himself and easily continued the conversation he's needed to have for years.

"Pop you would be so proud right now if you knew that Salvatore Bruno's is one of the most popular places around. About two years ago things really took off and we were able to expand. Now, we're booked solid on weekends and reservations are on a six-month waiting list." Tony hesitated and looked up at the sky. "I'll admit it though, I'm sure you wouldn't be pleased to know that some of the success is due in part to Carmine Esposito. He stopped by on a Friday night to see if the talk all over town was true and turns out he fell in love – not only with our new headline singer, but with the ambience and style of our place. You know, til then, he would only go to small Italian restaurants and bars that either he or his close friends owned. I really think that the music, cigars, and cognac kept him coming back. He's offered to buy the restaurant from Frank and me a couple of times, but we stuck together and politely declined his offer." Tony looked back at the headstone. "I know you wouldn't like Carmine even stepping foot into our place, but truth be told, you might've been worried over nothing where Carmine's concerned. He's been a loyal customer and has brought in many other customers like the mayor, several judges, lawyers, and even the governor, himself." Tony chuckled, "You know Frank is far more impressed by these people than I am. But the good thing is, he's always thinking of different improvements we can make to keep the V.I.P.'s interested in returning."

Tony lit a cigarette, "You know, Pop, the past few years have been good for Frank. Marrying Betty turned out to be the right idea and his gambling has taken a back seat to his role as a husband and father. Who would've thought that he would be the proud father of two sets of twins? The boys, Vinny and Jimmy couldn't be any different from Frank at all. At barely four years old, they're super smart. Vinny's passion is to read books and Jimmy is a pro at solving puzzles. His two-year old daughters, on the other hand, seem to be exactly like Frank. Denise and Nicole are a handful and often get into things they shouldn't. I say to Ruth all the time, 'God bless, Betty, she's an angel with the patience of a saint.'"

Tony put out his cigarette and took in the breeze that continued to surround him. "You don't have to worry about Louisa taking over the restaurant either. Frank and I started making monthly payments to her out of our profits. She now feels like she's getting her inheritance, and we're keeping the peace."

After a few quiet moments, Tony continued. "Mom, there's a lot I wanna say to you," he said as his voice broke. "Sometimes we feel so lost without you. The girls are growing up so fast. Janet is just the sweetest little girl there is. She loves to play dress up and walk around in Ruth's shoes, and Nancy's just like you. She's always at Ruth's side and loves to help her cook and bake. And, well, Rena. Rena's had a tough time of it these past four years. She's just not the same sassy little girl she once was. Mom, it just breaks my heart. When she first came to live with us, she was withdrawn and depressed. We were hoping going to a new school and making new friends would help, but it went deeper than that. It seemed like she was scared, and it took Ruth a long time to gain her trust. Rena won't talk about it much, but living with Louisa really did a number on her. Bob admitted that Louisa started getting severe mood swings after Sophia was born and they were getting worse as time went on. After you died she had a breakdown and hasn't been right since. Frankly, I'm having a hard time forgiving her for how she treated Rena. I know she's sick in the head, and I should cut her some slack, but it doesn't fix the damage that was done to Rena for having to bear the brunt of her explosive episodes. And now, Rena's seventeen and she's moody and tries to make herself up like she's a grown woman. I'm worried about her, and I just don't know how to help her."

Tony looked out over the green field of graves and pictured Rena as a little girl giggling and running in circles. Instantly, he was taken out of the memory by the sound of his son who stumbled over his feet as he toddled around in the grass.

"This here is Anthony, Jr.," Tony said as he picked him up. "Mom, Pop, this is your newest grandson. After the scare with Nancy's birth, the doctor was very cautious during this pregnancy. It was really tough for Ruth trying to take care of Janet who was five at the time, Nancy who was three and Rena who was fifteen, but you would've both been proud of our Ruthie. She came through it all like a true Russo. The doc said we shouldn't have any more kids, though. It's gotten to be too tough on her and she's lucky she's had four healthy kids. She still gets updates and pictures on Miriam through Ethan. Miriam's twelve now and went to live with Ethan and Rachel shortly after Ruth's father had a stroke and had to be put in a nursing facility. About a year ago, Ruth's mother died, they're thinking from pneumonia. I know deep down you thought she would eventually reconcile with her parents, but there's a lot of anger between them that I don't think could ever be healed."

Anthony wriggled his way from Tony's arms and started playing with a small stick.

"You know, I had so much anger in me the first few years after you died. It was Ruthie who suggested I go down to the gym and try to work through it all. I started lifting weights and doing some boxing, and now I'm in the best shape I have ever been. Ruth's really become the rock of our family. She continued our Sunday dinners, and Nancy loves to help. Vic and Mary are weekly regulars and have become close with the kids. Don't either of you worry, we're teaching them how important family is, and we talk about you both all the time."

Tony pulled a flask from his pocket. "I know you're watching over us, and I hope you know how much we miss you ... I miss you." He raised his flask up and said, "To our family, alla nostra famiglia," and took a long swig before he poured a bit on the grass in front of the headstone. "That's a sip for you, Pop."

Tony turned to his son and said, "So what do you say, Anthony? You ready to go get some ice cream?"

He looked up with his big brown eyes. "Yes!" he said enthusiastically.

"Ok, kiddo. Blow kisses up to heaven for Pop-Pop and Nonna."

THIRTY-ONE

APRIL, 1959
RUTH

RUTH HAD BEEN at the restaurant managing the books most of the afternoon. After the accident, she took on some of Sal's administrative tasks and came to find out that she not only enjoyed it, but she was also quite good at it too. She often felt like she channeled Sal's savviness when it came to bookkeeping, but she also attributed much of her confidence to Anna as well. Ruth knew she had to step up and be strong for the family, and Anna was an incredible role model.

She looked up from punching the weekend's receipts into the adding machine and saw Tony as he pulled out his handkerchief and wiped ice cream off of Anthony's face and fingers.

"Vanilla?" she smirked.

Tony looked surprised, "What do you mean?"

"Did Anthony enjoy his vanilla ice cream?"

"How did you know?"

"You did a great job wiping his face and hands, but there was nothing you could've done about the big stain down his shirt," Ruth answered as she gave Tony the 'I'm on to you' look she learned from Anna.

"Well, Anthony, I guess our secret's out. Mommy's just too smart to keep secrets from. Why don't you go sit at the table over there with your sisters. Maybe they'll let you help them with their homework." Tony winked.

"Really, Tony, ice cream this late in the afternoon? He'll never eat his dinner."

"Sorry. But we, I, needed to do something fun after visiting Mom and Pop at the cemetery."

"How'd it go?" Ruth asked, as she took off her glasses.

"I'm sure I don't have to tell you it wasn't easy. But I'm glad I finally went."

"How do you feel now that you've gone?"

"You know, when I was there, I felt a stillness pass through me. It felt good, and I realized driving over here that I don't feel the tension I usually carry around."

"I have to admit, you do look good today," Ruth said playfully.

"Maybe later we can find some quiet time together," he suggested as he walked around the desk and kissed her neck.

"Now, that would be a nice distraction from this paperwork." She giggled and pushed him away.

"Bad day?"

"No, not at all, just busy. I've been here most of the afternoon balancing the books, paying all the vendors, and writing out the payroll checks. It looks like we might be able to get that new refrigerator system sooner than we thought."

"Really? That'll be great. Frank'll be happy to hear that too."

"About Frank," Ruth sighed. "Betty tells me they've been arguing lately. Have you noticed anything?"

"Not really. He seemed fine here all weekend. He mentioned how Betty's been complaining that he doesn't do enough around the house, but other than that, he was his usual self, charming all the customers."

"Hmmm, she mentioned the same to me about him not doing enough for her around the house."

"Speak of the devil. Here he comes now." Tony nodded toward the front door as Frank sauntered toward the office.

"Hi Frank."

"Hey how's it going, Ruth? Uhm Tony, I just saw Rena walking down the street with what's his name. That young kid that works for Carmine."

"Which one, Joey or Dominick?" Tony raised his eyes.

"Dominick, that's it. They were just coming out of the soda shop down the block."

"Dominick? He's no young kid. He's gotta be at least twenty-five!" Tony raised his voice, put his hands on his hips and looked around the room.

"Wait? Who's Dominick?" Ruth asked as she looked back and forth between them.

"Dominick came in here with Carmine a few times. He seems ok, quiet. How do you think he knows Rena?" Frank answered.

"I'll tell you, it's those quiet ones you gotta watch out for. I don't care how he and Rena know each other; I'm putting a stop to this."

"Hang on. Let me talk to her tonight. See what I can find out. It may not be anything at all." Ruth placed her hand on Tony's arm to calm him down.

"She could be right. We don't need you going off on anyone."

"Ok, Ruth, you talk to her. But I don't want her getting involved with him."

"Alright," Ruth said. "So Frank, how's Betty and the kids?"

"Don't you talk to her every day?" Frank eyed her suspiciously.

Tony laughed. "What she means is, how are you doing keeping up with your wife and all those kids of yours?"

"Oh, that," Frank shook his head. "It's never ending. I miss the good ole days when I would come home from work and Betty would cook a nice dinner. Now all she does is yell and scream. If she's not yelling at the kids, she's screaming at me over something or other."

"I'm sure it's hard for her with them being so young," Ruth suggested.

"Hard? She has her mother or her sister helping her at the house all day, every day. Let me tell you about those two. All they do is whisper in Betty's ear how she should have this appliance or that appliance. They keep telling her that if I can't be home more often, I should at least be buying her the most modern conveniences. It's not enough that I bought her the house of her dreams. That mortgage alone is enough to strangle anyone. Now she wants to fill it with all the best. I keep telling her to slow down, we'll get there, but it's going to take some time. I'm working as hard as I can. But the in-laws, they don't see it that way. They start in with the questions, why am I not home at night? Why am I out late on weekends? Then they start filling her head with all kinds of crap and getting her thinking I'm up to no good. I might as well be out having fun for all they think."

"Gee, I didn't know," Ruth said.

"Yeah, I didn't realize it was that bad either," Tony added. "Doesn't Betty realize you've helped build this place from the bottom up? You're busting your ass here trying to turn a profit, and all your hard work is just starting to pay off."

"No, she just doesn't understand the restaurant business. She thinks we should have managers run everything while we sit back and spend the profits." Frank shrugged.

"Do you want me to talk to her?" Ruth offered.

"Thanks, but it won't do any good. I treated her like a princess before the kids and bills came along, and her family's opinions drive her thoughts."

"Well, let me know if you change your mind. You know we're here for you. But right now, I've got to get these kids home," Ruth said as she gathered her things and kissed Frank on the cheek.

Rena was sitting at the kitchen table looking through the latest *Seventeen* magazine as Ruth and the kids entered the door. Janet and Nancy went straight to their room, and Ruth led Anthony to the kitchen where she put him in his highchair. Ruth and Rena have developed a special bond, but it took Rena a long time to come around and start to trust Ruth. It's no wonder she was guarded. She'd had a tumultuous childhood living with Louisa and has had difficulty letting people get close to her. Anna and Sal's death had a huge impact on her. They provided a level of stability for Rena that she depended on. Tony tried to be there for her, but she held him at arm's length and maintained an emotional distance from him. Ruth worried that their relationship would never be as close as Tony would like, and she tried to bridge the gap with her own maternal instincts.

Ruth looked at Rena and tried to gauge the teenager's mood. "Hi sweetie, how was your day?"

"Good, nothing special," Rena said as she flipped the page and avoided eye contact.

"How does meatloaf sound for dinner?"

"Oh, I'm not hungry."

"You're not? Why not?"

"I already ate earlier."

"You know we eat dinner together as a family every day." Ruth tried not to sound annoyed.

"Well, I already ate with a friend."

"What friend?" Ruth asked as she unpacked groceries.

"No one you know."

"Was it Dominick?"

"How do you know about him?"

"Uncle Frank saw you coming out of the soda shop with him earlier."

"Oh, that's just great. Are you all spying on me now?"

"Calm down. No one is spying on you. He just happened to be driving by when he saw you." Ruth put her hand on Rena's cheek and kissed the top of her head. "Why are you so angry?"

She sighed and softened just a little. "I'm not angry, I just feel smothered sometimes. Everyone is telling me how to dress, how to act, what to do, what not to do. I feel like I can't be me."

Ruth sat down next to her. "I can understand that. We all have opinions on how to best look out for your wellbeing."

"I'm not a little kid anymore."

"No, No you're not. But Rena, don't be in such a hurry to be a grown woman either. This is the best stage of life for people your age. You can have fun going to sock hops and parties without being tied down by life's tough responsibilities. Right now, you have so many options and your adult life is just beginning. We all just want you to slow down some and enjoy this time and think hard about your choices so that your future is bright."

"I'm not interested in high school dances and parties. People my age are all nerds."

"Well, ok, tell me about this Dominick."

"There's really nothing to tell. We just met today." In a flash her attitude reappeared.

"Today? You said you ate with a friend."

"He's my friend now."

"I don't understand."

Rena rolled her eyes and sighed. "I went into the soda shop to have an egg cream, and when Dominick came in, he sat next to me at the counter. We started talking, and then he offered to buy me a burger, so I accepted. That's it. Now we're friends."

"Do you have plans to see him again?"

"No."

"So that's it? Dominick is just someone who struck up a conversation and bought you a burger?"

"Yup."

"Okaaaaay. You know, Rena, maybe you should stick to having friends closer to your own age. I know they aren't as exciting as someone like Dominick, but I don't want you to get hurt."

"Yeah, sure, ok." She picked up her magazine and started to walk out of the kitchen.

"Now, set the table. We have dinner every night as a family, and even though you ate already, you can sit with us and at least taste my food."

THIRTY-TWO

APRIL, 1959
TONY

TONY TRIED TO ease his fears of Rena getting too close to Dominick as he drove home. He seemed like a good guy from what Tony could tell, but he was just too old for her. Tony wanted so much for his daughter to have the same kind of lighthearted fun he had when he was in high school. Some of the best times of his life was back when he and his friends would go to football games and the soda fountain. Their biggest worry was whether the girls they had their eyes on would notice them.

He couldn't help but feel guilty every time he saw Rena moody and sullen. He wished he could erase the disappointment and betrayal she'd had in her life. If only he could go back and do it all over again. He never would've allowed Louisa to take her in. He would've tried to find a way to be a good father to her. But how could he have known that Louisa would turn on her, the little girl she'd loved like a daughter? He'd spent hours trying to figure out how he didn't see it all start to go wrong. Life for Rena wasn't always so bad living with Louisa. As a little girl she was always so happy and sassy. She doted on her little brother, Bobby, and was a perfect little mother's helper. Louisa even said it herself. But now, Tony saw that things started to change when Louisa became unexpectedly pregnant two years after having Bobby. She started to become more irritated, and often lost her patience. Anna tried talking to her about her moods and even went so far as to suggest that she see a doctor, but Louisa quickly got defensive, and Anna didn't bring it up again. He now realized that after Sophia was born it seemed that Louisa started to have very high expectations of Rena. She insisted that Rena behave more maturely and take on more responsibilities than the six-year-old was even capable of.

It didn't help that Bob turned into a somewhat absent husband and father and elected to spend most of his time at the deli rather than put up with Louisa and her mood swings. At the very least, Tony felt that Bob should have told him about Louisa's emotional episodes. But Louisa always had a strong, domineering personality and maybe Bob didn't realize the extent of pressure she put on Rena.

Now, all Tony could do is try to make things right for Rena. When she first came to live with them, both Tony and Ruth tried to help her talk through her emotions, but she was closed off. Ruth made some strides in getting closer to her, but it was Tony's relationship with Rena that had suffered greatly. When she thought he was her uncle, Rena was close to him and would even confide in him. Now, she had built a polite wall around herself where he was concerned, and nothing he'd tried to break through seemed to work. He'd worried about the path she seemed to be headed on. Tony wanted to provide the same consistent, loving family environment for his kids that he had growing up. He insisted on continuing his parents' tradition of eating dinner together every day. No matter how busy it was at the restaurant, he was certain to be home by 5 o'clock.

He walked through the front door and willed himself not to question Rena about Dominick before he could find out if Ruth had spoken to her yet.

"Is that meatloaf I smell?"

"Daddy!" Tony never got tired of seeing the excitement in his kid's eyes every time he walked through the door.

"Hey girls. Is Mommy making her special meatloaf tonight?" Tony winked at Ruth and bent over and hugged each girl.

Nancy nodded while Janet said, "Yes, and mashed potatoes too."

Ruth kissed Tony's cheek and said, "Dinner is almost ready. Girls, why don't you go wash up and give Rena the 10-minute warning. I need Daddy's help in the kitchen."

"What's going on?" Tony asked as he saw dinner was all set out on the table.

"I spoke to Rena when I got home today."

"I was hoping you did, what'd she say?"

"Well, she got defensive, but she said they just met. Dominick struck up a conversation and then offered to buy her something to eat."

"And she accepted?"

"Yeah, seems like she did."

"She doesn't even know this guy and he's buying her food?"

"She said it was just a friendly burger and she doesn't have plans to see him again."

"Do you believe her?"

"I'm not sure. I don't know what to think."

"I'll talk to her."

"When you do, keep your cool. The worst thing you can do is lose your temper. That won't help."

"Ok, ok, I got it. I can handle it."

Ruth put her hand on Tony's arm, "Please Tony, trust me on this one."

Tony never really knew when the time was right to talk to Rena. It always seemed to be a bad time when he tried, and he felt like he just couldn't get it right with her. He noticed that she was in a good mood during dinner so he decided that maybe it would be as good a time as any for them to talk.

"Hey kiddo, what do you say you and I go down to the corner and get some sundaes for dessert. Just the two of us?"

"I want to come," Janet insisted.

"Oh no, honey. This is a special date for me and Rena. But I'll tell you what. Tomorrow night, you and I will get sundaes just the two of us."

"What about me?" Nancy said.

Tony chuckled, "Of course Nancy, I didn't forget about you. You and I will go on Thursday. That is the day after tomorrow." Tony didn't think his plan through but actually liked the idea of spending some one-on-one time with each of his daughters.

"So, Rena, what do you think?"

Rena looked hesitantly at Ruth who smiled and nodded slightly at her. "Ok, I suppose so."

"Ok then, let's go," Tony said, feeling hopeful. As he kissed Ruth on the cheek she whispered, "Stay calm."

The silence felt heavy as they walked to the drugstore, took a seat at the soda fountain, and placed their orders. Tony wasn't sure what to say or how to say it, but all he knew was that he wanted Rena to know how much he cared and worried about her.

"Strawberry sundae, huh? Did you know that was your Aunt Carmella's favorite?"

"No," she said flatly.

"I've always been partial to hot fudge myself, but strawberry's good too."

"Uh huh," Rena looked around disinterestedly.

"I hear your school's having a spring dance. I used to love ..."

"What's this all about?" She cut him off. "Why are we here?"

"I just wanted to spend some nice time with you. I feel like we don't get to do that often enough."

"So, this isn't about my meeting Dominick today?"

"Not specifically, but now that you bring it up, don't you think he's a little too old for you to be friends with?"

"Oh geez, here we go. Be cool. I just met him today. He was a nice guy who bought me a meal. That's it. Case closed. Why is everybody making such a big thing of it?"

"We're not. At least we're trying not to." Tony took a few bites of his sundae, so he didn't say anything harsh. "I need you to know how very important you are to me. I worry about you."

"Yeah, you've said that before."

"Well, I mean it, you know."

Rena put down her spoon and looked directly at Tony. "You know, I don't know that."

Tony was taken aback for a moment and just stared at her. "I, I don't understand," was all he could say.

"You've told me many times that you love me, but if you really loved me, you wouldn't have let me live my life in a lie."

"Rena, honey, like I told you. That's my biggest life regret. I was so lost when your mother got sick and died. I could barely take care of myself, let alone a child. Everyone said it was for the best, and I thought they were right. If I could do it all over again, I would try to change everything. But I can't. All I can do is say, I'm sorry."

Rena turned forward and looked down.

"Just know this," he put his hand on her shoulder. "You deserve the best life has to offer, and I will stop at nothing to protect you." Rena continued to look down and nodded.

Three weeks later, Tony came upon Rena and Dominick talking near the coat check in the restaurant. Dominick leaned in close, and Rena reached out and put her hand on his arm. It was a quick encounter, and Tony couldn't hear their conversation. But he knew from Rena's blushing cheeks and Dominick's flirtatious smile that their conversation was intimate. Tony willed himself to keep calm and not punch Dominick. He could hear Sal's voice in his head.

"Take a breath son, punching this kid right here and now is no good. You talk to him direct, reason with him."

Tony stared at Dominick as he joined Carmine at his table and decided to bide his time and watch them closely. Just after they finished dinner, he brought over a bottle of their best brandy and three snifters.

"I hope you enjoyed your meals, I thought you'd like to join me in a nice brandy to finish it off."

"Well, that's very nice, Tony." Carmine nodded, "Please sit down."

"Have you met Dominick Trovato? He just started working for me a few months ago."

"We haven't been officially introduced. Hello Dominick, Tony Russo," Tony said as he passed a brandy snifter to him.

"Hey Tony."

Tony took a deep breath to stop himself from throwing the brandy in his face.

"Looks like business is good." Carmine smiled and looked around. "You know, my offer still stands. If you ever feel like getting out, you call me."

"I will, but gotta say right now, I'm still enjoying it."

"That's important, you've got to enjoy your work. Me, I love what I do. You could say I was born into it." Carmine sipped the brandy. "So, what really brings you to my table?"

"Well, I actually came over to talk with Dominick here."

"Me? What do you want with me?" Dominick narrowed his eyes.

"I've noticed you're getting friendly with my daughter, Rena."

"Rena? Rena's your daughter? Yeah, she's a nice girl." He took a sip of brandy.

"Dominick, do you realize she's only seventeen?"

"*Seventeen?*" Carmine said shaking his head. "Dominick, be careful there."

"Hey," Dominick raised his hands. "We're friends. Can't two people be friends?"

"Well, maybe you two don't need to be *close* friends. My daughter's young, she hasn't always had an easy go of things, and I just wanna make sure she doesn't get hurt or get into any kind of trouble."

"And you think she'll get in trouble with me?" Dominick said sarcastically.

"I guess you could say I'm just looking out for everyone. I'm quite protective of her."

"Are you threatening me?" Dominick leaned in toward Tony.

"Now Dom," Carmine put his hand up. "Tony here is just trying to look after his daughter. I would do the same for my Tina. I agree with him, why don't you take a step back from Rena. Find yourself another girl."

"Yeah, ok, whatever," Dominick mumbled and leaned back into his chair.

"So, Dominick, do we understand each other?" Tony asked

looking directly into his eyes.

"Yeah, I guess we do." he looked away.

"Very good." Carmine nodded. "Now if you don't mind, I would like to move to my table in the ballroom and watch my girl perform. I'm telling you, she's going to be famous."

"Of course," Tony said as he stood from the table, reached out and shook Carmine's hand. "Thanks."

Carmine nodded and gestured for Dominick to lead the way into the ballroom.

THIRTY-THREE

OCTOBER, 1959
RUTH

TODAY WAS THE day Ruth's been waiting for over the past eight years. Her hand shook as she applied her red lipstick, and she stared at her reflection in the mirror. She wondered if Miriam would recognize her. Eight years was a long time for a daughter not to see her mother, and Ruth was afraid that Miriam wouldn't remember her. It was only a week ago when Ethan called to say that Miriam wanted to meet her. Those words were music to Ruth's ears and she hadn't been able to eat or sleep since. Her initial elation quickly turned into anxiety as she pondered the thoughts, feelings, and questions Miriam must've had through the years. Although Ethan did all he could to be there for her, she must've felt a sense of loss not having her mother in her life. Ruth often thought of this every time Rena shut down at the mere mention of her own mother. Ethan told Ruth that Miriam had been asking a lot of questions since Rachel gave birth to their own daughter, Rose. Six months ago, he asked Miriam if she wanted to see Ruth, and although she didn't answer right away, last week she said she was ready.

Ruth must've changed her outfit at least five times wanting to look her best for her daughter. She finally settled on a blue polka-dot, bell-shaped skirt dress. On the drive over to the diner, Ruth reminisced about the little time she had in Miriam's life. The day she was born was one of the happiest and she still remembered how Miriam smelled, how her hair would curl around her small, narrow ears, and how her giggle would ease any tension in a room. Although Ruth saw her grow up through pictures and the occasional home movie Ethan would give her, she thought about all the ways Miriam's probably changed. She parked the car in the small lot on the side of the diner, and as she turned the ignition off, she realized that it was almost eight years to the day that Ruth had last seen her daughter in person. It was at this very same diner that Ruth last hugged and kissed her four-year-old daughter. She wondered if Ethan had chosen this diner to meet on purpose, and she made a mental note to ask him when the time was right.

As Ruth walked through the door, she briefly wished she had taken Tony up on his offer to come with her. She could've used his moral support to give her strength, but she knew this was something that she had to do herself. She immediately saw Ethan and Miriam in the corner booth and took a deep breath. There was her little girl. But she wasn't a little girl anymore, she was a twelve-year-old young lady. Ruth stood paralyzed as she took in all of Miriam's features. She still had her beautiful curly hair and dimples, but her face had matured from being round and cherub-like to being slender and oval like her own. In that moment Ruth realized that seeing how Miriam matured in pictures was very different than seeing her in person. Nothing could have prepared her for the overwhelming flood of emotions that overtook her. Her hands shook as she tried to straighten her dress, and she swallowed hard in an effort to calm her nerves and not run out of the door. She knew it was time to walk over to their table. A walk she'd been waiting to make for what felt like an eternity.

Ethan saw Ruth first and quickly stood. "Hi, we just got here." He then turned to Miriam and said, "Miriam, do you remember your mother?"

Ruth's eyes filled with tears as she smiled and said, "Hi Miriam. I'm so happy to see you." Miriam looked at her, and all Ruth could see was the sweet four-year old she left behind. "How are you?"

"Hi, I'm fine." Miriam answered as she stared at Ruth. Ruth could tell that Miriam was just as nervous as she was by the way she rubbed her hands together. Ruth had forgotten that Miriam did this every time she was nervous as a child.

"Why don't we sit down?" Ethan said as he slid into the booth next to Miriam.

Ruth slid in directly across from them and felt very self-conscious as she clumsily knocked a fork onto the floor with her purse. Both Ethan and Ruth reached down to pick it up. He put his hand on her arm and whispered, "Relax, it's going to be fine."

As they ate lunch, they engaged in small talk about the weather, school, and the quality of the french fries. Miriam didn't talk very much, but Ruth noticed she would steal glances at her every time she took a sip of her soda. The longer the sip, the longer the glance. It wasn't until the waitress cleared their plates that they started talking about the tough stuff.

"Why did you leave me?" Miriam blurted out.

"I, I didn't have a choice, Miriam. I didn't want to, but I had to."

"Grandma said you had a choice, and you chose a man over

our family."

Ruth took a deep breath and started to explain her side of the story. The side that had liberated her but caused Miriam so much pain.

"It was much more complicated than that. Your father and I didn't have a good relationship and had been separated since before you were born. I tried so hard to do things right. I tried to get a divorce from him, and I tried to reason with your grandparents. After three years, I met a man, Tony, who was the kindest person I've ever known, and well, we fell in love." Ruth took a sip of water. "I got pregnant. Some would say that was a mistake, but my daughter, your sister, Janet, is no mistake. Your grandparents did what they felt they had to because they were shamed in their community. They kicked me out of their lives and kept me from you all of these years." She searched Miriam's face for some kind of emotion.

"I have a sister?" she asked.

"You actually have two sisters and a brother, here I brought pictures to show you." Ruth quickly dug into her purse and pulled them out.

"Is this Tony?" she asked as she pointed to a picture of them in the restaurant.

"Yes, yes that's him."

"Why did you marry a gangster?"

"A gangster? Tony is not a gangster. Nothing could be further from the truth."

"Where did you get that idea?" Ethan asked.

"Grandpa told me. He said Tony killed my father."

Ethan and Ruth exchanged looks. "No, Miriam," Ruth said firmly. "That's just not true. Tony had nothing to do with your father's death."

"Do you mean Grandpa lied to me?" she looked at Ethan.

Ethan put his arm around Miriam and said, "Well, honey, Grandpa is a very angry man, and I think he's mistaken on this one."

"He said Tony's nothing but a no, good criminal," Miriam insisted as tears ran down her eyes. "He wouldn't lie to me."

"It's true they didn't like Tony, but he's a good person. Maybe if you met him, you'll see for yourself." Ruth reached out to touch her hand, but Miriam pulled it away quickly and started to cry harder.

"Ok, maybe we should head home now, Miriam. Today was a big a day, and I'm sure you have a lot to think about." Ethan said.

"Thank you for having lunch with me today," Ruth said feeling defeated but tried to sound positive. "You can keep these pictures if you'd like."

"Ok," she whispered.

As Ruth watched them leave the diner, a heaviness took over her body and that pain of losing her so long ago came flooding back.

THIRTY-FOUR

OCTOBER, 1959
TONY

TONY'S BEEN WATCHING the clock all afternoon as he waited for Ruth to come home from her lunch with Ethan and Miriam. He offered to go with her and even sit in the car if she wanted, but she was determined to see this through herself. He understood her point of view, but at the same time he wanted to be close by just in case. Through the years he's appreciated the incredible mother she was. She was always available for each of the kids and seemed to know exactly when they were feeling down or sick. It's usually only Ruth who was able to comfort Rena when she was in one of her dark moods. Tony hoped that Miriam would come to see the incredible sacrifice that Ruth made by not fighting harder for her. There have been many times when they considered different scenarios on how to get Miriam back into their lives, but they never wanted to bring the stress of confrontation and family hostilities into Miriam's world. They wanted her to have the happiest childhood she could possibly have. Even if that meant not having Ruth in it. So, rather than complicate her meeting with Miriam, Tony agreed it was probably best that he spend the day with the kids as he usually did on Saturdays.

"Daddy, when will Mommy be home?" Nancy looked at Tony with her big brown eyes.

"Mommy said she'll be home before dinner." Janet answered as she grabbed a Tinker Toy spool and handed it to him. "Do you think we can get this Ferris Wheel to work?"

"Well, I've never made one before, but it's looking pretty good, don't you think?" Tony raised his eyebrows at Janet. "Nancy, can you find five of these kinds of sticks?" He held up a medium size peg and she immediately started digging through the pile of wooden pieces that were strewn across the floor. Tony loved his Saturday time alone with the kids. The restaurant kept him away for long hours most days, and although they ate dinner together every night, he made sure every Saturday morning and afternoon was for the family. Usually, he gave Ruth some free time for herself and found some fun activities and projects to do with the kids, but every once in a while, they would all go on a family outing and have a picnic in the park or go to the zoo. Nancy was quite attached to Ruth and sometimes had a hard time being away from her for long periods of time. But Janet, she was Tony's little buddy. She was always excited for their Saturday time, and often started thinking up things for them to do the Sunday before. Anthony was too young to have a favorite parent just yet, and he seemed to be happiest following the girls around as he tried to do everything they did. Sometimes Tony could persuade Rena to join them, but most of the time she spent her Saturdays listening to music and reading her *Teen* magazines.

"Wait," Nancy said excitedly and dropped three Tinker Toy pegs. "I think I hear Mommy."

"No," Janet whined as Ruth walked in. "We didn't finish."

"Don't worry, Janet, we'll get it done." Tony took in Ruth's expression as she walked through the door. "But first I need some time to talk to Mommy. Why don't you and Nancy go check on Anthony."

"Girls," Ruth said as she crossed the room, "I need some big hugs before you go."

Janet and Nancy dropped the Tinker Toys they had in their hands and ran into Ruth's arms. Ruth smothered the girls with kisses and said, "Off you go."

"Ok, but don't be too long, we've got to finish this Ferris Wheel," Janet said as she led Nancy up to Anthony's room.

"Ruthie," Tony took Ruth's hand and led her to the sofa. "What happened? Are you alright?"

"I'm ok." She sighed.

Tony sat next to her and held her hand as she took in the Tinker Toy mess on the floor and stared at the half-built Ferris Wheel. After a few moments Ruth said, "You know Tony, I feel like I have taken you … the kids … our family for granted. After seeing Miriam today, I realized that we built a wonderful, simple life filled with daily routine and all of our moments together, even the smallest moments, are really big blessings."

Tony was confused at Ruth's epiphany. "Yeah, honey. You're right. But I have a hard time believing that you are only realizing this now."

"I have *always* known it, but seeing Miriam put things into perspective. I just saw my first-born child today for the first time in eight years …" Ruth caught her breath. " … And we were strangers." She turned and looked at Tony. "She is my daughter, and I didn't know what her voice sounded like. I didn't know she was close to my height, or that she bit her nails." She shook her head. "I now realize that I haven't been fully appreciating the little things, the little moments with our family that mean so much. Like how Anthony can't sleep without the baby blanket Anna made years ago when Janet was born, and Janet loves peanut butter and jelly but only if the crust is cut off, and Nancy loves her reading time. These details seemed so minor to me before today but are actually the big things that I need to cling to. I missed out on so much with Miriam."

"Oh, honey. I'm sorry." For the first time in their relationship, Tony didn't know what to say to Ruth to help her. "It had to be so hard for you. For you both actually."

"It was a lot of things. It was hard, it was polite, it was awkward, and yet, it was one of the happiest days in my life."

Tony narrowed his eyes in confusion.

"I got to speak to my daughter again."

Tony nodded and squeezed Ruth's hand.

"Things were going nicely with Miriam at first. At least I thought they were. I don't know now. Then she asked me why I left her and married a gangster." She looked down.

"A gangster?" What do you mean a gangster?"

"All these years she's been told you were a criminal. That I chose a criminal over her."

"You gotta be kidding me." He stood and started pacing the floor, his hands balled up into fists. "Ethan too? Ethan told her I was a criminal?"

"No, he was just as surprised to hear that as I was. I'm certain he had no idea. It was her grandparents who told her. Now she's confused and doesn't know what to believe. I guess I didn't really know what to expect. In my heart, I wanted her to run into my arms and everything would be perfect. I don't blame her for being cautious and shy with me, but I never even thought about what she would think of you."

After a few moments of silence, Tony sat down, relaxed his body, and started to think rationally. "I guess maybe in her grandparents' eyes I am a criminal. I came into your life and turned theirs upside down. If some guy comes in and steals away any of my daughters, I'll probably think of him as a criminal too. Give it time. Fixing relationships isn't easy. You can't give up hope."

Ruth nodded and let out a long sigh. "I've waited so long for this, but I suppose I have to be patient."

"That's exactly what Mom would say. Why don't you call Ethan during the week to check in on things?"

Ruth nodded again and curled into Tony's embrace. She knew she needed to set aside her emotions for the time being, especially for her other children. After a few moments she asked, "How was everything here? Where's Rena?"

"Rena went to the record store with some girlfriend. Can you believe that? She was in a great mood right after she got the phone call inviting her. She did her chores for the first time without me telling her, and I actually heard her singing while she was getting dressed. She even put on that new pink sweater and neck scarf you got her. Maybe we've turned a corner?" He shrugged.

"Wow, that's surprising. What friend? Who'd she go with?"

"I dunno, I think she said it was Sharon who called."

"Oh, Sharon, ok. She's a nice girl. She's the girl that used to come around here last year, Whisp of a thing, very outgoing. Always wore those poofy poodle skirts." Ruth smiled. "It'll be good for Rena to spend some more time with her."

"I remember her. Her father's an electrician, isn't he?"

"Yes, that's the one."

"By the way, Betty called for you. She said call back when you can. Nothing important,"

"She's another one that's been happy lately,"

"Really?"

"Yes, she said that Frank's been much more attentive. Even said he'll get her that new washer she wants."

"Ha ha, it must be that Friday night poker game he started going to."

"What? Is he gambling again? Betty'll never put up with that."

"He's not gambling like he used to. He just joined a poker game once a week. He says it takes the edge off. I figure it's not interfering with the restaurant, and if it keeps him happy and satisfied, it's probably good for everyone."

"Does Betty know about it?"

"He said he told her. She argued with him at first, but when he brings home his winnings, she stops arguing."

"I just think you need to keep an eye on him. You know how he used to be. It would be terrible if he went back to his old habits."

"Yup, I've got my eyes wide open."

"Daddy, are you done talking to Mommy yet?" Janet suddenly appeared with her hands on her hips and Nancy and Anthony at her side.

"Yes honey, we're done talking. I'm going to start dinner and you and Daddy can finish your project before he has to go into work tonight." Ruth walked over to kiss each of the kids and went into the kitchen.

"I'm going to help Mommy." Nancy announced as she ran into the kitchen and Anthony toddled behind her.

"Whelp it looks like it's just you and me, kiddo. Let's see if we can get this thing finished." Tony sat on the floor as Janet hurried over and collected the Tinker Toy pegs Nancy dropped.

THIRTY-FIVE

DECEMBER, 1959
RUTH

LIFE EVOLVED INTO a pleasant calm since Rena started spending more time with her friend Sharon two months ago. Ruth wasn't sure she'd ever seen Rena as upbeat and happy as she'd been recently, and she loved that Rena was starting to spend more time going to the movies and the ice cream shop with friends. Even Ruth's relationship with Miriam had slowly started to evolve. She's joined Ethan and Miriam on a few small outings, and each time they got together, Miriam seemed to be more comfortable and even told Ruth stories about her school and her friends. While Ruth wanted nothing more than to reach out and hug her daughter, she knew how delicate the situation was and she was cautious to follow Miriam's lead.

She and Tony decided to have the annual Russo holiday party before Christmas this year so that they could include some Channukah traditions. Ruth asked if Miriam would like to come to the party and meet her brother and sisters and was thrilled when Miriam said yes. She worried over minor details of the party and wanted everything to be just right. She felt like she was trying to make up for lost time with her daughter, but she did not want to overwhelm her either. With only a little more than a week until the party, Ruth made a mental list of things to do as she prepared dinner.

"Hi sweetie, how was school today?" Ruth asked Rena as she entered the kitchen.

"It was good. Nothing special." Rena smiled and began to chop the pepper that was on the cutting board. "I wanted to ask you. Do you think I can come home a little later than curfew tonight? Some of the kids want to go to the diner after the dance."

"How much later?" Ruth asked casually.

"I don't know, maybe twelve?"

"Midnight? Oh, Rena, I don't know." Ruth turned to look at her and Rena looked back with pleading eyes.

"Please? All the kids are going, and I don't want to be the only one left out. You, yourself, told me I should have some more fun."

Ruth pondered the idea for a moment. She'd been so very pleasant the last two months. There'd been no tension or arguing so maybe it wouldn't be such a bad idea to reward her with a little more freedom. "Well, alright, I'll talk to Tony and get it squared away but no later than twelve. Do you hear me?"

"Yes, twelve it is. Oh, thank you." She leaned in to kiss Ruth's cheek. "Do you mind if we eat dinner a little early? I want to have enough time to get ready for the dance tonight."

"That's my plan," Ruth said smiling. "I still don't understand going to a dance without a date."

"I already told you." She rolled her eyes. "None of us will have dates. We're just all going to meet up at the dance and have fun. This way we won't be stuck with the same person all night and can dance with whoever we want to."

"Well, things have certainly changed since my day. Now, can you go tell everyone dinner is ready?"

After Rena left for the dance, Tony and Ruth settled down on the sofa. They enjoyed the quiet after the tornado Rena left in her wake as she was getting ready for the evening.

"I'll tell you what, Rena looked beautiful. It's hard to imagine my little girl is almost an adult."

"I know what you mean. It's good to see her so happy these days."

"I have to agree with you on that one. So how are you doing with the plans for the party next Saturday? Don't forget to give me the menu so I can have the cooks prepare the food."

"I have it on the table. I added in a couple of traditional Channukah dishes, do you think that will be a problem?"

"No, not at all. Chef Amaro is the best we've had yet. You know, I think it's great you are trying to do all you can to make Miriam feel comfortable at the party."

"It'll be a big night for us but especially for her. She'll be meeting her half sisters and brothers for the first time and will probably be a little nervous."

"I'm sure she will be."

"I just wish Betty and Frank could come. I know how important it is for them to be on hand for the holiday parties at the restaurant, but if anyone can make a room full of people laugh, it's their kids."

Tony laughed, "That's very true. So, have you heard back from Louisa? Are they coming?"

"No. I haven't heard from her yet," Ruth said casually, hoping Tony would not get irritated over his sister.

"Maybe I should call her," he said impatiently.

"Let's leave it be. If she wants to join us, she will."

It's times like these that Ruth wished she could talk with Anna. She would know exactly what to do to help mend the rift between Tony and Louisa. Since that night when Louisa left Rena with them, Ruth honestly thought their relationship was beyond repair, but she included Louisa for every event and holiday. She felt that she should at least invite her. They were family after all. Anna always helped Ruth understand Louisa, and when even she couldn't understand her daughter's motives, Anna put a stop to her ugly behavior swiftly and easily. Secretly, Ruth would prefer Louisa not come to the party because the last thing she wanted was tension.

Tony played with the rabbit ears on the television set and finally succeeded in getting a clear picture just as *The Twilight Zone* came on the air. Watching him position the antennas reminded her of Sal and how he would spend a lot of time patiently adjusting them ever so slightly to get the best picture he could. *The Twilight Zone* wasn't Ruth's favorite program, she preferred comedies like *I Love Lucy*, but she was happy to snuggle with Tony and appreciated the rare opportunity for a romantic evening with her husband. After the show, Ruth lit candles throughout their bedroom while Tony poured two glasses of wine. They spent the rest of the night tenderly making love and falling asleep in each other's arms and never noticed that Rena came home over an hour late.

THIRTY-SIX

DECEMBER, 1959
TONY

THE PARTY WAS a bigger success than Tony imagined it would be. Ruth pulled out all of the stops, and by the end of the night everyone was singing and dancing. Tony was thankful that the kids came together easily, and they took such delight in simple things like decorating cookies. Tony was very nervous about seeing Miriam, but he was pretty confident that he made a good impression. He understood the hesitation she felt, and he only wished he could do something to bring Miriam and Ruth closer together. Miriam didn't remember the loving mother Ruth was. Instead, she'd heard conflicting stories from her grandparents that made her out to be a horrible mother and beautiful stories from Uncle Ethan about how much Ruth loved her. It's no wonder she was confused, and Tony knew all they could do was give her time.

Tony spent his entire commute to the restaurant thinking about Ruth and how happy she was after the party. He noticed that her greatest joy was hearing all four of her kids laughing and singing together, and her expression made it clear that the depth of her love was endless. He admired Ruth's tenacity, and wished he could be as level-headed and composed as she was whenever a complication arose. He was aware that his temper was his greatest flaw, and he'd done a lot to control it through the years. But when he was pushed to his limit, his passion to protect anyone and anything he cared about got the better of him. Tony knew how lucky he was when he met Ruth. She loved him completely and unconditionally, flaws and all. As he walked through the restaurant to the office, he made a mental note to be sure to do something special for her.

"Hey Frank. How'd we do last night?"

"Better than usual. We had a lot of people getting a head start on celebrating the holidays. The bartender and waitresses couldn't keep up in the ballroom and the dining room had over an hour wait for walk-ins. Even the party Betty was overseeing went longer than expected."

"Good. That's real good," Tony said as he skimmed through the receipts.

"How'd it go with Miriam at the party last night?"

"You know, I think it went pretty good. She was real quiet at first, kept staring at me. But she took to the kids right away. Ruth's Chanukah and Christmas activities really brought them together, and it took no time before they were all at the kitchen table playing with the Play-Doh Ruth got for each of them."

"Does she still think you're a gangster?" Frank laughed.

"I don't know what she thinks of me. I did get her laughing, though, when I tried to make a reindeer with Anthony's Play-Doh. So, I guess that's something. At the end of the night, she said she had fun and wanted to come back again sometime. Ruth's feeling real positive about it all."

"Oh boy, here comes Louisa." Frank nodded his head toward the door.

"Yup, it's payment day, you can set your calendar by her." Tony said as he shook his head and turned to face her. "Hey Louisa, Ruth missed you at the party last night."

"Hello Tony. Yeah, we couldn't make it. You know how busy this season is for us."

Tony knew Louisa was just making an excuse, and quite frankly was happy she didn't come to the party. "So, how are you?"

"I'm doing a lot better than you are, I'm sure," Louisa said sarcastically.

"What does that mean?"

"I see you have no better control over Rena than I had."

"What are you talking about?" Heat radiated up his spine.

"I'm talking about Rena being in a dance club in Manhattan last Friday night with some young man who looked much older than her."

"Wait, what? Who saw her there?" Frank asked before Tony could close his mouth from shock.

"Bob's younger sister, Ann, was there with her fiancé. As they were entering the club, they passed Rena and her date leaving. Ann locked eyes with her, but when Ann went to speak, Rena turned her head and sped away."

"You must be mistaken. There's no way that could've been Rena. She was at a high school dance with her friends. We took pictures before she left and everything," Tony insisted.

"Well, I don't know anything about a school dance, but what I do know is that Ann saw her. Tony, really! She has no business being in a dance club in the city."

"Do you really think I would give her permission to do that?

Come on! If anyone is to blame, it's you!" Tony yelled as he pointed his finger in her face. "If you had been kind to her when you had her, she wouldn't be acting out now."

"Don't you start blaming me," Louisa fired back. "You were the absent father!"

"Alright, alright. Let's all calm down." Frank quickly moved between them. "We've got customers in the dining room who can hear you. Besides, all this blaming each other isn't going to fix anything. Louisa, did Ann happen to say what the guy Rena was with looked like?"

Louisa took a step back. "All she said was that he was real Italian looking. Dark hair slicked back. He was dressed really nice with expensive clothes and had a gold chain around his neck with a cross on a shield pendant."

Frank and Tony exchanged looks, and Tony quickly sat down and put his head in his hands unable to speak a word. After a few moments, Frank took an envelope out of the desk and said, "Thanks for letting him know, Louisa. Here's your check."

"Thank you, Frank. Tony, you really need to take care of this," Louisa said sarcastically before leaving.

"I don't believe this. I *don't believe this*!" Tony slammed his fist on the desk. "I told that punk to stay away from her. I told him."

"Alright, let's calm down," Frank said. "You don't really know that it's Dominick she was with."

"Frank, with that description? It was him." He started pacing. "I've only seen that kind of pendant on one …" Before Tony could finish his sentence, he saw Dominick walk into the restaurant. "I'm gonna kill him," He said as he started for the dining room.

Frank moved swiftly and said, "Not in the restaurant. I'll go talk to him and bring him around back. You can scream at him as much and as loud as you want back there, and the customers won't hear a thing."

Tony marched through the kitchen and slammed open the back door. What did this guy want with Rena? He could have any young, sophisticated girl he wanted. Why her? Who did he think he was? He gave his word! It didn't take long before Frank and Dominick were outside with Tony in the back alley. He moved forward and quickly pinned Dominick against the wall.

"Didn't I tell you to stay away from her? Didn't I?"

"Yeah, but the way I see it, she's eighteen now and she can make her own decisions."

"She's just eighteen," Tony snarled as he moved in closer to his face. "She's too young for you."

"She's not as young as you think." Dominick smiled a broad sarcastic smile that released an anger inside of Tony that couldn't be tamed. He punched Dominick across the left cheek just before Frank pulled Tony back.

Dominick shook his head, lunged at Tony full on, and pushed him. "You think you can take me on, old man? You don't know who you're dealing with."

Tony blocked his right arm as Dominick swung toward his face and hit him square in the gut with his left fist. As Dominick doubled over, Tony punched him across his face again with his right fist and pushed him down on the ground.

"Obviously, punk, *you* don't know who *you* are dealing with," Tony said as he turned toward Frank.

"Watch out he's got a gun," Frank grabbed Tony and turned him around.

"Oh, come on, Mr. Big Shot needs a piece to fight?" Tony said disgusted. "Why don't you fight like a real man and use the weapons you were born with."

"Ok, old man, I'll tell you what. You and me we go at it. No weapons, and if I kick your ass, you leave me and Rena alone."

Tony looked at Frank and raised his eyebrows. "Fine, and if I kick your ass, you leave Rena alone and find yourself another girl."

"Fine," he said and gave his gun to Frank.

From that point forward, the kid didn't stand a chance. As soon as he released his hand from the gun, Tony stepped in and pummeled him. All Tony could see was Dominick's defiant, smart-ass smile and Tony wanted to wipe it from his face. Dominick got in a few good punches to Tony's face mostly, but by the time he was done Tony broke three of Dominick's ribs, smashed his right hand, and his face was almost unrecognizable. Frank had to pull Tony away before he killed him.

"Now leave my daughter *alone*."

THIRTY-SEVEN

DECEMBER, 1959
RUTH

AFTER PUTTING THE kids to bed, Ruth decided to relax on the sofa and allowed herself to become mesmerized by the brightly blinking lights on the Christmas tree. All day she was thinking about Miriam and how she seemed to have a good time at the party, and how happy and agreeable Rena had been lately. She would like to believe that their family had finally turned a corner, but she knew deep down that things were going a little too smoothly. She couldn't quite calm the nagging feeling that popped up, and she feared that the family harmony would not last long. She looked at the clock and realized that it was later than she thought. Every night she'd wait up for Tony to get home, and he has never been as late as this. She decided to try to read the romance novel she picked up at the drug store, but she couldn't concentrate. Finally, at two-thirty a.m., he came home and went straight to the kitchen, grabbed a bag of frozen peas, and sat at the kitchen table as he held the peas to his left eye.

"What happened?" Ruth asked as she entered the kitchen.

"You wanna know what happened? Ask Rena. Rena's what happened."

"I don't understand, you're not making sense," Ruth said as she took the peas from his hand and looked at his eye.

"Rena's big dance last week. It was all a lie. She was out in the city with that bum, Dominick. At a dance club of all places. Louisa's sister-in-law saw her."

"What?" she said as she shrank into a chair. "She lied to us about the dance?"

Deep down, Ruth expected some mischievous deception from Rena, after all, she was a very spirited teenager, but she thought it would have been something rather innocent like getting caught kissing a boy from school in the back of his car.

"She must've been seeing him this whole time. That's why she's been so happy. She's been getting one over on us," Tony said as he placed the peas back on his eye.

"I can't believe she would lie to us like that." Ruth shook her head disappointed that her fears were valid. She never should have dismissed her suspicions about Rena's sudden close friendship with Sharon and how easily she agreed to not see Dominick. But Ruth set aside her concerns for Tony's sake. He wanted her to be a typical teenage girl and was so happy with the peace in the house lately. She didn't want to get Tony alarmed and worked up over her skepticism.

"Who lied to you?" Rena asked rubbing her eyes as she walked into the kitchen and sat at the table.

Tony spun his head and stared at her.

Ruth quickly stood and put her hands on his shoulders to offer support but more importantly to keep him seated.

"Rena, now is probably not the best time to talk, why don't you go back to bed," Ruth said firmly. Ruth didn't want Tony to say anything he might regret and thought it would be best if he had a chance to calm down before having this conversation.

"Don't you dare move a muscle," Tony hissed. "Who lied to us, you ask? *You*," he yelled. "*You lied to us*! Every time you said you were going out with your girlfriend, you were going to see *him* weren't you?"

"You wouldn't have let me see him if I told you the truth, so I had to lie."

"Oh, Rena," Ruth said irritably.

"And that big dance last Friday. There was no dance was there?" Tony demanded.

"There was a dance, but I didn't go." She looked down.

"So it's true? You really were in Manhattan with Dominick?" Tony asked furiously.

"Yes, he wanted to take me to a real dance club. Not some high school gymnasium decorated with paper streamers." She looked up and searched Ruth's eyes for support.

"But Rena, you *are* in high school. You're too young to be going to those kinds of places," Ruth snapped. "And Dominick is obviously not the right boy for you."

"Boy?" Rena raised her voice. "He's not a boy, he's a man. And I may be in high school for now, but I'm eighteen and if I want to see him, I will."

"Oh no you will not," Tony bellowed. "I'm locking you in that room of yours from now on. You're to come straight home from school, go straight into that room and nothing else. No television, no radio, no telephone, nothing. You can come out for meals and chores and that's all. You see this shiner on my face? This is what Dominick did to me. I'm not even gonna tell you how he looks right now. Just know, I mean business."

"You can't do that," she cried and screamed at the same time.

Tony stood, he put his hands on the table and leaned in close to Rena's face. "Watch me. You'll be trusted to go straight to school and back, and if we find out you're lying, going anywhere else, or skipping school, we'll have someone personally escort you there and back. Follow you around the school if we have to. Now get to your room. NOW."

Rena ran up the stairs to her room and slammed the door. While Ruth took out the first aid kit and started to clean Tony's face, he grabbed her hand and placed it against his cheek.

"How could this have gotten so bad?"

Ruth felt like she'd been holding her breath for hours and let out a large sigh. "I don't know. I just don't know."

"We trusted her."

"I know, I feel just as betrayed as you do. Hell, I helped her style her hair that night." She sat next to him and pulled his head up so their eyes met. "How bad is Dominick hurt?"

"A couple of Carmine's guys took him to the hospital."

"Tony!"

"He'll be alright."

"That doesn't make it right."

"No. I suppose it doesn't. But I'm not sure I wouldn't do it all over again. I'm trying to save my daughter and I just don't know how." Tony said raising his voice.

"Violence is not the way."

"Violence is the only way to get through to people like Dominick." Tony threw the bag of peas into the sink and stormed out of the kitchen.

Ruth slammed her hands down on the table. She didn't know

who she was angrier with, Rena for her deceit or Tony for letting his temper get the better of him. She took her time cleaning up the kitchen. She knew she needed some breathing room before she tried to talk to him calmly.

"Here, I thought this might help." Ruth handed Tony a cup of tea as she entered their bedroom.

"Thanks."

"I know you don't really want to hear this, but getting into a fight with Dominick was not the right way to handle this. You know that I've endured violence throughout my life, and I've got to say that it's wrong. *You* were wrong." She paused for a moment and hoped Tony started to see how serious his actions were.

When he bowed his head and ran his fingers through his hair, she knew she was getting through to him.

"I know you're trying to protect your daughter."

Tony nodded. "I did get carried away, but he disrespected and lied to me. He gave me his word he wouldn't see her, and what does he do ... he encouraged her to lie to us and took her out dancing."

"Quite frankly, I never did trust this Dominick." Ruth admitted. "I just hope it doesn't all backfire on us and make them even more determined to see each other."

"Well, we'll just have to make sure that doesn't happen. I meant it when I said I want her to come straight home from school. Even if that means we'll have someone there to bring her home personally."

"I'll call the school first thing tomorrow. Hopefully, they can help keep a close eye on her."

"We need to keep her busy so she doesn't have any opportunities to sneak off and see that bum. I would put her to work down at the restaurant, but I think that would be a recipe for disaster."

"Oh, I've already started making a list of things that need to be done around here, and I think after the holidays I'm going to talk to Mrs. Esposito and see if she needs any help looking after her grandkids."

Tony chuckled. "Now that's exactly what Mom would do to keep us in line."

"Where do you think I got the idea?" Ruth sighed, "I sure do miss her. Especially at times like these where we could use her wisdom."

"I miss them both too." Tony pulled her into a deep hug.

Ruth gently pulled away and put her hands on his. "I'm serious about the fighting. It's not the answer. It will only break this family up, not pull us together."

"Ok, Ruthie." Tony kissed her hands. "I promise you I will try to keep the fighting to just in the boxing ring down at the gym."

"Thank you."

"Our family is the most important thing to me. When you came in, I was just thinking that I should cut back on the amount of time I spend at the restaurant."

"I think that would be good for us."

"Yeah, I don't like spending so much time away from you and the kids. And I wanna spend some more time with Rena."

"I think she might like that, and frankly, I think she needs that."

The next morning, Ruth knocked on Rena's door to have a heart-to-heart talk before she went to school. "Hey, can I come in?"

"Sure, if you want." Rena glanced at Ruth as she brushed her hair.

"I think we need to talk."

"Look, I'm sorry I lied. But I knew there was no way either of you would let me see Dominick."

"So, you thought it was a good idea to sneak around?"

"I didn't have any other choice." She shrugged.

"The way I see it, you had choices. You could've honored your promise not to see him or you could've come to us and talked to us."

"Talk to you? Tony just makes demands on what I'm supposed to do and there is no conversation."

"You should've come to me. Have I ever given you a reason to feel like you couldn't come to me and talk to me? Have I ever betrayed you?"

Rena looked down. "No," she whispered. "You're the one person that's never lied to me."

Ruth lifted Rena's face up by the chin. "And I never will. But you've betrayed my trust and I am disappointed in you."

"I really am sorry for that." Rena hugged Ruth and cried on her shoulder. "He's not a bad person, you know."

"Maybe he's not. But did you ever really stop and think about why we're so adamant about you not seeing him? Your age difference is really too big right now. He's an adult with far more experience and opportunity to do things that you're not ready for."

Rena pulled away and wiped her eyes with a tissue. "I'm eighteen. So really, I'm an adult too, and who says I'm not ready to experience life like he does? Just because I'm still in high school doesn't make me a child. I'm not like those kids at school."

"Rena, you've had a difficult time growing up and have lost a lot of your childhood innocence far sooner than you should have. Your father and I wish to God we could change that, but we can't. What we can do is help and protect you now."

"I don't need protection. Not from Dominick." She adamantly shook her head.

"You don't see it now, but you do. You're not ready for such a mature relationship."

"Dominick loves me. He's not going to hurt me."

"Is it really love if he's encouraged you to sneak around and lie to us? Is he really thinking about what's best for you?"

"I don't want to lose him." Rena started to cry again. "I've never felt this way before. I'm just so happy when I'm with him, and when I'm not, I feel so lonely."

"Look at me. Don't ever lose yourself to any other person. You are a strong, smart young woman who has the world at her fingertips. Have the confidence to trust and love yourself and don't ever depend on anyone else for love and happiness."

Rena put her head into Ruth's shoulder again and cried uncontrollably. "How can I love myself if I've never felt loved before?"

"Never felt loved?" Ruth couldn't hide her surprise. "Don't you feel loved living here with us?"

"I suppose I do. I mean I know you love me and all, but I don't really feel close to anyone. Sometimes I feel like an outsider."

Ruth's heart sank. "My God. I'm so sorry. I know it was difficult for you when you first came here, and I guess I didn't really understand everything you were feeling. It's true I had my hands full with Janet and Nancy being so young, and then Anthony came along, and things got crazy again. But I guess that's no excuse."

"It's ok, it's not anyone's fault. It's not easy being the person no one wants around."

"That's just not true."

"Isn't it? I spent most of my life thinking my Aunt was my Mother because my Father didn't want me around. And then she dumped me here the first chance she got."

"I can't speak for Louisa. Truth is I don't really understand her much. But I know your Father always loved you. It was just difficult for him to be able to raise you. If circumstances were different, he never would've let any of this happen."

"But it did happen. And if he really loved me, he wouldn't forbid me to see someone I care about."

"Rena, look at me." Ruth softly put her hands on Rena's cheeks. "Don't ever doubt that your father's love for you runs very deep. You're his first-born, and he'll always try to protect you. I know it may not seem like it, but everything he does is out of love for you. Try to see things from his point of view."

"I've tried. I just don't always understand him."

"He can be a complicated man and I'm sure he doesn't understand you completely either. He's going to work on finding extra time to spend with you. Hopefully, you can both get to know each other and start forgiving each other."

"I think I might like that."

"I know he will too. In the meantime, Rena, no more lies and no more sneaking around."

Rena swiftly looked down and said, "Ok."

THIRTY-EIGHT

DECEMBER, 1959
TONY

TONY THOUGHT IT would be best to let Ruth talk to Rena after the last shouting match. He found himself at a loss on how to talk to her – how to fully communicate how much he loved her and how much he regretted not being there for her in the past. He'd always blamed himself for the wall she built around herself, and now he also blamed himself for the bad decisions she'd made. But for the life of him, he didn't know what else he could do for her. He hoped spending more time at home would help, but he was afraid it was too late. He called Frank and asked him to meet at the restaurant to see if they could figure out a way for Tony to be able to spend more time at home.

"Hello, Tony," Carmine said as Tony walked through the door.

"Hi Carmine, I guess you heard about what happened last night?" Tony was sure he would get a visit from Carmine Esposito sometime soon, but he didn't expect him to be at the restaurant drinking coffee with Frank as he entered.

"I did," he said flatly as he nodded his head and looked at his cup.

"Carmine was just saying that Dominick may never get full use of his hand." Frank's worried expression told Tony there's more he's not saying.

"Oh. Oh wow. I'm real sorry about that. I didn't mean to hurt him that bad. I just found out he's sneaking around with my daughter and taking her out to dance clubs. I thought he and I had an understanding. Turns out, he lied."

"I understand. He gave you his word, and a man's word is everything in my world. I will say, if it were my daughter and he and I shook hands on an agreement, I probably would've done the same, if not worse. But you see, I now have a problem." Carmine turned in his chair and looked Tony in the eyes. "Dominick played a very important role in my business. He kept people in line and delivered consequences if the need should arise. And now, I need to replace him." Carmine lifted both eyebrows and nodded his head at Tony.

"Like I said, I'm real sorry. I'm sure there's lots of young guys who could fill his shoes."

"No, that's the thing. You need to 'fill his shoes' as you put it."

"*Me.* Oh no you've got the wrong guy. I wouldn't be of any good use to you."

"The way I see it, you nearly killed that kid with your bare hands and only walked away with a black eye. I could use that kind of muscle. Besides, you owe me for Dominick. He was one of my men you took down. Usually there would be consequences for that type of thing. But I like you, and I'm willing to forego the retribution just so long as you take on some of his jobs."

"What type of jobs are we talking about?" Tony shifted nervously.

"Let's just say that, from time-to-time, you will be called on to use your talent and exert your strength. Whenever the need arises, one of my guys will contact you with the details. But, Tony, I need to make myself very clear, this is not negotiable. You must follow orders as instructed each and every time." Carmine put his hand on Tony's shoulder. "If not, there will be a price to pay, and I would hate to see a member of your beautiful family punished for the sins of their father. Capisce?"

Tony nodded his head, "I understand."

"Good." Carmine tapped his shoulder, put his overcoat and hat on and headed for the door. "Have a good day, gentlemen. Oh yeah and Merry Christmas."

"Oh my God, Tony. What are you going to do?"

"What can I do?" Tony walked behind the bar and took a shot of whiskey. "I don't have any choices right now."

"What are you going to tell Ruth?"

"Nothing, and don't tell Betty any of this either. I don't want Ruthie finding out."

Tony slammed the whiskey glass on the bar and locked himself in the office. "Well, you've really done it this time. Didn't I tell you not to get involved with people like Carmine? This is just no good." Tony could hear his father's words in his head. He put his head in his hands and thought to himself, "Oh, Pop, what am I gonna do?" He realized just how right Sal was about Carmine all along. He never should've encouraged Carmine to spend so much time at Salvatore Bruno's. None of this would've happened if Carmine and Dominick weren't around so much. But Tony just wanted the restaurant to be successful. He wanted to give Ruth and the kids security, he wanted to make his family proud, and he got caught up in Frank's enthusiasm over the business Carmine brought in with his associates and friends. Tony shook his head, inhaled a deep breath and exhaled slowly. No. He thought, it's not Carmine's fault. He should've handled things differently himself. He never should've let things get so out of hand last night and he should've just walked away from Dominick. It's easy to look back and think about what you should've done, the hard part was dealing with the consequences of what had been done.

"I've made promises to Ruth," Tony muttered as he started to pace around the office. "But she can't know about this. Not until I find a way out." Tony sighed as he thought about Ruth and the kids. "All I've ever wanted to do is protect my family."

THIRTY-NINE

DECEMBER, 1959
RUTH

"HOW LONG WILL I be locked up in this place? It's been over two weeks," Rena whined as she dried the dinner dishes.

"It's going to take a long time to win back our trust," Ruth casually handed her a wet glass.

"Well, things are definitely over with Dominick now," Rena snorted.

"I'm sorry, but I just don't think he was good for you. I'm certain you'll meet lots of other young men, closer to your age, that you'll like just as much. Maybe even more."

"I doubt it."

"So, what exactly is it about him that you like better than any other boy?"

"He's so much more interesting and nicer than the boys my age. He's not all goofy like they are, and he's really interested in *me*. He respects me and doesn't try to get me in the backseat of some car.

When we're together, we laugh and talk about so many different things. You know, he has a difficult relationship with his family too, so he understands me and everything I've gone through."

"Well, I do like that he shows you respect, but I don't like how disrespectful he's been to Tony."

"I think they don't get along because they don't trust each other."

"You're probably right about that. But do you blame Tony for not trusting him? He's twenty-six."

"But that's only eight years difference between us."

"Eight years is a lot, especially when you're young. Maybe if you were a few years older things could be different."

"How would things be so different?"

"I think right now, you're smitten with the excitement of an older man. If you were older, you may have a better idea of what you want in a relationship. Maybe Dominick isn't the right one for you."

"But maybe he is."

"Rena, you've got to let this go. No one is worth lying to your family over. This relationship of yours nearly ruined your relationship with your family. Is that what you want?"

Rena put down the dish towel and wiped her eyes.

"Oh, come here sweetheart." Ruth took her in her arms and hugged her tightly. "Everything is going to work out. I know it doesn't seem like it now, but I promise you it will."

"I hope you're right."

"You know what, tomorrow is New Year's Eve. I think we should spend it as a family, just the six of us. We can get some Chinese food, make some ice cream sundaes, watch Guy Lombardo, and maybe after we put the little ones to sleep, we can play Monopoly or Clue."

"But you always spend it working at the restaurant."

"Nope. Not anymore. It's time we make some new traditions,

and this is going to be the first."

"What about Tony? He won't want to be away from the restaurant."

"Don't you worry about him. I'll take care of it. So, what do you think?"

"It sounds like it could be fun. Maybe I can make something like a cake or a Jell-O mold?"

"Why don't you go and put cold water on your face, and then we can sit down and plan it all out. And then we can watch some television together, just the two of us. I think we can relax that part of your punishment."

"Ok," Rena nodded and started toward the bathroom but stopped after taking a few steps, smiled, and said, "Thank you."

That was the first genuine smile Ruth had seen on Rena's face in a long time, and she slowly shook her head. She knew how hard it was to have faith that life would get better when it seemed like your world was crashing in. Rena has had more than her share of emotional turmoil in her life, and sometimes Ruth felt helpless on how to comfort her. One thing she was sure of was that it was going to take a long time for Tony and Rena to trust each other and mend the cracks in their relationship. Ruth just hoped that they would give each other the time that it'll take.

———

Tony wrapped his arms around Ruth's waist as she put Rena's Jell-O Mold on a platter. "This was a great idea. I've gotta admit, I didn't love the thought of being away from the restaurant on such a busy night but I'm glad you convinced me."

"It was a spur of the moment idea, and once I saw how much Rena seemed to like it, I realized that we absolutely had to make it happen. I think bringing in a new year, heck a new decade together will be good for us all."

"Come on, guys. We have our New Year's reservations ready." Nancy ran into the kitchen.

"I think you mean resolutions, Pumpkin." Ruth laughed.

"We're all waiting," Nancy insisted.

"Ok, ok," Tony conceded. "Let's go Mommy. They're all waiting."

"Who wants Jell-O?" Ruth sang as she placed the platter on the table.

"I do," Janet answered.

"Meeee," Anthony squealed.

"Me too," Nancy added.

Rena sat up proudly and said, "I'll serve. Dad, do you want some?"

Tony choked up and nodded his head quickly not sure if he actually heard his daughter call him Dad for the first time since she was a toddler.

Ruth closed her eyes and tried to will tears of happiness from running down her face. She cleared her throat and finally said, "Why don't we share our resolutions. Who wants to go first?"

"I do!" Janet exclaimed. "During this new year I want to try to keep my room clean so Mommy doesn't yell at me, and I want to practice my hula hoop every day."

"I like that, Janet. Great job." Ruth laughed.

"Me next." Nancy cleared her throat and held up her paper. "I want to sing a new song to everybody every week."

"How are you gonna learn a new song every week?"

"You're going to teach me, Daddy." Nancy said so seriously that everyone started to laugh.

"What about you Anthony? What do you wanna try to do this year?" Tony asked still amused over Nancy's resolution.

"I wanna eat cookies," he said smiling with a mouth full of whipped cream and Jell-O.

"I bet you do." Ruth said as she wiped his face.

"My turn." Rena seriously looked around the room. "This year I want to try to do better and be better."

"You *are* good, Rena." Janet said looking at Rena confused.

"Thanks, Janet." Rena hugged her tightly.

"We love you, Rena." Nancy pushed her way into the hug.

Ruth and Tony exchanged glances and squeezed each other's hands.

"Love Rena." Anthony yelled across the table.

"Yes, buddy. We all love Rena." He caught her eye before he added, "A lot."

"It's your turn, Daddy," Janet said as she returned to her seat.

"This year, I am gonna spend less time at the restaurant and more time on what's important." He lifted his soda glass in a salute. "Mommy, what about you?"

"My New Year's resolution is to plan more family nights just like this one." She looked around the table as the kids started clapping and cheering and she took a snapshot of this moment in her mind.

This was a night she wanted to remember.

FORTY

APRIL, 1960
TONY

IT'D BEEN THREE months since Carmine threatened Tony to take on muscle jobs for him. Although Tony hadn't had to rough anyone up to the point of hospitalization, he hated everything about the situation. Most of the jobs had been to threaten people who owed Carmine money, and Tony noticed how quickly people produced cash when he just stepped closer to them in a threatening way. Yet, after nearly every job, he got physically sick to his stomach. Although he realized he had a bad temper, he hated having to inflict fear and pain on people when he himself didn't have a personal problem or gripe with them. Tony took Carmine's threats against his family very seriously and he felt like he had no choice but to comply. He felt guilty lying to Ruth, but he felt like the best way to protect her physically and emotionally was to keep it from her. He'd rather break his promises to her than have her live in fear every day of what could happen at the hands of Carmine Esposito.

He'd conditioned himself to separate the many facets of his life. When he was at the restaurant, he was an outgoing, charming host. When he got a call to go on a job for Carmine, he turned into a menacing goon, and when he arrived at home, he transformed into the man he liked best, the loving husband and father. Tony found that he couldn't spend as much time at home as he originally wanted because a call would come from one of Carmine's guys at any time day or night. Getting called away from the restaurant was not as bad as getting the call when he was home. The look of disappointment on his girls faces crushed his spirit every time, and he hadn't been able to bond with Rena like he wanted. She started to pull away from him again, especially when he was called away. He tried to reason with Carmine and even offered to make amends for hurting Dominick through a financial payout to both Dominick and Carmine. But Carmine wouldn't even consider the proposal. He liked Tony's maturity and demeanor and had stated on multiple occasions that his decision was final. For now, Tony reasoned he had to make this way of life work until he could figure a way out.

 On Saturday he was able to spend the day at the park with his family. He got lucky that most of Carmine's collection calls were finished during the week. Usually, the people who owed money anticipated their collection visit and made themselves scarce during normal business hours. But this week they were able to make most of the collections without any problems. Tony and Ruth decided a picnic in the park was a great way to get the kids out in the fresh spring air. Rena was not as thrilled with the idea of a family outing as everyone else was, but her mood lightened when Tony spent the entire day playing cards and tossing a frisbee with her. He had asked Ruth to keep the other kids entertained so he could get quality time with Rena.

"This has been a great day." Ruth said. "We all really enjoyed it. Saturday afternoons together have become so rare."

"I know, and I'm sorry for that. Things have been so busy at the restaurant and it's getting tough to take off." Tony avoided Ruth's eyes. He's never been good when it came to lying and he knew she would see right through this one and start asking questions if she saw his face. "Frank volunteered to cover today so I could spend the day with you."

"I think maybe on Monday, I will try to come up with a solid schedule that will guarantee some family time for both you and Frank. I know Betty would like that too."

A specific work schedule would make it even more difficult for Tony to explain his absence while he worked for Carmine, so he quickly looked at his watch and called out, "Hey, Rena, *Perry Mason* is about to come on. Let's watch it together."

"Really? Ok," Rena smiled brightly as she entered the living room.

Tony was relieved to have been able to change the subject. "Why don't you go get us some of that pie I saw in the refrigerator before the show starts?"

"None for me tonight," Ruth called out. "Just bring in some for both of you."

"Put extra whipped cream on mine," he added as the phone rang. Dread filled his body as he answered, "Hello?"

"Yeah hey, Tony, it's me, Tommy. We're gonna need you to come downtown with us tonight and pay a little visit to the barber on 18th Avenue."

"Tonight? I'm just settled in with my family."

"Tony, Carmine gave instructions. It's got to be tonight. I'm on my way over. Meet me outside." Tommy hung up before Tony could answer.

"I'm sorry, I've gotta go. Gotta get down to the restaurant." Tony stood and started to change his shoes by the door.

"Now, Tony?" Ruth leaned forward.

"But I thought we were going to watch TV?" Rena, clearly disappointed, put down the two slices of pie.

"It can't be helped, something came up," Tony said abruptly as he put on his jacket.

"When will you be back?" Rena looked back and forth between Tony and Ruth.

"I dunno, probably late. Don't wait up for me. Maybe we'll watch tv next week."

"Again? It seems like you're always having to leave at a moment's notice." Ruth said and didn't hide her annoyance.

"Ruthie, I have no choice." He looked pleadingly into her eyes and willed her to understand.

"What's wrong with Frank that he can't handle these things that come up at the restaurant?"

"Nothing. There's nothing wrong with Frank. Sometimes he needs my help when things get real busy. You know we're short staffed."

"You've been short staffed since Christmas. When are you going to hire some people?"

"We're trying. Now I gotta go. I love you." He kissed her cheek and raced out the door. Tony's body tensed as he waited outside for Tommy. It was hard for him to lie to Ruth, but he realized the lying was getting easier. What *was* even harder were the nightmares he had after each encounter. Just when he's able to shake it off, he got called in for another round.

Tommy's car pulled up and Tony quickly got in.

"Hey Tony, how's it going?"

"Just great," Tony said sarcastically.

"It's probably tough for you, not being a part of this thing of ours. But if it makes you feel any better, Carmine's impressed with the work you've been doing. That's really saying something."

"Oh, good." Tony stared out into the night and tried to will himself into a bad mood to help make it all a little easier.

"Here we are," Tommy parked the car in front of Bensonhurst Barbers. Inside, Tony saw a man in his fifties who had no idea what was about to happen.

"Angelo, my friend," Tommy said as he opened the door. "Do you know what today is? It's payday." He walked over to Angelo and took a broom from his hands.

Angelo looked at Tommy and then over to Tony and was unable to hide the fear in his eyes. "Tommy, I'm a little short this month, but I promise I'll make it up next month."

Tommy gripped Angelo's shoulder. "Short, huh? You were short last month, the month before that, and in fact, you've been short the last six months. Now, didn't I tell you that if you didn't come up with all the money you owe, there would be a problem this month?"

"I know. I tried to get all the money, you've got to believe me, I tried. Business is slow, my mom's sick, providing for six kids, it all adds up. I just can't seem to get ahead." Angelo nervously looked back and forth between Tommy and Tony.

"Well, now, that's not good, Angelo. Today's tab is four thousand dollars. If I go back to Carmine with nothing, he's going to be unhappy, and it's never good to make Carmine unhappy."

"Look, here, look." He quickly moved across the room and opened the cash register. "I've got twenty-five hundred." He emptied the cash register and shoved the money toward Tommy. "It's all the money I got."

Tommy took the money and counted it. "As it is, your next

month's tab will be another four thousand, what with interest and all. I'll bring this back to Carmine, but I know he won't be happy. Now this here is Tony," Tony moved forward and rubbed his right fist with his left hand. "Tony's here to deliver a message from Carmine."

"I'm real sorry about this," Tony whispered in his ear as he punched Angelo in the stomach and folded him over like a piece of paper. Tony looked to Tommy, who nodded and gestured for him to continue. He punched Angelo in the face and looked to Tommy again.

"Keep it going, Tony. I'll tell you when to stop." Tommy insisted. Tony shook his head, took a deep breath, and punched Angelo two more times dropping him to the floor. Tony kicked him in the stomach twice before Tommy said, "That's enough."

"Hopefully, you understand Carmine's message because if you don't pay in full next month, you're not going to be as lucky as you are tonight."

Tommy stepped over Angelo carefully and avoided the stream of blood that pooled on the floor and walked toward the car.

"I can go for a burger, Tony, how about you?"

"No, I'm good," Tony said feeling sick. "You can just drop me off at home."

"Are you sure? That new place around the corner is pretty good."

"Yeah, I'm sure."

"Hey, honey. You're up." Tony said as he slid into the bed next to Ruth.

"I couldn't sleep," Ruth said flatly.

"Come here, maybe I can help you," Tony said teasingly as he reached out to Ruth.

"Are you serious?" Ruth pushed Tony away. "You up and leave us suddenly to go into work, don't come home for hours, and then expect me to be all lovey-dovey?"

"I'm sorry Ruthie, but I had to go."

"What was so important that you had to leave us so abruptly? Do you know Rena went right to her room after you left and stayed there the whole night? She didn't want her pie, didn't want television, all she wanted was to spend time with you."

Tony chose to focus the conversation on Rena so he didn't have to come up with another lie about work. "But we had a great time at the park today."

"Yes, but she feels like she can't depend on you. How would you feel if you got excited to spend time with her and then she gets a phone call and leaves without much explanation?"

"I would like to think I would understand that sometimes important things come up."

"Ok, *sometimes* important things do come up, but do you realize you've done this to us, to Rena, at least four times this month alone? It's becoming more and more frequent."

Tony sighed and looked down. He knew only too well that it was happening a lot.

"Each time you disappoint Rena, she retreats into herself a little more. Do you want things to go back to the way they were with her?"

"No, I don't. I'm trying to do the best I can for this family."

"Well, maybe you need to try harder." Ruth rolled over and turned out the light.

Ruth's words cut Tony like a sharp blade. He slid over and pressed his body against her. As he put his arm around her waist he said, "I love you and the kids more than my own life. You know that don't you?"

"I know," she sighed, and they both barely slept the rest of the night caught up in their own fears and worries.

FORTY-ONE

APRIL, 1960
RUTH

THE NEXT MORNING, Ruth woke up to the smell of pancakes, bacon, and coffee. She put on her robe and slippers and made her way to the kitchen. She found everyone busy making breakfast. Rena mixed the batter, Tony flipped the pancakes, Anthony and Janet sat at the table and sampled the bacon, while Nancy supervised the whole production.

"What's all this?"

"Dad woke me up and asked me if I wanted to help him make blueberry pancakes like he used to do with Nonna." Rena smiled at Tony as he handed Ruth a cup of coffee.

"Well, this is a nice surprise," Ruth said as she sat down next to Anthony and took a bite of the bacon he had in his hand.

"Daddy, the pancakes are gonna burn," Nancy commanded.

"Yup, I see it, Nance." Tony moved the pancakes from the skillet onto a platter and looked at Rena. "So, I see that that new movie *Psy-*

cho is playing downtown. Wanna go see it today with your old man?"

"Really?" Rena said excitedly, "Don't you have to work?"

"No. I already called Frank. No work for me again today. What do you say?"

"Yes!"

"I want to go," Janet said with her mouth full.

"Sorry kiddo, not this time. You're not old enough for this movie."

Janet sighed, "I'm not old enough for anything."

"Why don't we work on that jigsaw puzzle you got for Christmas? We can set it up on the dining room table?" Ruth offered.

"Ok." Janet smiled, easily appeased.

Tony winked at Ruth, and she mouthed the words, "Thank you" to him. The smile on Rena's face filled her heart with joy.

JUNE, 1960

The strain that had developed within the household over the past two months began to weigh heavily on Ruth. Tony said he was going to start doing better about spending time at home and not working so many long hours. At first, he stayed true to his word. He planned various activities, mostly on Sundays, but slowly things started to change. He was away from home more than ever. If he wasn't working, he was boxing down at the gym. There had even been a few times where he had gotten a phone call in the middle of the night and left. His absence affected Rena more than anyone. Instead of getting to know her father better, she's been disappointed over and over again, and her moods swayed between happiness and distance. Ruth told Tony how important Rena's high school graduation was, and he said he would be there right after he picked up a special locket he had engraved for her.

Ruth rushed around the house feeling excited and anxious at the same time. "Come on girls, we've got to get going. We can't be late," she called out while she wiped a smudge from Anthony's shirt. "Anthony, how did you manage to do this, I just dressed you not five minutes ago? There you go, now sit on the sofa and don't move a muscle." She kissed his forehead, checked her watch, and got ready to call for the girls again when Janet and Nancy appeared in the living room as they awkwardly tried to put on their white gloves. "Oh good, go sit on the sofa with your brother. Rena are you ready?"

"I need help pinning this into my hair." Rena flipped her graduation cap around in her hands.

"Oh." Seeing her in her graduation gown momentarily took Ruth's breath away. "I'm just so proud of you."

Ruth tried to give her a hug, but Rena shrugged away and held out the cap and bobby pins.

"Let me see if I can help you with this. Everyone's going to meet us at the school and hopefully we'll get good seats," Ruth said as she straightened the cap on Rena's head.

"Not everyone." Rena looked in the mirror, "Mom won't be there, or should I call her Aunt Louisa?" she said sarcastically.

"I'm sure she wants to be there tonight," Ruth said trying not to look at Rena. "So. Are we all ready?"

"I'm not so sure she wants to be there tonight, but whatever." Rena turned from the mirror. "I'm ready to go and get this over with."

"Wait a minute, before we go, I just want to tell you how much we love you and we really are proud of you. These past six months have been tough, and I know you don't see it now, but we really want you to be happy."

"Yeah ok," she said rolling her eyes and held out her hand to

Anthony. "Let's go squirt."

When they got to the high school field, Ruth found Ethan and Miriam sitting in the third row keeping watch over a block of seats.

"Hey, great seats, you must've made it here early," Ruth reached out and hugged Ethan and smiled at Miriam. Although they've been spending more time together, Ruth still felt awkward. She could see that Miriam was not ready for a lot of affection, so Ruth respected her boundaries and was grateful for every little smile and touch she got from her.

"It was all Miriam, she wanted to be able to see everything," Ethan pointed in Miriam's direction, and her wide grin and nod lifted Ruth's spirits.

"Well, you've certainly found the best seats." Ruth reached out and placed her palm on her cheek.

"Thank you." She looked around worriedly. "Where's Rena?"

"She's in the school with her class getting ready for the ceremony. Why don't you sit here next to me?"

"Ok, but can Anthony sit next to me on the other side?"

"That would be great. You can remind him to stay quiet." Ruth anxiously looked around and checked her watch every couple of minutes as she waited for Tony to arrive. Just as the band began to play the opening song and the graduates started marching in, Frank quickly sat down and kissed Ruth's cheek.

"Tony's going to be a little late. He's got something he's got to take care of."

"What? Are you kidding me? Now? Couldn't you have taken care of it?"

"Uh, no, Tony really needed to take care of this. Don't worry Ruth, he'll be here." In a flash Frank moved to a seat next to Ethan. Ruth sat back and let out a frustrated sigh and continued to look toward the entrance throughout the ceremony. Tony finally arrived just as the graduates were about to receive their diplomas.

"Where have you been?" Ruth demanded.

"I'm sorry. I had to take care of a few things."

"This is your daughter's graduation. You missed most of it."

"I know, I know. It couldn't be helped. I'm here now though." He shook his right leg up and down.

"We'll talk about this later. Now you need to focus on Rena, they're about to call her name."

After the ceremony, everyone gathered at Salvatore Bruno's for a celebration dinner. Ruth put on a happy face while she laughed and mingled. She found that she actually enjoyed the evening despite her anger at Tony.

At the end of the night, Tony tapped his glass of wine and called for everyone's attention. "Excuse me everyone. I can't let tonight end without saying a few words to my beautiful daughter, Rena."

Rena looked up confused.

"Today's an important day. Your graduation from high school signifies a new beginning. You've got a whole future standing before you and I couldn't be prouder of you than I am today. As you start this new chapter in your life, I want you to carry all of my love with you. Rena, honey, I know I haven't been the best father to you. I've made a lot of mistakes that I wish I could change. Someday, when you're a parent, you may understand that everything I've done, was to protect you." Tony reached into his jacket pocket and handed a gift-wrapped box to Rena. She unwrapped it and stared at the inscription on the locket that read, 'You are My Heart.' She looked at Tony as a tear fell down her face.

On the drive home, Ruth's anger toward Tony intensified. What could've been so important that he couldn't make it on time to the most important event of his daughter's life? He certainly couldn't blame it on the restaurant. Not this time. Even Frank made it to the graduation on time and he was notoriously late for everything. Her mind had been spinning all night with different scenarios of what Tony could've been up to and her biggest fear was that he was involved with another woman. That's the only thing she could come up with that would possibly explain the many months of strange phone calls, late nights, and Tony's increased irritation.

After putting the kids to bed and locking up the house, Ruth marched up to the bedroom, and stood next to the bed with her hands on her hips. "What the hell happened today? And don't give me that crap about something came up at the restaurant."

Tony looked up from his *Time* magazine, removed his reading glasses, and let out an impatient sigh. "Nothing's happened. I stopped off at the jewelry store to pick up that locket for Rena. They didn't have the inscription done, so I had to wait." He put his glasses back on and continued to read.

Ruth grabbed the magazine and threw it across the room. "Well, that's a convenient excuse. I don't buy it."

"What do you want me to say, Ruth?"

Not wanting to wake the kids, Ruth tried to keep herself from shouting. She grit her teeth and forcefully demanded answers. "I want to know what's going on. I just don't understand what's gotten into you lately! You're never around, you're moody, and you seem nervous a lot. What were you really doing that made you miss most of Rena's graduation?"

Tony sat up straight and answered very slowly, he clearly enunciated each word, "I was at the jewelers."

Ruth's frustration mounted. "Ok, so let's say you're telling the truth about today. What about the other times you were late or had to leave in a hurry, huh? What about those times?"

"It's a very busy time at the restaurant, I've had to find some new vendors, licenses need to be renewed, and we have to get ready for inspections."

"None of that is new. You change vendors all the time, and licenses and inspections haven't been a cause for concern in the past." She leaned into his face and asked, "Are you having an affair?"

"An *affair*? What would ever make you think that?"

"Well, let me see, you've been absent a lot, you leave after getting late night phone calls, and let's face it we haven't been intimate in some time."

Tony reached out for Ruth's hand and pulled her onto the bed. He softened his voice and put his hand on her cheek. "Ruthie, I promise you, I've never even looked at another woman since you came into my life. Hand to God." He wrapped his arms around her and kissed her. "I know I haven't been attentive lately, and I'm sorry for that."

Ruth's anger softened just slightly. "I miss you. Not just physically, but emotionally too. We all miss you."

"I'm right here. I haven't gone anywhere." He gently ran his finger across her cheek.

"But that's just it, even when you're physically here, you're distant." Ruth turned her head so she didn't have to look at him. She hadn't felt his arms around her in weeks and she wasn't ready to break away yet.

"You promised you would spend more time with Rena, but you keep letting her down, and she's become even more withdrawn. You haven't been yourself lately. I know you're hiding something, and we promised to always be honest with each other." She turned her head to face him again. "Should I be worried? Are you in some kind of trouble?"

Tony was silent for what felt like an eternity. He took Ruth out of his embrace and held her hands, his face aged within an instant.

"You're right. We did promise to be honest, and I haven't been honest with you. So here it goes." He took a deep breath and braced himself to tell Ruth everything he's been hiding for the past six months. "Back when I had the run-in with that punk Dominick, I did damage to his hand. His dominant hand."

"Damn it, Tony, your temper!"

"The kid is fine, he just doesn't have the strength in that hand like he used to is all. Because he doesn't have his strength, he can't protect Carmine Esposito and his business like he used to. So, I've been stepping in from time to time."

"What do you mean?"

"It's no big deal really. I just flex my muscles to scare people into acting right. Every once in a while, I'll have to throw a punch or two and that always does the trick."

"Tony, that sounds dangerous."

"Carmine always sends one or two guys with me. Kinda like bodyguards." Tony chuckled.

"This is not funny at all. You're putting yourself into risky situations. Why don't you just tell Carmine you're done and can't do it anymore?"

"It's not that easy. Because I damaged Dominick's hand, it's my duty to step up and fill his place."

"You and your sense of duty." Ruth said as she rolled her eyes.

"It wasn't my idea. Carmine insisted that I do it and wouldn't take no for an answer."

"So now you're caught up in Carmine's business? This is exactly what your father didn't want to happen."

"I really know nothing of Carmine's business, and he certainly isn't involved with the restaurant. Every now and then I get a phone call or one of his guys comes by and tells me they need a little extra muscle. Usually, it's when people owe Carmine money, but I don't know specific details, and I don't wanna know. We go meet up with someone and scare them a bit. That's all it is."

"I don't like it. Not only is it tearing up our family, but Carmine is a dangerous man. There's no telling what he's capable of."

"I don't either, really, but I have a plan. There's this young kid I know from down at the gym, Donny. Great boxer. I've been working with him, teaching him everything I know. When the time's right, I'm gonna set up a situation where Donny can show Carmine just how good of a threat he is. I'll make the proper introductions and recommend to Carmine that my young trainee would be a great replacement for this old bag of bones."

"That sounds like a long shot. Do you think that it'll work?"

"Well, it'll take a little time to set it up right. Donny needs more training, and I wanna have him down at the restaurant a few times so Carmine can get a feel for him before I set it all up, but I think it could work."

"You've got to make it work. I'm serious. The sooner the better. Wait a minute, were you doing a job for Carmine tonight? Was that why you were late for the graduation?"

"Yeah, that was it. I already picked up the locket earlier. They came by to get me just when I was about to leave. There was nothing I could do."

"Thank God Rena doesn't know you were late. Why didn't you tell me all this sooner?"

"I was trying to protect you, Ruthie."

"*Protect* me? Am I in danger? Oh my God, what about the kids?"

Tony looked down and hesitated. "Not so long as I do what Carmine tells me to do."

"Oh Tony, you've got to fix this and fast!"

Tony rubbed his face with both hands. "I've been trying to fix this since the day it started. You've got to believe me, this whole thing has been destroying me. Every day I've been living with fear, guilt, and shame." His voice cracked, "I just don't know how much longer I can keep this up. I've kept it from you to protect you and keep you from worrying. I just wanna keep my family safe and secure and it's killing me."

Ruth took a long look at Tony's face. She saw how much he's aged in the lines and creases brought on by stress and anxiety. As she looked into his eyes, she saw the endless amount of love he had for his family. She now understood the lengths he would go to keep them safe without any hesitation or consideration for himself. His greatest quality was also one of his greatest flaws. She knew she needed to let go of her anger toward him. Tension between them wouldn't do anyone any good. Now she needed to find a way to come to terms with this horrible situation.

"I worry about you." Ruth leaned into him, and they fell into a warm embrace.

"Please don't worry about me. I am worrying enough for all of us." He kissed her passionately. "Now promise me you won't talk about this to anyone. Not Joan, not Betty, no one. This is not the kind of thing people should know about."

"I won't, just so long as you promise me that there will be no more secrets between us."

"You have my word."

"And please, Tony, you've got to find a way to make things better with Rena before it's too late. She's very unhappy and unsettled."

"I know. You're right. Do you think she liked the locket?"

"I think so. The locket is lovely, it's a beautiful sentiment. Maybe you should also do something special with her for her graduation."

"I can take her to see *Bye Bye Birdie* on Broadway, and then maybe to a nice dinner after."

"That would be wonderful."

"Don't ever doubt how much I love you, Ruthie." He kissed her gently, and they made love with the warmth and tenderness like they did when they were young.

The next morning, they felt three little bodies jumping on their bed laughing and giggling. "Get up, get up. We're hungry."

Tony and Ruth looked at each other, grabbed the kids, and started a tickle fight.

"Alright," Ruth said as she tried to catch her breath from laughing, "who wants Egg in a Hole?"

"Egg in a Hole?" Tony sat up. "Only if there's sausage on the side."

"Oh Mommy, please, please can we have Egg in a Hole and sausage?" Janet fell on her knees and begged.

"I don't see why not." Ruth started to put on her robe. "Janet, go wake Rena and ask her if she wants some."

"Can I help, Mommy?" Nancy asked.

"Sure honey, and uhm, Daddy can you see about getting Anthony cleaned up? I smell a situation."

"I'm on it." Tony carried Anthony to the bathroom with his arms extended.

"Mommy! Come here." Janet called out from Rena's room.

"What is it, Janet?" Ruth asked as she entered her room.

"She's not here." Janet waved her arms.

Ruth looked around and noticed that her room was in perfect order. The bed was made up and there were no clothes strewn about, but there was an envelope on the dresser with the locket Tony gave her on top. Ruth grabbed the envelope and locket and raced to the bathroom.

"Tony, *Tony*, Rena's gone."

"What? Where is she?"

"I don't know, she left this on the dresser." Ruth shoved the envelope and locket at Tony. "Janet, can you do Mommy a big favor? Can you please finish taking care of Anthony for Daddy, and fix some cereal for the three of you?"

"Sure." Janet sensed Ruth's alarm and quickly stepped into her role as a big sister and took control. "Nancy, help me get Anthony dressed and then we'll have breakfast."

Ruth found Tony in the living room where he sat on the sofa and turned a piece of paper from front to back over again. The envelope and locket were sitting on the coffee table.

"What's it say?" Ruth leaned in and looked over his shoulder. "Tony?"

"She ran off with him," Tony said flatly in shock.

"With who? *Dominick*? Where'd they go What's the note say?"

"See for yourself." He handed her the note and picked up the locket and stared at it.

Ruth read the note out loud.

I've gone away with Dominick to start our life together. I know you've tried to protect me from what you think is a mistake, but I think being with someone you love can't be a mistake. I tried it your way and now it's time for me to do it my way.

"You've got to find her, Tony."

"I'm gonna," Tony said lifelessly, as he stared at the locket.

"Are you ok?" Ruth had never seen him so detached. He didn't flinch when the phone rang, and she reached over him to answer it.

"Hello?" She said anxiously.

"Yeah, this is Tommy. I need to speak to Tony."

"Just a minute."

"It's for you, it's Tommy." Ruth shook him. "Tony you've got to snap out of this!"

He took the phone and came back to life. "Tommy?" There was a pause, "Now? No, I can't now, I'm having a family emergency." Tony started to shake his right leg. "Ok, Ok, I know. I understand."

"I gotta go. I got no choice. But I'll get to the bottom of this and find that punk." He looked at Ruth with sorrow in his eyes and went off to get dressed.

FORTY-TWO

JUNE, 1960
TONY

TONY PACED IN front of the apartment building as he waited for Tommy and contemplated many questions in his mind. How could he not have seen this coming? Where'd they run off to? What're they gonna do for money? A father's job was to protect his children, and he felt like he's completely failed her. Was he too hard on her? Was he too soft? How could he make this right? He didn't notice the car pull up and Tommy had to honk to get his attention.

"What's up with you today?" Tommy raised his eyes.

"Got family problems."

"Oh, yeah?" Tommy said alarmed.

"Yeah, my daughter Rena. Hey, you know that Dominick Trovato? Do you know where he is?"

"No, I don't know much about him. I don't see him much since he stopped working muscle for Carmine and started managing junk on the streets."

"He's *dealing?*"

"Not dealing directly. More like managing the dealers. From what I hear, he's pretty good at it. He's a smart kid."

Tony was so caught up in his head that he never asked Tommy what the job was, and when they pulled up to an abandoned warehouse, he looked around confused.

"What're we doing here?"

"It's the job today, come on." Tommy got out of the car, put his hand on Tony's shoulder, and led him to a far corner where there were a group of five men standing in a semi-circle around another man who was beaten and tied to a chair. As they got closer, he saw that Carmine, himself, was standing in the center of the semi-circle. Tony's heart started to race. He realized this wasn't a typical job where he just scared someone into compliance, and he knew he would soon be involved in something that would change him forever.

"Ah, Tony, you're here. Good." Carmine said as he nodded. "I think you know our friend here." He gestured to the beaten man in the chair.

Tony instantly felt lightheaded, and the room began to spin as he saw Frank sitting in the chair. "What, what's going on?" Tony whispered.

"Frank here had a few too many to drink and lost his cool last night at a card game. Didn't you Frank?" Carmine stepped closer to Frank who looked at Tony with fear through his swollen lids.

"I'm sorry, Tony." Frank gurgled as blood spilled from his mouth.

"Carmine, I'm sure Frank didn't mean any disrespect. I'm sure we can take care of any damage he might've done." Tony stammered.

"Oh, Tony, no. The kind of damage Frank caused can't be undone. You see, our friend here stabbed and killed one of my top guys. Do you know what that means?"

"I, I'm not sure that I do."

"He killed a member of *my* family, which, in this thing of ours, means that there must be grave consequences."

"Can't we figure something out? Maybe it was all just a big misunderstanding, an accident?"

Tommy interjected. "If it makes you feel any better, it probably was an accident." He looked to Carmine for a nod of approval before he continued. "Frank lost quite a bit of cash last night at the game. Vito had been provoking him all night, and by the fourth hand he was on edge. Frank took a break and started cutting up some hard salami to make a sandwich." Tommy shook his head. "Vito never should've gone up behind him and pretended to put him in a choke hold. Frank wouldn't've gotten startled and accidentally stabbed him as he turned around if he hadn't." Tommy shook his head again.

Tony looked over at Frank, whose head was now hanging low into his chest, and he feared for what Carmine was about to ask him to do. He looked at Carmine, who took a gun from Tommy and held it out to him.

"Carmine, please!" Tony begged. "Isn't there something, anything to make this right?"

"I'm sorry, Tony. This is the way it has to be." Carmine moved the gun closer to Tony's hand.

Tony shook his head slowly and whispered, "I can't."

"You must." Carmine put the gun in his hand.

Tears flowed down Tony's face as he looked at his best friend, his brother. How could he possibly end his life? Tony lifted the gun, but his arm was shaking badly, and he lowered it back down. He suddenly felt the cold end of a gun barrel against his own temple.

"It's time."

Tony lifted his arm again but couldn't see through the tears in his eyes. He whispered, "God forgive me," and with a trembling hand, pulled the trigger.

Tony fell to his knees, dropped the gun, and let out a cry from his gut when he realized his shot missed. "Tommy," Carmine commanded. "Do it yourself and let's get this over with." The shot to Frank's head was deafening, and the image of his brain splattered throughout the floor was embedded into Tony's mind.

"Come, Tony, take a walk with me. The rest of you, take care of this." Carmine pulled Tony to his feet, put his arm on his shoulder and led him outside to the fresh air where Tony began to vomit. Carmine gave him a handkerchief and said, "It had to be done. There was no other choice. Just like that accident that killed your parents had to be done."

"What?" Tony looked up at Carmine in disbelief.

"You heard me. It's a shame really, they seemed like nice people."

"Why would you ever do such a thing?" Tony screamed.

"Your father, Salvatore Russo ... he stole quite a bit of money from my uncle, Marco, back in Naples. The family just couldn't let that kind of thing slide."

"How did you know it was him, my father, who took the money?"

"I had my suspicions. Once Frank got a few drinks in him, it was easy to coax him to tell me your family history. It wasn't long before we put the pieces together, and I got the order from Naples." Carmine lit a cigar. "Now, I meant what I've said in the past. I like you. I really do. But you've seen something here today that could make you a liability. That is, of course, unless you step up your responsibilities and start carrying out jobs like the one we had here today." He puffed on his cigar. "Your aim was off, I suppose that's to be expected, but you have to hit your mark every other time from here on out." He patted Tony on the cheek. "I'm sure you now know what could happen to you and your family if you choose not to accommodate my requests."

Tommy came out of the warehouse as Carmine's driver opened the back door for Carmine.

"Tommy here will take you home. Tony, go get some rest and remember I expect you to be discreet and keep my business to yourself." He said and got into the Cadillac.

As Tommy got in the car with Tony he shook his head. "Sorry about Frank. It's a shame, really. He was a nice guy. Everyone thought so. Even Carmine liked him. He never would've done that favor for Frank and took care of that Harvey Goldberg back in '52 if he hadn't. But Vito was a 'made man.' There's rules about that kind of stuff."

Tony slowly looked at Tommy and whimpered.

FORTY-THREE

JUNE, 1960
RUTH

RUTH'S NERVES WERE frayed as she tried to figure out where Rena and Dominick were. She called Mrs. Scardino to see if she knew anything, and she said Rena hadn't been babysitting on weekends for the past month. She assumed Ruth knew, and that Rena told her she had to spend more time studying for her final exams and preparing for graduation. She said that the kids really missed their trips to the park every weekend with Rena and how Rena's friend would buy them ice cream or cotton candy. Now it made sense, Ruth thought to herself. They had told Mrs. Scardino all about Dominick and asked her to keep an eye on things with Rena, but apparently, Rena was able to outsmart her. She really couldn't blame the woman, Rena could be a very good actress.

Ruth grew even more overwhelmed and decided to call Joan, hoping their conversation would help to calm her nerves.

"Hello?" Joan answered the phone on the third ring.

"Thank God you're home. Do you have a minute to talk?" Ruth asked shakily.

"I've got some time before Paul comes home. Are you ok, what's going on?"

"Rena ran away with Dominick. We woke up this morning and she was gone."

"No! I don't believe it. Everything seemed fine at her graduation dinner last night."

"I thought so too. Before graduation she was a little moody, but I didn't think anything of it. You know how she gets. I keep going over last night in my mind for some clue that this was going to happen."

"How did they manage to communicate? I know you both were working hard keeping tabs on her."

"We had no idea they were seeing each other. Apparently, Rena was slick enough to pull the wool over Mrs. Scardino's eyes while she was helping to babysit the kids. Mrs. Scardino thought she was talking to a girlfriend on the phone while the kids napped, and from what I can gather Dominick must've been seeing her in the park when she would bring the kids to play."

"Well she certainly did a great job hiding it from you. How's Tony taking all of this?"

"Actually, I'm even more concerned over Tony right now than I am over Rena. When we found her note, he didn't explode at all. I kept waiting for his temper to flare up, but it didn't. I think he was in shock. He kept staring into space."

"That's not like him at all. How's he now?"

"I'm not sure. He was called away on an emergency for the restaurant. That seemed to help bring him back, but he's just not right." Ruth really wished she could confide in Joan about Tony working for Carmine, but she agreed that it was best for people not to know. At least for now. "He's been under a lot of stress lately, and I'm not sure how much more he can take."

"You know, I noticed he seemed tense the last few times I've seen him."

"It's a lot worse now."

"I have an idea. Why don't I have Alan call his cop friend, Jack, and have him look into finding them. Maybe there's something he can do to keep an eye out for them."

"That'll be great, thank you. Listen, I hear Tony coming through the door. I'll call you back later."

"Ok, love. We'll talk later. Please give Tony a hug for me."

Ruth gasped when she saw Tony walk through the door. His face was gray, and he was breathing heavily. "There's my girl," Tony struggled.

"Let me help you." Ruth quickly moved to his side and took his hat from his hand. "What's happening? Do you need a doctor?"

"Frank." He whispered as he looked at her, his eyes pleading.

"Do you want me to call Frank?" She started to reach for the phone, but Tony whimpered and shook his head.

"Can't. Dead. Carmine. My parents. Harvey." Tears formed in his eyes as he looked at her.

Ruth began to shake as she tried to make sense of what Tony was trying to say. "Let's get you to the sofa; we can talk there," she said nervously. She wrapped her arm around his waist.

When they took their first step together, he quickly grabbed his left arm. He turned his head, looked pleadingly into her eyes, and said "Ruthie," then he fell to the floor.

"Nooooo," she screamed. "Tony! Nooooo!"

EPILOGUE

AUGUST, 2004
ANTHONY

ANTHONY STOOD IN the party room at Villa Romano admiring the decorations for Tony and Ruth's 50th wedding anniversary party. He noticed a picture of his parents with their arms around Rena and wondered to himself if it should be part of the display.

"What's that?" Nancy asked as she put her hand on his shoulder.

"Look. A picture from Rena's high school graduation."

"Mia must've added that one. It's the nicest picture she has of her mother and grandparents."

Anthony sighed. "Yeah. I get it. But do you think it will stir up too many emotions?"

"Well, it's been a long time since everything happened. Why don't we move it to a less prominent place in the collection of pictures. This way Rena's memory is here with us, but it won't be the first picture everyone sees." Nancy rearranged the pictures and placed a picture of Tony, Ruth, Sal, and Anna in front of a Christmas tree front and center with Rena's graduation picture off to the side.

Anthony nodded as he scanned the pictures. He was reminded of his parents' tenacity to recover from the darkest time in their lives, and also of their determination to be the most loving and supportive parents they could be.

It had been forty-four years since Tony collapsed in Ruth's arms and suffered a heart attack. Although Anthony doesn't remember much from back then, Tony and Ruth have always been upfront and honest with all of the kids about the events of their past. Anthony had always thought that his father's heart had broken from the stress of Frank's murder, Rena's running away, and the truth of Sal and Anna's death. The doctors said he was very lucky to have survived, but they insisted that changes be made to prevent another attack from occurring. The day after Tony was released from the hospital, he sold Salvatore Bruno's Ristorante to Carmine Esposito at a lower price than what it was worth. After he received assurances from Carmine that his retribution debt was paid-in-full and no further harm would come to him or his family, Tony paid Betty and Louisa their share from the sale and used the rest to move his family to a comfortable house in Lyndhurst, New Jersey. Tony often told Anthony that both he and Ruth needed a fresh start, and this small town was a perfect fit for them. Tony took a job as a manager at Villa Romano, a very popular Italian restaurant and catering hall. The Romanos, who owned the restaurant, appreciated his personality and experience, and in time, gave him free reign to manage the place as he saw fit. In turn, he received an attractive salary to do so. Late in the evenings, Anthony would sometimes find Tony sipping wine as he stared out of a window. When he asked Ruth about it, she told Anthony that although his body recuperated from the stress of that day, Tony never fully recovered emotionally from seeing Frank killed. He was often plagued with the memory and only Ruth could set his mind at ease and give him peace.

It was no secret that Ruth loved living in Lyndhurst. But she admitted that the early years after Tony's heart attack were tough on her. She often worried about him, and it became a running joke in the family that it took her a while to not panic every time he so much as sneezed for fear of him having another attack. As the kids grew up, she enjoyed being a Cub Scout Den Mother, member of the

PTA, and a Girl Scout Troop Leader, and she often helped out with other activities each of the kids became involved with. Her family was always her top priority, and there was never a Sunday where they didn't have a houseful of people for dinner.

As he gazed at the picture display, Anthony thought about the people that he wished could have come to his parents' anniversary party. First and foremost was his sister Rena. She touched his heart, and he wished he could've changed her difficult, sad life. After she ran off with Dominick, they married and quickly had a child, Mia. They really named her Carmella after Rena's mother, but everyone had taken to calling her Mia after Anthony couldn't say Carmella. Five years into their marriage, Dominick was arrested and sent to jail for his role in the drug business. It was rumored that he was going to testify against Carmine, but he was killed in prison before that could happen. After Dominick died, Rena fell into a deep depression and in the end of 1966, she was hospitalized for nine months where she underwent Electric Shock Therapy. When she was released, Anthony was thrilled when she and Mia moved in with the family permanently. She confided in Anthony that she always felt guilty for Tony's heart attack and there was nothing anyone could say to relieve her anguish. She started drinking heavily and there were some nights where Tony would get a phone call from a local bar asking him to pick Rena up. One night, she was hit by a car when she drunkenly stepped off a curb. As a result of the accident, she became addicted to painkillers, and on her thirty-fifth birthday, Rena accidentally overdosed on a combination of pills and alcohol. She died wearing the locket Tony gave her.

Anthony would've also loved it if his Uncle Ethan had been able to attend the party. But pancreatic cancer had a mind of its own and took Ethan in May. Although he knew she would be happy to see his wife and daughter, Rachel and Rose, Anthony knew Ruth's heart ached for her brother just as much as it ached for her daughter, Miriam. Within a year of Tony's heart attack, Miriam was very disappointed that Ruth converted to Catholicism. She just couldn't understand how Ruth came to embrace the faith and wanted to raise her kids within the church. Miriam held her Jewish beliefs in such high regard that she chose to cut ties with Ruth, just like her grandparents did. Ruth had told Anthony that she respected Miriam's beliefs, but she was heartbroken once again.

Although all of Frank's kids and their families were expected to attend the party, Frank's wife, Betty, passed away over three years ago. She remained close to Tony and Ruth, and it was no surprise that she had spent her share of the money from Salvatore Bruno's swiftly. She paid off the mortgage on her house, bought new furniture, a new car, and a new wardrobe that came in handy when she went out on the town in her quest to find a new husband. She vowed to never marry another man who drank or gambled. It didn't take her long before she met and married a quiet, meek postman named Sam. Until the day she died, Betty never believed the story she was told that Frank was a victim of a mugging gone wrong.

The one person Anthony knew better than to invite to the party was Louisa. Tony never hid the fact from his children that he completely cut his sister out of his life right after giving her money from the sale of the restaurant. To this day, he had not forgiven her for being cold and callous to both Rena and Ruth. Anthony had speculated often with Janet and Nancy that Rena's life could've turned out differently if Louisa had been more stable.

Nancy startled Anthony out of his thoughts as she whispered, "Look. Joey Scardino is here. We didn't think he would make it."

Anthony turned around and saw Mrs. Scardino's youngest son

smiling as he made his way across the room toward them.

"Anthony, Nancy," he exclaimed. "It is so nice to see you both. It's been such a long time. I wouldn't have recognized you if your mother didn't send a family picture each year with her Christmas card."

"Hey, Joey." Nancy leaned in and gave him a big hug. "We're so glad you could come."

"I wouldn't have missed this party. Both your grandparents and parents were always so good to my mother. Even after your parents moved here to Jersey, they continued to look out for her. Did you know your Dad would drive all the way out to her apartment to pick her up every Sunday for dinner with your family and then drive her all the way back?" Joey smiled and shook his head at the memory.

"Yeah, I remember. I would join him on some of the drives to pick her up. Although sometimes I think it was to get me out of my mother's hair." Anthony chuckled.

"That's exactly what happened. You were always getting in the way." Nancy jabbed Anthony in the ribs and looked around the room. "Oh look at that, I should really help everyone find their tables. Anthony, why don't you fill Joey in on our lives while I greet the rest of our guests? I will catch up with you in a bit."

"Yes. I would love to hear what's become of the Russo children."

"Well, I'll try to give you the condensed version," Anthony said as he led Joey to a nearby table and poured two glasses of Cabernet. "Let's see. Janet became a hairdresser and married her high school sweetheart, Ryan. They've worked hard to build their businesses and raise their two children Gabe and Julia. After moving to Nutley, they were able to open their own shops right in the center of town called *Main Street Cuts* by Janet and *Main Street Florist*. Now, Ryan is considering the idea of running for mayor."

"Oh that's wonderful." Joey took a sip of wine. "And Nancy

looks fantastic. How is she doing?" Joey asked.

"Nancy became a private caterer and when she's not working, she volunteers at the animal shelter near her home in Montclair. Her husband, Richard, is a very busy lawyer and spends a large amount of time working and entertaining clients." Anthony sat back in his chair and smiled at his wife. "As for me, I married the girl of my dreams, Susan. We decided to settle in Lyndhurst, where we met."

Joey followed Anthony's gaze and nodded at Susan. "She's lovely. How did you meet?"

"That's a long story. I started to learn the plumbing trade while I was in the service. Dad helped to set me up with a local plumber he had gotten to know from work, Arthur Rubinetti. Arthur not only helped me with an apprenticeship and my plumbing license, but he took me under his wing and taught me the business from the ground up. One morning, I went to his house to pick him up for a job and I met the most beautiful girl I've ever seen. I was so smitten that I could barely speak."

Joey laughed. "Ah, love at first sight."

Anthony nodded. "Every day after, Arthur insisted that I come pick him up and I was only too thrilled to do so. Finally, he asked if I was ever going to take his daughter out on a date. It turned out that Arthur set it up so that I would meet Susan on that day and see her every day after. He liked me from the start and knew I would make a good husband for his daughter. We were married within the year."

"That's a wonderful story. Are you still in the plumbing business?"

"Yes, as a matter of fact I am. Susan's family has been very good to us and when it was time for him to retire, Arthur handed over his plumbing business to me. Someday, I hope to hand it down to my son John and his wife Amanda. They're all here tonight. I will be sure to take you around and introduce you to everyone.

"I would love that. And how are your parents?"

"They're really doing well. They sold the house in Lyndhurst and moved to a retirement community down the shore."

"Good for them. They've certainly endured their fair share of adversity throughout their lives. Just like your father's parents, your parents truly are wonderful people."

Anthony nodded in agreement as Janet's daughter, Julia, rushed into the room and warned of their arrival. "They're here, they're here. Shhhh everyone, they're coming."

All of the guests fell silent, cameras and phones in hand ready to capture the moment where Tony and Ruth acted surprised as they entered their anniversary party. It was Anthony's decision to tell them about the party. He didn't think yelling surprise at a seventy-eight year old woman and an eighty-three year old man was a good idea. When the door opened, they walked proudly into the room holding hands as everyone cheered, "Surprise!" They lit up as they gazed over the crowd and started to recognize the many faces that played an important part in their lives. Janet had told them the party guests would be the close family only, and they were surprised to see Alan, Joan, their son Paul, and his family, Joey Scardino, and Aunt Betty's kids and grandkids.

Anthony smiled proudly at his parents. He realized that if anyone documented the events of their early life together, some might not believe them to be true. The 1950's was a time of conformity, and his parents did anything but conform. They faced many challenges head on and did not give in to the expectations of the time. He admired them for being so devoted to those they loved that they would do anything to protect them – even if it went against their principles. Life wasn't always easy for them, and they always tried to be the best people they could, in spite of the turmoil. Anthony learned to live his life with honor and integrity by their example.

Tony and Ruth proudly walked around the room and greeted all of their guests. Just before dinner, Tony insisted on making a toast with Ruth at his side.

"Fifty years ago, I got to marry the girl of my dreams, my best friend, and my soul mate. I can honestly say, I wouldn't be standing here today if it weren't for my Ruthie." He turned to her, smiled, and kissed her cheek. "Together we have endured more than any couple should in life and we came out stronger and better for it. For this, we are blessed. In spite of it all, we have made a wonderful life together filled with precious memories and precious people. Thank you all for coming." He raised his wine glass and said, "To our family, alla nostra famiglia."

THE END

ACKNOWLEGEMENTS

So many people helped me in this journey of writing my debut novel. Whether it was the little things like giving thoughts on design or big things like reading and re-reading my drafts, I appreciate you all.

To my life-long friend and chosen sister, **Nancy Maldonado Harrison**. I thank you for inspiring me when I was feeling low, for cheering me on throughout the process, and your constant support and enthusiasm about this book. This would have never happened without you.

Jodi Sheridan, thank you for being a good friend and for all of the brainstorming sessions, editing, proofreading, advice, and belief in my talent.

Sue Walsh, you have helped me more than you know. Your encouragement and friendship helped to boost my confidence, and I am so very grateful for you.

To my wonderful sister, **Denise Fedorchak**, thank you for all of your support, advice, and for being you. I don't know what I would do if it weren't for you. The best is yet to come.

Thank you, **Shari Hofbauer**, for being a friend. Your belief in me is so very much appreciated.

Thank you to **Cathy Housman** for sharing your dream and insisting that I write.

Thank you to everyone who lent a hand in editing, proofreading, and design. Your talent, skills, and professionalism was second to none: **Cara Stevens, Kelly Carter**, and **Elina Vaysbeyn**.

To my extended family **Rosita and Moses Card, Robin, Sheryl, Tyrone, Damaris, Sequoria, Andrea, and Jasmine Brown, Joan Mingo, and Cheryl Phelps**, I thank you all for opening your hearts to me, loving me, and accepting me. You lift me up.

And finally thank you to my amazing nephew and nieces, **Jonathan, Nicole, and Amanda Fedorchak**. You are one of my life's greatest blessings, and your love and support is everything to me.

ABOUT THE AUTHOR

Born and raised in New Jersey, CYNTHIA COPPOLA holds a BA in English and an MA in Education. She has spent much of her career teaching High School English and now lives in Michigan with her wife and two dogs. She is grateful to have the opportunity to tap into her creativity and do something she loves ... storytelling. *In the Name of Family* is her debut novel.

Made in the USA
Middletown, DE
05 August 2024